In A Pig's Eye

by

Viggiani

 Epimetheus Press, Inc.

NEW YORK

Address all inquiries to:

      Epimetheus Press, Inc.
      P. O. Box 565
      Gracie Square Station
      New York City 10028

Library of Congress Catalog Card Number: 81-67765

ISBN: 0-88008-000-0

This book was set in Vevey by TYPE SYSTEMS, INC., New York City.

For Evelyn

Introduction

Only man is more human than the pig.

Back in the old days, when alcohol was still legal, men and pigs were the only creatures that would willingly become addicted to it. Then there's the matter of body hair. Both the domestic pig and man have lost most of theirs, and their naked hides aren't pretty. The few patches of fur remaining on the human head and body are no help, since they only make the blighted areas more repulsive by contrast. Finally, like man, the pig has an ambiguous image. No one has ever been certain whether it's sacred or unclean. Especially now, after the revelations. Or, rather, after the Second Coming, if you can believe the fundamentalists.

So, since pigs are interesting, I'm doing my thesis on them. The last ruined arch of the last university here in the East collapsed a month ago, but it doesn't matter. I'm just at the fact-gathering stage now. By the time I've had the whole thing written up, someone will have built another university in the neighborhood. I guess.

While it's certainly not necessary for a farmer like myself to have an advanced degree, one can be useful. Things go easier at the feed distribution depot if the overseer is a fellow Harvard man. Naturally, as I said before, there's no longer a Harvard. But I heard a bunch of people got together and pitched a very large tent in Cambridge. Rumor has it that they're slipping a little philosophy in with the animal husbandry courses, so maybe there's hope. Supposedly, the philosophers are even agitating for a tent of their own, since something always seems to moo or bleat just when a great mind is about to cleave the veil of ignorance. The veil isn't cleft very often, needless to say, but they've managed to get it a bit threadbare in places.

The subject I've chosen for my thesis is peculiar, I admit, since I won't be raising pigs at all. I don't like them very much, even though they're interesting. Anyway, you need a special license to be a pig keeper, and the authorities aren't about to give one to me. Probably I'll grow corn and keep chickens and a few cows and goats.

To tell the truth, I'm writing about pigs because of my father Frank. He found salvation in a pigpen, or so he claimed in the last letter he sent me, mailed while he was on his way to join Guido Mocha and his band of insurgents.

I never heard from him again. Now I only know what I read in the newspapers. Every time I see another story about how they've once again swept down on the Potpourripolis Social Sanctuary complex, flaying some of the country's best social scientists and dragging the skins away behind their motorcycles like obscene trophies, I could die of humiliation and grief! How could my own father, a former police officer and good citizen, do these monstrous things?

I feel sorry for him, though, because I know he's a sick man. I feel sorry for him, even though he destroyed me. I was supposed to become a Social Sanctuary official myself until he ruined everything. I'd completed my preliminary therapy and had already gone all the way to the Middle Provinces, where the Social Sanctuary complex is located, to begin advanced training. A thousand miles I rode, on the back of a mule!

Everything was wonderful in Potpourripolis. Just as I dreamt it would be. The Social Sanctuary doesn't have a formal university situation there. It's more of a potential-realizing learning environment. They really know how to maximize and facilitate the information induction process.

My father spoiled all of this for me when he joined that rabble. Oh, the SS people were very empathic and caring. But, naturally, they couldn't let me stay on.

I just don't feel good about myself anymore. I don't know why he did this to me, but as I draft my thesis, I'm going to try to figure the whole thing out and hopefully emerge a more knowledgeable person.

Even if they build another university, I don't think I'll send my thesis there. I'll send it to the Social Sanctuary. Maybe they'll be impressed by my careful research and penetrating insights into myself and others. Maybe I'll turn up enough information to enable them to find my father and kill him. Maybe they'll take me back then, and I won't have to milk goats after all. Doing it upsets my stomach.

I'm trying very hard to be objective. As sources, I'm using *The Revelations of Our Savior Pie* (even though I'm not a fundamentalist); the excellent Social Sanctuary publication, *History for the People: Interpreted;* interviews with my father's former partner, Hilly (a magnificent person who has triumphed over severe disabilities to become an open, giving, functioning, emotionally whole human being); and my father's twisted diaries, which reveal that his deterioration had begun long before he started behaving in an overtly antisocial manner. I've even included the absurd rantings of a deranged fertilizer salesman in the next town, who claims to be God's brother-in-law and who has a large following, even though everybody knows that it was the Reillys' handyman and not God who got to his sister.

I'm going to start at the beginning, when everything suddenly went wrong. It's absurd to do it that way, I know. Why include events that are common knowledge in my account, especially since it's destined for the Social Sanctuary? The SS people are well aware of the story. Didn't they put America back together when everyone else was being extremely counterproductive and self-defeating?

But I keep thinking of an old man who told me about a book he'd found. It wasn't a sociology or law book, but one of the other kind, that you have to buy in Canada. I didn't see it, so I'm not sure it even really existed. The old man could have been lying. Or hallucinating. Senility can do that.

The book was supposedly about the Black Death, an epidemic disease of ancient times. There was a man whose friends had all died. He knew that he didn't have long to live and suspected that the entire population of the world was doomed. But just in case someone survived, he wrote, he wanted the people of the future to know what had happened.

I feel like that man, and I don't know why. From now on, things are going to get better and better. Nothing bad is going to happen.

I have a very full schedule. My goat-milking lessons alone take up a good deal of time. I don't seem to have the knack. These hands were made to hold Rorschach and Thematic Apperception

Tests, not goat teats. And the silly way an udder is constructed doesn't help matters. Ideally, all you should have to do is give a little yank for the milk to come squirting out. But, instead, you have to grab hold way at the top and force it down. The whole concept is disgusting.

Obviously, anyone as busy as I hasn't time to do stylistic justice to a thesis of this importance. I plan to send my reference material and first draft to an acquaintance of mine in Potpourripolis, who's a secretary at SS headquarters. He has access to a typewriter, and he reads a great deal, especially those strange old books that they reproduce in Canada. I can't say I approve of their subject matter, but reading them seems to have given him a feeling for words.

Since my acquaintance hasn't any legs, he should have plenty of time to polish up my thesis. Mutilation keeps one close to home, and he has to do something to pass the time.

The Social Sanctuary ordered his legs cut off an inch above the knees to discourage his habitually aggressive behavior. They hated to do it, but therapy had been ineffective. When they were certain he'd been rehabilitated, they very generously gave him a job that didn't require legs and that kept him where he could be watched for any sign of a relapse into psychopathy.

I'll write to him tomorrow, asking him to type my thesis and submit it to the Social Sanctuary in my name. I'm sure he'll be delighted to help me, since when I was in Potpourripolis, I spent many hours consoling him and explaining to him why he's really much better off now that he's part of the SS family. Also, for his own good, I reported certain hostile statements of his to the authorities. This enabled him to work out his negative feelings with a therapist and become a better person.

He told me he'd never forget what I'd done and would repay me if he ever had the opportunity. I'm happy to be able to provide him with one. I'm sure he'll do a wonderful job on my thesis.

Entered in my diary on
December 31, 2701

Part One
Wormwood

Chapter One
Pie Meets God

-1-

Around 1985 a feverish millenarianism gripped America. Everyone was preparing for beginnings and ends, but no one was sure of what. Religious and political movements dizzily formed, splintered, and disbanded. People expected tribulations, but they were thinking in terms of starvation and nuclear holocaust. Nobody anticipated anything as quaint as pestilence.

-2-

According to revelation, we were visited because God was upset with our Savior Pie. Pie was a hairy, smelly, rather stupid little man, who lived in a tenement in what was left of Manhattan. Actually, his name was Pizzadisanantonio, because he was born in a pizza parlor on the feast day of St. Anthony the Hermit. But compassionate friends and relatives shortened it to "Pie."

When Pie was seven years old, his mother became very sick. He made a vow to God that if she recovered, he would never again wash his balls. She died almost immediately, but Pie thought God might be testing him and decided not to wash his balls anyway.

In 1986 Pie was twenty years old and still had not washed his balls, although his mother continued to be dead.

-3-

Despite his limited intelligence, Pie was somewhat of a mystic and given to trances. The first one occurred when he was nine years old. As he lay on his bed, picking his nose, a strange paralysis seized his body.

The room swam before his eyes in a golden haze, and a majestic voice flowed from the light. "Pie. It's been two years. Your mother is very happy here. So please wash your balls."

"Who?" Pie asked. His finger was still in his nose, frozen there by the sudden paralysis.

"This is God," the voice continued. It sounded less majestic now, almost tired. "I repeat, please wash your balls. Even a minor disaster, like your unhygienic scrotum, can have repercussions throughout the universe. All is one."

"Bullshit!" Pie said indignantly, his common sense violated. "One is one. All . . . that something else."

There was a trace of irritation in the voice now. "I'm not here to argue eternal verities with you. The fact remains, I've been getting complaints from other planets, not to mention the woman who lives in the apartment above yours. She prays constantly, and it's beginning to get on My nerves. You'd damned well better wash your balls!"

Now Pie understood. "You devil," he said calmly. "Evil devil from Hell. My balls given to God. I no wash, mother be alive again. Like with Lazarus. So devil fuck off."

"Pie," the voice went on, mildly shocked, "do you realize how privileged you are to hear My voice?"

Pie didn't look as if he realized it at all. In fact, he seemed distinctly unimpressed.

"Blessed! You're blessed, Pie! Saints, mystics, ascetics, brilliant and odorless human beings meditate for years and practice brutal austerities, yearning for a glimpse of Me. Or a word from Me. And you've achieved what most of them could not, merely by stinking up the entire universe."

Pie simply repeated, "Fuck off, devil from Hell." He would have made the *cornuto*, but he still couldn't move his hands.

"Let me waste him, Resplendent One," said a new voice.

In his dim way, Pie was confused. "Who? More devil?"

"No," the first voice answered. "That was the archangel Michael. You can't waste him, Michael. He's not fated to go until he's ninety-one."

"Then let's take him into the bathroom and throw him under the shower."

"No good. We can't force him to wash his balls. We can only ask. Free will. Remember?"

"Yeah, yeah. How could I forget!"

"Why don't you try to reason with him? Maybe I'm too overwhelming. He might be struck senseless with awe."

Pie made a rude noise with his mouth.

"I don't know, Lord," the second voice said. "I'm not picking up a feeling of awe from him. In fact, I'm not picking up much of anything from him. I think You've managed to create someone too stupid for us to understand."

"I don't need any nasty cracks from you, Michael. It's not like you could come up with something better, so just lay off. Now will you please try to get through to him?"

The second voice sounded barely under control. "Listen, you," it said carefully. "I speak for the Lord of the Universe. If you wash your balls, He'll give you something nice."

"Send mother back."

"For your information, your mother doesn't want to come back," the first voice snapped. "When I suggested it to her, she became hysterical and nearly tore Heaven apart. I was willing. I almost performed a miracle for you. An honest-to-God miracle! An actual resurrection! You know, once I got this mess of a planet functioning by itself, I cut out miracles, for the most part. And I was ready to make an exception and perform one for you. Is it My fault your mother hates your guts?"

"Devil eat shit," Pie answered placidly. "No wash balls. Balls holy. Belong to God."

"Heaven forbid!" the first voice groaned. "Come on, Michael. Let's get out of here. The smell is even getting to Me, and I'm supposed to be above all that."

"Well, You had to have free will," complained the second voice peevishly. "You were bored, You said. Even after Satan, You still had to have Your damned free will."

"But don't you understand? Once I've given it, I can't take it back."

"Oh, hogwash!"

"What was that?" the first voice snarled. "Are you calling Me a liar? Me?"

"Take it easy. I didn't mean it that way. Maybe You can't take free will back, but You can at least stop the dominant life form on this planet from reproducing. You got rid of dinosaurs, didn't You? This place has become the slum of the universe."

"Really? Maybe you'd like to stay down here and rectify things for Me, since you're so smart."

The second voice was faint with horror. "You don't mean that! Do You?"

"Don't push your luck, Michael. Just because you're My favorite now doesn't mean you're going to be forever. You'd better remember your place and keep in mind Who created whom. Now come on."

The glow faded, and Pie was able to move again. He went off to school, proud at having resisted an assault from Hell.

Chapter Two
The Floor Plan and Fauna of Heaven

-1-

God had done a good job on the entire cosmos, but, of course, Heaven was His chef-d'oeuvre. It was a largish room at the very edge of creation. God had made it trapezoidal in shape, because He thought a rectangle would be too monotonous to look at for all eternity.

The longest wall was actually a video screen which could be tuned in to any part of the universe. God was able to focus it for anything from panoramas to extreme close-ups. His favorite throne, with the purple cushion, was directly in front of it. Although God watched the vast screen as intently as the rest of Heaven did, He was still aware of what was happening everywhere else, while the others were not.

One of the two side walls of Heaven was mirrored. God, the angels, and the Elect, once they'd passed over, were shape shifters. Newcomers to Heaven spent most of their time in front of the mirror, assuming different forms and giggling at the results.

The other side wall was also popular with the lately dead. It was blank, and they could project visible manifestations of their thoughts onto it. But after a few hundred years, they tired of both this and the mirror, and stayed by the screen, watching.

The wall at the narrow end of the room, parallel to the screen, was covered from floor to ceiling with Venetian blinds. Right after He created the angels, God warned them that if they ever raised the blinds, they would be annihilated. As He spoke, He seemed frightened, and the sight of His fear chilled them. What horror, they wondered, could be gruesome enough to scare God Himself? The warning was repeated each time a member of the Elect passed over, and everyone stayed well away from that part of the room. Only God would occasionally stand beside the blinds, move them a bit to the side, and peer out. He always looked queasy after He'd done this.

-2-

While the members of God's court lounged on the thick bed of feathers in front of the screen, they feasted. Naturally, they didn't eat duck or roast pig or cupcakes, since their bodies were too subtle for such coarse food. They gulped and gnawed at the emotions that spurted into Heaven through the screen. As something was being killed, they drank its sour terror. They watched young things a lot so they could chew at their crunchy green hope. Things having sexual intercourse produced a meaty stew with a rancid aftertaste. Jealousy was clotted and bittersweet, like orange slices in cream. They had hatred frequently, because they enjoyed the way it seared their jaded palates, and followed it with a soothing empathy treacle.

They made love as they watched the screen, usually looking at it instead of each other. On the anniversary of their deaths, the Elect got a chance to do it with God. The angels could have God any time, but most of them didn't, because they knew Michael would sulk. They all loved God, but not the way Michael did. They felt sorry for him. He really had it bad.

-3-

It was traditional for the heavenly beings to take on the appearance of the creatures they were watching on the screen. But whatever shape they assumed, God was always the most beautiful of all. And Michael, because he was closest to God, always looked the most like Him.

When the screen was tuned in to earth, God generally took the form of a man, even when He was watching women. This was in deference to the Judaic/Christian/Islamic theology that dominated the planet. Long ago He'd just as often been female. But He believed in giving people what they want.

As might be expected, in His human guise, God was tall and exquisitely proportioned. His skin was so white that the slightest excitement caused a delicate flush to spread over His entire body. Sometimes He would cut Himself for the delight that the bright blood trickling over His snowy flesh gave the angels.

His golden hair was softer than the down that carpeted the floor of Heaven. It was barely visible on most of His body and made Him seem to glow with a warm radiance. On His head, though, it curled in lavish tendrils around His handsome face and down to the soft nape of His neck. The angels loved to touch His hair. Some slipped their hands into the neck of His jewel-colored gown and coiled the luxuriant growth in His armpits around their fingers. But only Michael would reach under the skirt of His gown and stroke the feathery pubic hair that grew in a triangle up His flat belly.

God's nose, chin, eyebrows, mouth, and ears were the most perfect of their kind, but they weren't that much better than those of the average male model. It was His eyes that were exceptional. The irises were made up of lavender, blue, and silver flecks and were outlined by a thin band of silver. The flecks moved, as if they were floating in a little sea, and no one could look into God's eyes for long without getting vertigo.

God's hands were also abnormally beautiful and so white as to be luminous. When the angels turned out the lights in Heaven once, just for fun, the hands were still visible. Several feet above them the uncanny violet eyes swirled in the darkness like pinwheels. It was very unsettling, and the angels turned the lights back on immediately.

There were no lines anywhere on God's hands, and the long fingers, which He adorned with rings of ivory and moonstone, didn't seem to have knuckles. His fingernails were jagged, and there was something blackish underneath them.

Michael was a watered-down version of God. His hair was a darker blond, slightly coarser in texture and given to cowlicks. His eyes were a lovely blue, but they didn't shimmer at people out of the night. He was a bit shorter than God. His hands were rather pudgy. But, as looks went, he was still the second best creature in all the universe.

Chapter Three
Pie Remains Steadfast

As Pie grew older, the Satanic attacks which had begun in his tenth year became more intense. But pleas, threats, and bribes were all equally ineffective, and Heaven was desperate. Michael had developed nervous eczema. Gabriel suffered from a continuous migraine. Israfel had psychosomatic laryngitis. And the Elect held perfumed handkerchiefs to their noses.

Only God was unperturbed and, in fact, seemed to be finding the whole thing rather exciting. Despite the complaints of the others, He stubbornly kept the screen focused on Pie about eighty percent of the time. And even when they were looking at something else, the stench managed to find its way across the universe and into Heaven.

"I don't understand you," God teased His court. "Dead things are rotting on a billion worlds, and you're carrying on about one lousy pair of rancid balls."

"Dead things are supposed to rot," Michael told Him. "And they stop when they've finished. This is unnatural."

"Yes," added Gabriel. "It's backwards. If live things can rot, dead things will be able to get up and walk. There have to be rules."

"In the first place, he's not rotting, he's reeking," God said. "There's a difference. And, besides, I don't know what you're worried about. He's twenty now, so he only has seventy-one more years to live. What're seventy-one years, *sub specie aeternitatis?*"

"Seventy-one more years of this is longer than eternity," Michael told Him angrily. "If You don't do something, I'm going to defect!"

God did such an excellent job of seeming appalled that He almost convinced Himself. "You mean you'd actually go down there? With him?"

"Yes."

"You can't be serious!"

"I am," Michael said firmly.

"You'd trade bliss for an eternal steambath?"

"Bliss isn't supposed to stink."

God sighed. "Oh, all right. Have it your way. Screw fate. Screw free will. What's the use of being God if You can't break Your own rules once in a while. I'll get rid of Pie. I'll even send him to Hell."

"That's not enough anymore," Michael pouted. "Get rid of them all."

"The entire human race?" God asked with mock astonishment.

"Yes." Michael's exquisite lips quivered, and tears filled his eyes. "Ever since You created them, You've been ignoring us."

God seemed touched. He drew Michael to Him and kissed his wet eyes. "You know they're nothing to Me," He said gently. "Just toys. I assumed you found them amusing too."

Michael thought he detected an undercurrent of sarcasm in God's voice, but when he searched His face, he was, as usual, too distracted by its beauty to read its expression. "You were wrong," he told God. "I'm not at all amused."

The sarcasm was unmistakable now. "Oh. I was wrong. Thank you so much for letting Me know, Michael. What would I do without you to keep Me in line?"

God stretched His shimmering arm through the vastness of the universe to earth. There, He reached a slender, jeweled hand into the vagina of a Chicago prostitute, who squealed at the utter novelty of the sensation, and rearranged the genetic makeup of a certain bacterium.

He smiled crookedly at Michael. "It's done. I guess I had to give you what you wanted, or you would have left Me. You did say that, didn't you?"

Michael nodded uneasily.

God pulled him down beside Him on the throne and kissed him until his lips bled. "Watch with Me," He said and licked the blood from Michael's lips. "Their removal will be an artistic coup—protracted, yet with sustained drama." Again He swept His tongue over Michael's lips and thrust it deep into his mouth so he tasted his own blood.

"You know, you're the one who's going to be doing this,"

God whispered after they'd finished kissing.

"What? I don't even know how!" Michael protested.

"I'm doing it because I love you. So you're the real cause. Not I."

Michael had never known God to sweat before, but now he noticed that His flesh was clammy with excitement.

Chapter Four
All Fall Down

-1-

Everyone had known for years that venereal diseases were becoming resistant to penicillin. But doctors thought they'd be able to cope by using other drugs in place of penicillin, or in addition to it, while hopefully developing new and more effective antibiotics. Nobody had foreseen the sudden mutation of the syphilis spirochete into a form that thrived on penicillin and ran its fatal course in months rather than decades. It couldn't be cured, but only controlled to some extent by constantly increasing doses of all the other antibiotics.

Although this virulent form of the disease originated in Chicago, it soon spread throughout the American continent. Precautions were taken. Genitals were examined along with luggage during customs inspections. Still, by 1988, two years after the first appearance of the disease, Europe, Africa, and Asia were also infected. Nearly all humans had it. Most babies were born with it. And it had begun to be found among flocks of sheep and goats in rural areas and among the majority of house pets in New York and Los Angeles. It had even been identified as the cause of leaf mold on some of the foliage in the Brooklyn Botanical Gardens. Life as we know it was doomed.

-2-

As if the ravages of this pestilence weren't horrible enough, mankind also had to contend with the dread killer flea. These insects were the descendants of a few brought from Africa by a South American scientist for use in experiments. But the scientist was careless, and they escaped, soon becoming incredibly vicious in their wild state.

For years they'd been working their way northward. It had been hoped that they wouldn't be able to get a foothold in the United States because of the scarcity of coconuts, which were where they laid their eggs. But, unfortunately, they proved to be adaptable, laying their eggs on oranges, lemons, and pineapples when there were no vacant coconuts.

Alarmed, Washington sent an entomologist to South America, where the killer fleas had penetrated as far north as Rio. If he were able to find a way of interfering with their breeding process, their relentless advance might still be halted. But although he was the most highly skilled man in his field, his attempts were futile.

After six months he admitted defeat and prepared to return home. Exhausted and depressed, he decided to take a nap before he went to the airport. All the beds in Rio had been equipped with extra-fine mosquito netting, which enabled people to sleep without the voluminous protective clothing they had to wear during the day. For the first time since he'd arrived, the entomologist neglected to fasten it. He was too tired to think clearly. He just pulled off his clothes and sprawled naked on the bed, falling instantly asleep.

A pregnant killer flea was in the room, hovering indecisively around the ceiling. Instinct told her that it was time to deposit her eggs and that she needed to find a roundish, nourishing thing for them to cling to. Then she spied the oddest plant she had ever seen. It was big and leafless, and between two of its branches hung a double coconut with a shriveled pink root. Like most fleas, she didn't have an inquisitive nature. Without wasting time on idle speculation, she flew down and deposited her eggs on the entomologist's scrotum.

Killer flea eggs are visible, but only barely, and the groggy entomologist didn't notice them when he finally awoke and pulled on his underwear. With scrupulous care, he dressed himself in the protective clothing that he would only remove after decontamination in the boarding area of the airport. This decontamination procedure destroyed any killer flea eggs on the outer clothing, but could not be used on the skin without injuring it. Travel to killer flea-infested areas was severely restricted, and it was assumed that anyone sufficiently important to have security clearance would have enough sense not to let the insects near his balls.

Once on the plane, the entomologist began to drink heavily. There was a great deal of turbulence, and he'd never felt really comfortable in the air. Too, he was aware that he'd failed not only his superiors, but the entire human race. Soon no one would be able to venture outside without swathing himself in layers of plastic. He'd seen the few pitiful survivors of killer flea attacks, doomed to spend the remainder of their lives suspended in vats of dilute calamine lotion with only their snorkels and the needles through which they received intravenous nourishment linking them to the outside world. Mercifully, people attacked by the swarms usually died.

When he began to feel weak, he attributed it to the liquor, not realizing that deep within the recesses of his jockey shorts a mass of rapidly growing killer flea larvae was feeding on his scrotum. He might have experienced pain if he hadn't been so drunk. But he managed to sleep fitfully throughout most of the trip, his hand straying now and then to his crotch, as if to brush something away.

He was giddy and disoriented when they landed at Kennedy Airport, but still able to walk. His bladder was swollen with all the liquor he'd drunk on the plane, and he staggered through the terminal, looking for a restroom.

Some picnickers who'd come to watch the planes take off and land were just uncorking a large thermos of lemonade. At this point, the entomologist's ravaged brain was capable of processing only the most minimal information. To him, the thermos was a container, and a container was something to piss in. He reeled over to the happy, unsuspecting group, unzipped his fly, and released the now fully grown swarm.

Instead of diverting the killer fleas from the United States, the poor entomologist had imported them months, maybe even years before they would have arrived on their own. He collapsed in a state of severe shock, his devastated balls flopping out on either side of his open fly like deflated balloons. By the time the astonished picnickers found a doctor who'd believe them, the entomologist was dead.

Now that they'd discovered something softer, warmer, and tastier, killer fleas wanted nothing more to do with fruits and vegetables. Since a determined pregnant killer flea could find her way through even the plastic protective garments if she smelled a healthy pair of balls, the government was forced to take stringent measures. A special task force locked every man's penis and scrotum into a leather codpiece with a lead inner shield that prevented any enticing odor from escaping or any killer flea from getting in. Drugs which suppressed orgasm and turned urine into earwax were administered so the codpieces never had to be removed.

As had been the case with killer syphilis, it was impossible to stop the killer fleas. With their new rapacity and altered breeding habits, they spread throughout the world. Since the codpieces and the drugs taken to suppress sperm formation caused permanent sterility, it looked as if the human race would become extinct.

-3-

There was only one person in America who managed to profit from all this anguish and disruption. Dr. Niemand Lurk was a sleek, well-fed man of early middle age, who, while everyone else starved, somehow ate well enough to have a bit of a weight problem. His round face and padded body glowed with health. No matter how chaotic his surroundings, he always took excellent care of himself. Even though his beard was light, he shaved twice a day. If he had so much as a cup of coffee, he'd brush his fine white teeth immediately afterward. At a time when it was impossible to find any barber at all, since no one had money to spend on such frivolities, Lurk found an expert. The man had been plodding through the streets with a cart, trying to sell junk he'd scavenged from deserted buildings. Lurk recognized him as a former employee of one of the best salons in the city and made a standing appointment to have his thick dark hair trimmed every other Tuesday afternoon.

After the codpieces had been mandated and all the apples and oranges in the country destroyed, leaving the killer fleas unable to breed, a frost got rid of most of the adults of the species. Thorough spraying eliminated pockets of them remaining in tropical areas, and Americans could remove not only the codpieces, but the ugly plastic protective clothing as well.

When the plastic came off, the rest of the country was in rags, but Lurk was a fashion plate. He'd had the foresight to make sure his assistant, Simon, to whom he'd given a list of sizes and preferred colors, was in the mob that sacked department stores during the Great Deodorant Riots that occured at the height of the killer flea panic. Frenzied mobs, sweating and stinking at one hundred times their normal rate because of the plastic protective garments, erupted into violence when faced with deodorant rationing. At first they only raided toiletries counters, but when the supply of deodorant ran out, they stripped other parts of the stores bare as well.

Simon hadn't bothered to get any clothes for himself during the raid. He was perfectly content with his ancient blue polyester suit, a pair of dungarees, a few shirts, and a fleece-lined jacket. In his attitude toward clothes, as in most other respects, he was his employer's opposite. Although he was around ten years younger than Lurk, his wizened little face made him seem the older of the two. He was short, and as sallow and bony as the other man was robust. His eyes were small and black, and the tight curls of his hair, which was the same dark brown as Lurk's, had a greasy sheen. The few badly discolored teeth that were left in his mouth ached. He never went anywhere without a pocketful of codeine tablets to ward off the pain.

Simon had once hoped to be a doctor himself. But he was kicked out of medical school when he made a minor error one night in the lab and the next day twelve people whom he'd been supplying with illegal drugs died in agony. Nothing could be proven, but the university administration was able to use his low grades as a pretext for expelling him.

Simon had originally answered an ad Lurk placed for a secretary. His talents were soon recognized, though, and he was made an assistant. Most patients assumed he was a doctor too. He lived in a room in Lurk's house and followed him everywhere, like a shadow that had gone slightly askew.

When he'd graduated from medical school in 1982, Lurk had become an abortionist. It had been a good business in those days, when there was still a surplus of humans. But times changed, and Lurk prided himself on being a man who could change with them. As soon as he realized that his branch of medicine was becoming obsolete, he began to search for a new way to apply his talents.

In 1995, using money he'd accumulated running his profitable abortion mill, Lurk took Simon with him to various remote areas of the world, where they managed to find a total of thirty men who had neither contracted killer syphilis nor been subjected to the sperm-suppressing drugs. It was easy to smuggle them back into the States, since the entire world was in chaos. Most of the bureaucracies, among them customs and immigration, had all but collapsed.

Lurk kept these thirty men locked in his clinic under absolutely sterile conditions and milked them daily. His patients paid exorbitant sums to be artificially inseminated, even knowing that the children would be born deformed from their mothers' killer syphilis and probably wouldn't live long. Soon Lurk was a rich man and becoming ever richer.

Chapter Five

Heaven Gets Mad at God, God Gets Mad at Heaven, and Everyone Sulks

Heaven was extremely impatient.

Everybody but Pie was dying. He'd never had sexual intercourse, so he escaped killer syphilis. And the fungus growing on his balls discouraged even the most avid killer fleas, since it had a tendency to eat them.

He'd managed to avoid the codpiece as well, though not intentionally. Because he didn't like to see anything go to waste, he made frequent trips to the basement with a pail to gather ashes from the furnace. In his fifteen years as super of an upper East Side tenement, he'd filled nearly an entire room of his apartment with his treasure.

On the day the National Guard had attached codpieces to the males in his neighborhood, he'd made the error of standing up inside the furnace and getting his head stuck in the flue for three hours. The National Guard was gone by the time he worked himself loose, and since everybody avoided him because of his smell, no one even told him what had happened. He did notice that people were wearing plastic, so he started throwing a shower curtain over himself when he went out to shop for groceries, just to be polite.

The angels and the Elect beseeched God to make special arrangements for getting rid of Pie quickly—a bolt of lightning, for instance. Otherwise, it looked like he just might live to be ninety-one after all, and they didn't think they could take it when they'd had hopes of an early deliverance. They reminded God that way back in 1986 He'd promised them only one more year of Pie's balls, and that was nearly fifteen years ago.

God was obstinately deaf to their pleas. He was in a rotten mood, in fact. At first He'd found the extermination of the earth people great fun, especially when He could still make Michael cringe squeamishly by reminding him that he was to blame for all that suffering. But Michael's qualms were short-lived. He'd never liked humans, and now he couldn't help taking a delighted interest in their misery. Many parts of the globe had not yet rid themselves of killer fleas, and he had a disconcerting way of shouting "Got one!" every time a swarm attacked somebody.

God thought this was in very poor taste. He was beginning to miss the soap opera the humans had once provided. They were too feeble now to do much but lie around in a very uninteresting way. He switched the dial to other worlds, looking for diversion, but nowhere did He find the total baseness that had so amused Him when He used to watch the earthlings.

"I think I'll save them," He announced one day, to the consternation of all Heaven.

Michael turned on Him furiously. "I was right! You do like them better!"

"Maybe I do, you damned twit!"

With this, God rolled Himself up into a seamless golden sphere and refused to talk to anyone.

Heaven was aghast.

Michael gathered his courage and knocked on the sphere, only to have a jet of black, brackish liquid squirted into his face.

"God is dead," ventured Nietzsche uncertainly.

"No," Michael said, wiping his face on his sleeve. "He did this once before, a long time ago."

"During that nasty business with Satan?" Nietzsche asked.

"No." Michael looked nervously at the sphere and dropped his voice to a whisper. "When you-know-who was born."

Nietzsche shook his head. "I'm afraid I don't know who."

"You know," Michael said, stretching his arms out to the sides and letting his head fall forward.

"Oh. But I thought that was His son."

"Shhh!" Michael cautioned. "Don't ever say that again! Everyone is always trying to pin things like that on Him, and it makes Him furious. He not only didn't do, you know, *that* with that woman, He didn't even create what's-his-name."

"I thought He'd created everyone," Nietzsche said with surprise. "By indirect means, of course," he hastened to add, glancing apprehensively at the sphere. "I didn't mean to imply that any hanky-panky was going on."

"Well, He didn't create that one. They did." Michael pointed a disdainful finger at the screen, where earth was in its death throes.

"People?"

"Yes. They decided what a god should be like and actually summoned one up. No one knows quite how they did it. Not even...." He shrugged in the direction of the sphere. "Of course, it didn't work out. He was dealt with."

"But what about all those churches?"

"Haven't you ever noticed how the unluckiest wretches are always described as 'a wonderful person who served his community and was active in his church'? I don't need to remind you who passes out the luck, good or bad."

Nietzsche shook his head sadly. "It's ironic. They're so absolutely certain they're right."

"If they were," Michael said with a wink, "you wouldn't be up here now, would you?"

The Elect had begun to grumble.

"How long is He going to stay like that?"

"He has certain obligations as a host, after all."

"That scum down there is nearly eliminated, so what's His problem? He wasn't serious about wanting to save them, was He?"

"I'm afraid He was," Michael told them. "He has a vulgar streak. Now that there's almost nothing disgusting left, He's bored."

"You mean we're not enough for Him?" one of the Elect asked indignantly.

"Apparently not. If we don't let Him keep a few of those...." Michael looked contemptuously at the image of earth on the screen. "... or maybe even Pie himself, He's apt to bring Satan and his crew up here."

"What?"

"With us?"

"The very idea!"

"I wouldn't put it past Him," Michael said. "He's threatened as much before."

"Well, let Him keep the horrid things then," one of the angels sighed.

A member of the Elect gingerly approached the sphere and circled it, examining it with interest. "Can He hear us when He's like this?" he asked Michael.

"I'm still omniscient," the sphere snapped, "so watch your ass!"

Everyone, even Michael, backed well away from the thing.

God resumed His quasi-human form. "I'm going to save humanity," He announced, "and if any of you holier-than-thou types object, I'm busing in the entire population of Hell."

Many faces were less than radiant, but no one dared protest openly.

"Come on!" God told Michael. "We're going to see Pie."

Michael's nose twitched with disgust. "What on earth for?"

"He's going to be the savior of the human race."

"You've got to be kidding!" Michael sniggered.

"Not at all. Outside of thirty men in a certain Dr. Niemand Lurk's clinic, Pie is the only man in the world who's still fertile. Also, the fungus on his scrotum is a new and powerful antibiotic. It's the only thing that can cure the devastating strain of syphilis I invented."

"But if we tell him to save the world, he won't listen to us," Michael said. "He never listens to us."

"Leave it to Me," God told him smugly.

Chapter Six
Pie Receives His Mission

Pie was in his bedroom, cataloguing ashes. Since he was illiterate, this involved separating darker ones from lighter ones and making neat piles of each shade in various parts of the room.

He'd just made the momentous discovery that rat shit was mixed in with the ashes and had stopped work to ponder the question of whether or not this was desirable. So preoccupied was he with the rat shit dilemma that God and Michael had to glow very energetically before he noticed them at all. When he did, he merely said, "Devils fuck off," and continued his meditations.

"I told You so," Michael said. "How do You propose to get him to save the world when he thinks You're a devil?"

"I'm going to materialize."

Michael gasped. "What? A theophany? Why, the sight of You will sear his mortal eyes and blast his puny brain! I don't think he could even take You through a glass darkly."

"He could if it's polarized," God said. "Just watch."

A pair of polarized cool-ray sunglasses appeared in the air above Pie and dropped into his lap. He picked them up and looked at them with mild interest.

"Put them on, Pie," God commanded majestically, lowering and slowing down His voice so that it was audible to human ears. "You have resisted the wiles of the devil and have earned the right to see Me face to face."

"Very clever," Michael told Him.

"I'm not God for nothing."

"You real God?" Pie asked the glow suspiciously.

God's voice was impressive yet benign. "Put the sunglasses on to protect yourself from My radiant countenance, and you shall see and be convinced that I am truly the Lord thy God."

Pie put the sunglasses on, and God materialized as an elderly, white-robed man with a snowy beard and a triple-tiered halo.

Michael recoiled at the sight. "Yecchh! You look like hell!

Don't come anywhere near me until You've done something about Yourself."

Pie had sunk reverently to his knees and was gazing at God with adoration.

God nudged Michael. "See? They expect it." He addressed Pie in a rolling voice that sounded like muted thunder. "You have done well, My son, to have withstood the Tempter."

"Devil come and come!" Pie sobbed. "Want me wash balls. But I save for You, Dominus Vobiscuit." He unzipped his fly and pulled his rancid balls out through the opening.

Michael choked and withdrew his luminance to a distant corner of the room, near the ceiling.

But God was made of sterner stuff. "You've done well, Pie," He repeated, only gagging slightly.

"Take!" Pie insisted. "They Yours!"

God shook His head. "I can't, Pie, as much as I'd like to. Your balls belong to the world."

The patch of brightness that was Michael took on a distinctly greenish hue.

"I no wash balls, You send mother back," Pie said tremulously. "We have deal."

"I'll send her back to you," God lied. "I don't welsh. But first you must save mankind."

"How do that?"

"With your balls, which, by My benediction. . . ." God raised His hand in a blessing. " . . . I have made sacred."

Pie looked from his balls to God with a puzzled expression.

"Now you must go forth and join with all the women in America," God continued.

"Huh? What You mean?" Pie asked.

"You must have relations with them."

"All my relations in Brooklyn and Newark, New Jersey."

God sighed impatiently. "You must fuck them, Pie."

"Oh, no!" Pie said with horror. "Fucking sin! Fucking dirty!"

"It wouldn't be, if you'd wash your damned balls," Michael grumbled from the ceiling.

"You shut up!" God snapped. He pulled a parchment from His robe and handed it to Pie.

"What?" Pie asked, taking it and holding it upside down a couple of inches from his face.

"It's a special dispensation," God said. "See? It's in Latin. You can fuck all the women in America with impunity . . . that is, without going to Hell."

Pie carefully rolled up the parchment and put it in his pocket. "How many women in America?"

"Hmm, with the plagues and all," God said thoughtfully, "I guess around ten thousand."

"No can do!" Pie gasped. "Five hundred, maybe. But ten thousand? No can do."

"Ah, but you can." God raised His hand again in blessing. "I have just given you the power to have twenty ejaculations a day."

Pie stared at Him blankly.

"To come, Pie," God explained. "You'll be able to come twenty times a day."

Pie looked down at his cock dubiously, but God gave him an encouraging pat on the shoulder. "You can do it. Now go forth and fuck this nation!"

Pie nodded. "I fuck it good, Dominus Vobiscuit! You see! Just wait!"

"There is one thing you must remember," God added. "This is very, very important. Before you stick your cock in a woman, you must rub some of the, uh, stuff that's growing on your balls on the tip of it. Do you understand?"

Pie nodded again.

"So, get to work!" God commanded as He dissolved back into a patch of light.

Chapter Seven
Mission Accomplished

"What was really written on that parchment You gave him?" Michael asked God as they soared back to Heaven.

"I don't know. I didn't bother to read it. I just thought it into My robe pocket from the ruins of the nearest library. It was chosen completely at random."

"If it was chosen at random, how come it happened to be in Latin? That's very convenient randomness."

"My kind of randomness usually is," God said with a trace of bitterness in His voice.

They sailed into Heaven through the screen, and God called everyone over. "Something good is coming on," He announced. "Pie is going to save the world."

They all crowded eagerly around the screen while God focused it on Pie's bedroom. After the picture was nice and clear, He sat on His throne and drew Michael down beside Him.

Pie had taken off the sunglasses and was standing in the middle of his bedroom, holding his cock. He knew he was supposed to do something with it, but he wasn't quite sure what. Although his teachers in parochial school had told him fucking was a sin, they'd never described how to commit it. And he'd begun to stink around the time his peers were finding out about sex, so they didn't want to spend enough time with him to discuss it at any length.

As he stood there trying to piece scraps of information into a coherent idea of exactly what fucking was, the voice of a female meat vendor drifted in through his open window. "Horse meat! Dog meat! Choice cuts!"

Her voice seemed to awaken a response in Pie. He looked toward the window, then at his cock, which was gradually stiffening. When it was fully erect, he walked out of his apartment, down the stairs, and into the street.

The few passers-by and the squatters in the largely gutted buildings watched curiously as Pie approached the meat vendor with his penis thrust out of his open fly. It had been so long since the women had seen one that some of them weren't any more certain than he had been what he was going to do with it.

Meat vendors were the only people in the city other than Niemand Lurk who got enough to eat. This one was enormously fat, and her bulk was further increased by the three dresses she was wearing. She didn't want to leave her extra clothing in her hovel for fear it would be stolen.

Pie had a difficult time finding his way, but he somehow managed to blunder through layers of clothing and flaps of skin to complete an act he knew only through instinct and hearsay. It wasn't at all bad, he decided, and he wondered why it had been a sin.

The meat vendor didn't try to stop him. She was a little puzzled, but not very, and yawned a few times while it was going on. When he'd finished, she got up, straightened her clothes, and continued along the street without a backward glance.

"The idiot forgot," God sighed. "Well, I'm not going back down there."

A fearsome voice that seemed to come from the sky was heard on Pie's street. "Hey, stupid!" it boomed, rattling the few windowpanes that were left and shaking leaves from the trees. "Didn't I tell you to rub some of that gunk from your balls on the head of your cock before you fucked?"

Everyone trembled and stared with dread at the empty sky.

Pie fell to his knees in anguish. "Sorry! Sorry! Bad sin!" He pulled the lace out of one of his shoes and began to flagellate his cock with it.

"Oh, will you stop that!" God told him irritably. "The damned thing has to be in working order. Now go do the rest of the women that are standing around."

Pie got up, but when he tried to walk, his shoe fell partially off, tripping him.

"Put the lace back in your shoe," God groaned.

Pie sat down and put the lace back in his shoe. Then he looked up at the sky for further instructions.

"Now tie it," God said patiently.

After a few false starts, Pie got it tied.

"Now go fuck," God told him. "I'm signing off." He rested His head wearily on Michael's shoulder. "The meat vendor's child will be deformed," He said, "but as long as Pie follows My instructions, the rest will be okay. The antibiotic action of his scrotal fungus will cure the potential mothers of killer syphilis at the same time they're being impregnated."

Pie started on the other women. They didn't object, but only turned their faces away as he pulled them to the ground so as not to breathe his stench head-on.

"Look at them!" the angel Gabriel said priggishly. "Right in the street! They're no better than animals!" He grabbed one of the Elect and soon was rolling around with her on the feathery carpet.

As they watched the screen, the rest of the Heavenly Host began to rub against one another during the good parts. God and Michael were kissing. Michael's eyes were closed, and his arms were twined around God's neck. But God embraced Michael almost absently. His attention was on Pie.

Chapter Eight
Lurk Presents a Problem

-1-

Some months later, Dr. Niemand Lurk was sitting in his office, drinking a chocolate-flavored antibiotic cocktail. Usually he had strawberry, but the ice cream truck that serviced his neighborhood had been out of it.

At the beginning of the killer syphilis emergency, the government had converted all ice cream trucks in the country into MDVs, or Medication Distribution Vehicles. Lurk was galled that he, a doctor, as well as a man of wealth and position, had to stand in the street and wait on line for his antibiotic like any common slob. But in the early days there had been profiteering in antibiotics, and now government regulations were so stringent that even doctors like Lurk weren't allowed to maintain a private supply.

Around this time of the morning Lurk always listened very carefully for the tinkling of the bell, since the trucks went through each neighborhood only once a day. Anybody who missed the truck had to pick up his dose at the government depot, where there were long lines, numerous forms to be filled out, and energetic interrogations to discourage those who might be trying to get extra medication to sell on the black market. It wasn't enough simply to require that everyone swallow his dose in the presence of the official distributor, since people had been known to go to great and disgusting lengths to recover the drugs before they were absorbed by the stomach lining. A good deal of money could be made smuggling antibiotics into Canada and Mexico, where there wasn't enough to treat the entire population.

Lurk would have liked to increase his already sizable income in this way, but he had too much to lose. He didn't want to do anything that might jeopardize his business, which was booming. From where he sat, he could see his waiting room reflected in a mirror he'd installed for that purpose. Even now, two hours before clinic was to start, all the chairs were occupied by nervous women, fidgeting and thumbing through his brochures.

The artificial-insemination racket was okay, he supposed. The money was good. And he enjoyed knowing that the future of the entire human race was in his hands. It gave him a feeling of potency that he sadly needed, since his genitals were as atrophied as everyone else's from the codpiece and sperm suppressant. But still, something was missing. He'd been happier as a simple abortionist, because then at least he'd had a dream.

It had been a long time since Lurk had allowed himself to think about his dream. But now, suddenly, it filled his mind with all its original sweetness. It would have been a way for him to satisfy the creative side of his nature, and Lurk felt himself to be a very creative man.

He'd planned to open up a suicide parlor, where people could either end their lives quickly, by some means designed by him that would combine appalling violence with a witty personal statement, or slowly, by handpicking a fatal illness. Lurk had worked out a deal with a nearby hospital, which had agreed to trade him diseased organs for healthy ones. If one of his customers opted to die of cancer of the liver, for instance, he could swap his healthy liver for somebody else's cancerous one. It had been a brilliant idea, but the disasters ruined everything. When everyone was dying, no one wanted to anymore.

Now Lurk's only creative outlet was photography. The walls of his clinic were covered with his work. His favorite pictures were of ritual circumcisions, taken back in the good old days when people still had something to circumcise. Lately, the only subjects he was able to find were starving beggars and ruined buildings. There weren't even any animals to photograph, since they'd all been eaten.

-2-

As Lurk was finishing his antibiotic drink, Simon came into the room, carrying a rack of test tubes.

"How was the yield?" Lurk asked.

"Pretty good. They were all able to come up with at least a test tube full, and Windooga managed two." Simon set the rack down on a white metal table and began placing stoppers in the test tubes. He glanced out the office door at the waiting room. "Full house, I see. I'm glad the boys were up to snuff."

"Did you give them their steaks and orange juice?"

"Yes. They're all happy as larks, eating and looking through your illustrated gynecology texts. They should be ready to make another donation after lunch."

Outside, a meat vendor was calling her wares. "Dog meat! Cat meat! Choice cuts!"

"I could sure go for a cat meat patty," Simon said.

Lurk made a face. "I don't know how you can eat that crap. It's half rotten. She doesn't have refrigeration or even a block of ice in that filthy cart of hers."

"It doesn't matter. She comes here first thing in the morning, before it has a chance to spoil."

"But maybe it's left over from yesterday."

"No," Simon protested. "She butchers the stock for the day every morning. I've noticed that the blood under her fingernails is still pretty wet."

"So go get your cat meat patty. But just don't eat it in here," Lurk said.

Simon left through a side door so he wouldn't have to parry a lot of anxious questions from the women in the waiting room. He trotted across the lawn, calling to the vendor, who was already a way down the street.

She stopped and let him catch up with her. "Help you, sir?" she asked.

"Let me have a portion of cat meat," Simon told her.

"Will that be raw, sir, or shall I fry it for you, like always?"

"Fry it up, please. I can't cook it back at the clinic, because my boss doesn't care for the smell."

"Some people don't know what's good," the woman replied. She turned on a gas grill at the front of her wagon, formed a patty from some ground cat meat, and slapped it on the griddle.

While the patty was cooking, Simon idly examined the vendor. He noticed that she was even fatter than usual, particularly in the abdomen. "You look like you're expecting," he joked.

She glanced down at her bulging gut. "Yeah. Six months gone."

Simon was stunned. True, she made a few dollars. And, because of her job, she ate regularly. But she couldn't have anywhere near enough money to afford Lurk's clinic. Besides, he acted as receptionist and would certainly have recognized her in the waiting room. And she him. He was one of her steady customers.

He took the cooked patty, which she offered him on a small square of waxed paper, and paid her. While he ate, he walked very slowly back to the clinic so he'd finish before he went inside.

"I didn't know you took charity cases, boss," he teased Lurk as he stepped into the office.

Lurk was puzzled. No one had ever accused him of charity before. "What do you mean?"

"Don't tell me the meat vendor paid the going rate."

"The meat vendor?"

"Yes. She's six months pregnant, and this is the only place in the country she could have gotten that way."

Lurk jumped to his feet, glaring at Simon. "It didn't happen here! How do you know she's pregnant?"

Simon traced a wide arc over his own flat abdomen to suggest an enormous bulge.

"Maybe it's a tumor," Lurk said desperately.

"Maybe," Simon conceded. "I never thought of that."

"You didn't leave the dormitory door unlocked, did you? I mean, you don't think one of the fellows got out for an hour or so?"

Simon was offended. "I never forget the doors, boss. You know me better than that."

"You've always been very careful," Lurk agreed. "But how did it happen then?"

"Like you said, it's probably a tumor."

"But it could also mean someone's poaching on my territory," Lurk told him grimly. "And if the meat vendor can afford his services, he's underselling me as well." He opened a desk drawer and took out a gun, which he placed in a shoulder holster under his suit jacket. "I have to check this out. Which way is she heading?"

"North on First Avenue. But, boss, what about all those women in there?" Simon glanced toward the waiting room.

"Take their names, and if I'm not back by the time clinic is due to open, inseminate them for me. They all think you're a doctor, so they won't give you any trouble."

-3-

Lurk stepped out into the cool morning air. He walked to First Avenue and spotted the vendor some distance away. At first he followed swiftly, until he'd nearly caught up with her. Then he paused. He planned to throw a scare in her by pulling his gun in case she was reluctant to answer questions. But there were still too many people around, and you couldn't predict what the rabble would do if they saw his gun. They might run away. On the other hand, they might jump him for threatening one of their own. He decided to follow the meat vendor at a distance until they were in a more isolated area.

Although Lurk tried to be unobtrusive, he couldn't help but attract attention, since he was the only person on the street who didn't look half dead. His fat little feet were well shod, and his fat little hands glittered with rings. As the people he passed gaped at him, he stared defiantly back. And made a horrible discovery. About half the women he saw were visibly pregnant, despite their bare feet and ragged clothes, which made him quite certain that they couldn't even have afforded the registration fee at his clinic, much less an actual insemination. It was worse than he'd thought. Obviously, someone had organized a vast, well-planned operation, similar to his own, only cut-rate.

Pie was just returning from a walking tour of New England, where he'd gone to do God's work as the Johnny Appleseed of sperm. He'd entered the city limits around dawn and was trudging wearily toward his apartment for a few hours of sleep before he resumed his labors.

Lurk became aware of a nauseating odor. So did the other people on the street, but they didn't seem to find it offensive, he noticed. They moved to the curbs and knelt devoutly. Lurk did the same to avoid attracting even more attention than he already had. But he placed a handkerchief under his knees so he wouldn't soil his neatly pressed pants. The smell grew to a stomach-wrenching intensity, and he was glad he hadn't eaten a heavy breakfast.

Three women, two of them pregnant, were kneeling close to Lurk. They were whispering together, their pinched faces flushed with excitement. As Pie plodded into view, they became even more agitated. Lurk watched as the two pregnant ones pushed and encouraged their companion until she got up and went to stand in the middle of the street, facing Pie. When he reached the woman, Pie drew her to the ground.

As they coupled, Lurk burned with hatred. He knew he was looking at his financial ruin. When they'd finished and the woman had returned to her friends, Lurk got to his feet. He stalked over to Pie and planted himself in front of him, his hand inside his jacket, wrapped around the gun.

Pie gave him a bored look. "No do men. Screw off, faggot." He pushed past Lurk and continued up First Avenue.

Lurk stared after him, and his hatred grew to murderous fury. He began to walk, following Pie now instead of the meat vendor. As soon as they reached an alley, he decided, he'd drag his competitor into it and put him out of business. He trembled with indignation. The unmitigated nerve of the man! He was giving it away! For free! Lurk smiled coldly. He knew where he was going to aim the gun.

Chapter Nine
God Sends Michael to the Devil

-1-

Michael tugged at God's robe. "You'd better do something, or Your repopulation project is going to come to an abrupt end."

"You have a point," God agreed. "There's an alley just a couple of blocks ahead, so I'll put them on hold for the time being." He turned off the universe and continued. "I'm going to offer Lurk a deal. In exchange for getting out of the pregnancy business, I'll give him exclusive rights to the V.D. cure. He can harvest the fungus from Pie's balls. It's so potent that he'll be able to manufacture vast quantities of antibiotic from it.

"And it must be pointed out to him that it's to his advantage to change businesses. Only fifty percent of the population can become pregnant, but one hundred percent will buy his killer syphilis cure."

"What are You going to do?" Michael asked. "Appear to Lurk and tell him all this?"

"No. From what I've seen of him, I don't think I'm his type. You'll have to do Me a favor, Michael. Run down to Hell and tell Satan I want to see him."

"Run down to Hell!" Michael complained. "Just like that! What do You care about my sensibilities?"

God licked Michael's nostrils with His long pink tongue. "Please? For Me?"

"I'm going," Michael sighed.

God waved His hand in the air and produced a shiny yellow asbestos poncho with a hood. "You'd better put this on. You know how it is down there."

"I sure do," Michael said glumly. He put on the poncho and disappeared through the screen.

-2-

Although there was only one Heaven, every world had its own hell. This was because the Reprobate greatly outnumbered the Elect. The hells were located in the centers of their respective planets and were presided over by fallen angels.

Satan, ruler of earth's hell, was a thin angel with narrow shoulders, a bad complexion, and a bald spot. When Michael arrived, he found him sitting next to his torment machine, an enormous electric corn popper. It sizzled angrily, spattering Michael's poncho with butter and brimstone. The Reprobate were spewed briefly out of its maw, only to fall back again with piteous cries.

Satan raised his hand in a listless greeting when he saw Michael.

"How's it going?" Michael asked him politely.

"Can't complain."

"I guess it's less work for you since God made that thing electric," Michael observed, looking at the corn popper.

"I don't know. At least when there was coal to shovel, I had something to do," Satan told him. "Now I get kind of bored. But I have the television set, and I just got a bunch of really good horror-movie cassettes."

"Great. So things are pretty comfortable down here now."

Satan looked around critically. "Do you think so? It seems too antiseptic, in a greasy sort of way. Too bare." He patted a book which lay next to him. "I've been reading this *Inferno* by a guy named Dante, and he has some nice ideas. Maybe I'll redecorate."

"Good for you. You should never let your job become routine," Michael said. "Why don't you tell His Grace about your plans when you see Him," he continued, by way of easing into the reason for his visit.

"I don't intend to see Him," Satan answered firmly. "He's always criticizing me. Nothing I do is ever enough."

"You shouldn't feel that way. You just caught Him in a bad mood a few times. He really likes you a lot."

"I'll bet!" Satan sneered. But he looked slightly mollified.

Michael pressed his advantage. "He talks about you all the time."

" "I can imagine," Satan said bitterly. "Whenever He needs a bad example."

"He sent me here to invite you for a visit. Would He have done that if He didn't like you?"

"Who knows why He does anything!"

"Look, do you really care why He wants to see you?" Michael argued. "Isn't it enough just to get out of this place for a while?"

Satan looked around at the greasy cement floor and walls, the spluttering corn popper, and the television set, whose picture was never quite in focus. "You're on," he told Michael.

Chapter Ten
God Sends the Devil to Lurk

-1-

God's eyes glittered with excitement when Michael and Satan flew in through the screen. "Ah! Satan! My Adversary! I suppose you've come with your mouth filled with blasphemies to heap abuse on Me."

Satan groaned. "Oh, please, not that! I can never think of anything to say."

"Would it kill you to prepare a little something and memorize it?" God snapped.

"How was I supposed to know You were going to send for me? It doesn't happen very often, after all."

"Okay, okay. Forget it." God looked closely at the pimples on Satan's face. "There must be a lot of pus in some of those," He said with interest.

"Sorry. I squeezed them all this morning."

God's eyes glazed over with boredom, and He sank back into the cushions of His throne. "I have a job for you," He told Satan.

"Oh, no!" Satan whined. "Not another rebellion!"

"Nothing like that," God assured him. "Get the makeup boys!" He ordered Michael.

Michael went to fetch two of the Elect who had been connected with the theater during their earthly existence. They'd remained obsessed with the mirror longer than usual and weren't with the others around the screen.

Satan backed apprehensively away from God. "I know what it is! I know what You have planned! You want me to play the heavy with some of Your scummy earth people, right?"

"Come on," God coaxed. "I'm only asking you because you're so good at it."

"Hah! You're only asking me because You know how much I hate it! You always make me visit the most disgusting people imaginable. Why can't I ever go to see somebody nice?"

"Oh shut up!" God told him. "What makes you think that somebody nice would want to see you?"

Michael had returned with the makeup men, who were setting up their tools and pots of color near Satan. He looked as if he were about to dive back through the screen.

"Sit down!" God commanded, discerning his intention.

Satan sank to the floor and sat there miserably while the makeup men used black paint to extend his eyebrows and the corners of his eyes nearly to his temples.

"Very sinister," God said approvingly. "Maybe put a little red under his eyes. And be sure to powder his lips."

"Would you like to see yourself?" one of the makeup men asked Satan when they'd finished.

He shook his head glumly.

"You know, you have a choice," God told him.

"I do?" he asked hopefully. "You mean I don't have to . . . "

"Between black and red leotards," God continued with a nasty smile. "Now strip!"

Satan wearily pulled off his grease-stained robe and stood naked before God, shivering more from embarrassment than cold. After the Fall, God had afflicted him with knock-knees and a protruding navel. He could hear the Elect and even some of the angels giggling as they looked at him.

God dangled two pairs of leotard tights, one black and one red, in front of him. "Well?" He asked. "What's it going to be?"

Satan grabbed the red ones, just to get something on. After he'd struggled into them while the Heavenly Court chortled with delight, God gave him a long black velvet cape with a red silk lining. He put it on and clutched the two ends together over his skinny chest. "Who am I supposed to see on earth?" he asked dully.

"A Dr. Niemand Lurk," God told him. "He's in New York City, at First Avenue and Ninetieth Street. You won't have any trouble recognizing him. He's a tallish, piggy-looking man, and he's wearing a hand-tailored, three-piece suit. That's two more pieces than anyone else down there has."

"What do I tell him?"

"First you have to stop him from killing Pie. That's a dirty little fellow who's walking a few paces ahead of him. You won't have any trouble recognizing him either. He has this certain smell. So what you have to do is jump out in front of Lurk or something. You know. Get his attention. Then give him this message."

God explained the message several times in great detail, since Satan wasn't very bright. Finally, He gave up and wrote it out on a piece of paper with His silver Boss pen. He handed the paper to Satan. "Don't exert yourself. Just make the introductory spiel and give him this."

–2–

God turned the universe back on, and Satan hurtled to earth, wrapped in a shell of multicolored lights. It was decided that under the circumstances he should make a grand entrance. He landed at Lurk's feet and climbed out of his ball of light, smiling uncertainly. "Hi!" he said.

Lurk stared at him in mute astonishment.

"I'm Satan, the Dark Angel," he explained.

"Do you have any I.D.?" Lurk asked him suspiciously. "I don't even believe in God, much less Satan."

"Oh, well . . . " Satan wondered what to do next. He'd never appeared to an atheist before. "Well, I dropped from the sky," he offered lamely. "I bet you couldn't do that."

"That's true," Lurk acknowledged. "I don't know if you're a devil, but obviously you're something."

"Then you'll listen to me?"

"I guess so." Lurk looked in Pie's direction and saw that he hadn't gone far and was moving slowly. "For a while anyway."

Satan followed his glance. "That must be Pie."

"Is that his name?" Lurk asked. "What else do you know about him?"

"You mustn't kill him," Satan blurted out. "He hasn't completed his mission yet."

"His mission?"

"Yes. He's supposed to repopulate the earth. Or a lot of it anyway. And he's only just started. If you don't interfere, I'm prepared to make it worth your while."

Lurk thought about this. Then he shook his head. "It's not just a question of money. Maybe I'm a crazy romantic, but I like earth the way it is now. It's so . . . I don't know . . . nice and barren. My babies don't ruin it. Killer syphilis gets them before they're old enough to take up much room. But from what you tell me, Pie's are going to be built to last."

Satan was at a loss. "Excuse me for a couple of minutes," he told Lurk. "Stay where you are. I'll be right back. I have to check something in my files." He climbed into his ball of light and shot up to Heaven.

–3–

"I heard," God told Satan when he repeated Lurk's words. "I was watching the whole thing, after all. And I like that man's style. Marvelous! He thinks the world is 'so nice and barren.' Why don't you ever say anything like that?"

Satan was offended. "Because I'm not a psychopath," he said bitterly. "Some of the people that turn You on are absolutely disgusting. Lurk's sick! He actually wants his own species to be annihilated! He'd be a social pariah in my corn popper. Even the Reprobate have better taste than You."

Although God was becoming annoyed, He knew that once Satan worked himself into a really intense whine, there was no stopping him. So He decided to try diplomacy. "Look, I'm doing this for you," He told Satan in a wheedling voice. "Lurk has talent. If you convince him to play ball with us, I just might let him take over Hell for you when he dies. Then you could come back up here."

"Do You mean it?" Satan asked carefully, torn between hope and skepticism.

"I give you My word," God promised, "and you know I never lie."

Satan seemed dubious.

"People get the wrong idea sometimes," God added hastily, "but that's not My fault."

Satan figured he didn't have anything to lose and might possibly have something to gain. "Okay, I'll do my best with him," he told God. "But what do You want me to tell him he'll get as a bonus for giving up all his precious waste and desolation?"

"Tell him that after the population has been increased to a viable level, monsters will emerge from the bowels of the earth and strike terror into mankind. He ought to get off on that."

"What monsters?" Satan scoffed. "I live right in the center of the earth, and I've never seen anything like that."

"They exist," God assured him. "Some have been there since the Creation and some were swallowed up by a couple of My super spectacular cataclysms."

Satan was beginning to feel very nervous. "You mean there are . . . things . . . down there with me? Crawling around?"

"Relax. They don't get down that far."

"Are You sure?"

God fixed him with a stare of icy contempt. "Of course I'm sure, you damned fool. I'm God. Now get back to Lurk."

Satan's chin trembled. "All right. I'm going. But I just want You to know it wasn't very nice of You to use that word."

"What word?"

" 'Damned.' You needn't rub it in." Satan climbed into his ball and disappeared in a huff.

"Say you'll send the monsters," God called after him. "Don't mention Me. It wouldn't look right."

-4-

Satan skidded to an angry stop in front of Lurk. "You're getting monsters," he said abruptly as he stepped out onto the street.

"Huh?"

"If you don't kill Pie," Satan explained, "after the population's adequate again, I'll send hideous monsters. They'll slither up out of the earth. It'll be really disgusting, and you'll be there to see it."

Lurk's face brightened. "What kind? What'll they look like?"

"Oh . . . " Satan tried to remember some of the horror films he'd seen, but his mind went blank. "Oh . . . hideous . . . awful," he said desperately. "I couldn't even describe them to you without making us both sick."

"Well, that part of the deal sounds interesting," Lurk said, "but what about the money angle? If I let Pie live, he'll ruin my business. Let's face it. He's turning out a better product. And for free, damn his soul!"

"You won't lose a dime," Satan promised him. "In fact,

you'll come out ahead. I'm going to set you up in an entirely new business."

"Like what?"

"There's a fungus growing on Pie's scrotum. From it you'll be able to make a new antibiotic, which will be effective against the dread killer syphilis."

"The entire world would have to come to me," Lurk mused, rubbing his chubby hands together.

"Yes. Male and female both. You'd make twice what you're making now. Even more. Because pregnancy is a luxury item, but health, if you can get it, is a necessity. Right?"

"Right," Lurk agreed. "But how do I make this antibiotic? I was never much good at chemistry. Surgery's my thing."

"No problem. I wrote the formula down for you." Satan handed Lurk the piece of paper God had given him.

Lurk stared at it. He turned it upside down, then sideways, and stared at it some more. "I can't read this," he said finally. "Your handwriting is atrocious."

"Oh, hell, wouldn't you know!" Satan muttered. He snatched the paper away and hopped back into his ball. "I'll be back in a moment," he called to Lurk as he shot upwards.

Lurk shrugged and walked over to a building so he could lean against something while he waited. If that character really was Satan, he reflected, it was a miracle that the world was as nasty as it was. He seemed extremely inefficient.

-5-

Satan stormed back into Heaven. "Why don't You type these things," he told God crossly. "You know Michael's the only one in the entire universe who can read Your handwriting."

"Oh, so have a scribe take care of it," God drawled. "Why do you get hysterical over every little thing?"

Michael took the paper from Satan and carried it off to translate it for one of the scribes.

While they waited for Michael to return, God and Satan didn't speak. Satan's silence grew out of resentment, but God was deep in thought. Lurk intrigued Him. He intended to watch him closely.

-6-

"Is this better?" Satan asked as he delivered the typed formula to Lurk.

"Yes," Lurk said, studying it with interest. "I think you have something here. I have to grab that stinky little fellow and take him back to my clinic right away." He tucked the formula in his pocket and pulled his gun from its holster, flicking off the safety catch.

"Put that thing away," Satan told him. "He won't go with you willingly, and if you shoot him, you'll spoil everything. Fungus doesn't grow on a dead man's balls. Not for very long, anyway."

Lurk was annoyed, but he saw the logic in this and reholstered his gun.

"He'll be told he must cooperate with you and sent to your clinic," Satan continued. "So go back there and wait."

Chapter Eleven
The Damnation of Lurk

-1-

Lurk had just inseminated his final customer when Pie appeared at his clinic later that day. He didn't seem very happy to be there. In fact, God had been forced to make another personal appearance, complete with beard, white robe, and triple crown, before he could be persuaded to come. But he sat quietly enough while Lurk and Simon scraped the fungus off his balls and into Petri dishes. Then he left, saying, "Back next week."

After Lurk had manufactured a large amount of the new antibiotic, he saw his government connections and made sure he'd have exclusive rights to its distribution. He didn't want anyone trying to cut himself in on humanitarian pretexts.

At first, his friends at the capital were reluctant to get involved. But when he cured them and their families for free, they became more tractable and passed a special law, turning him into a monopoly. All legal obstacles having been removed, Lurk closed down his insemination clinic and launched his new business.

Only the very rich could be cured in the beginning, since the prices he charged far exceeded the ones he'd asked in his insemination days. When accused of exploitation, he contended that the antibiotic, whose chemical composition was, of course, known solely to him, could be made only at great expense and in very small batches. In reality, Pie's scrotum fungus was so potent that Lurk collected enough each week to provide antibiotic for ten thousand people.

After the rich had all been cured at premium rates, Lurk dropped the price and went after the poor. By the time killer syphilis had been eradicated, Lurk was the richest man in the world.

-2-

God watched Lurk's meteoric rise with approval. He'd become infatuated with His protégé and longed to meet with him face to face. But He was certain Lurk would reject Him if he knew who He was.

Finally, when He could no longer restrain His ardor, He made up His mind to visit Lurk in disguise. He transformed Himself into a nearly exact replica of Satan, even including the pimples and the bald spot. Then He had Michael help Him into the same red tights and black cape that Satan had worn.

Michael, already half mad with jealousy, knew this was done to humiliate him, since God was perfectly capable of thinking Himself into the cape and tights. He gritted his teeth and wished it were possible for God to catch killer syphilis.

-3-

The last patient had left, desyphilized, and Lurk and Simon were having coffee while they counted the day's take. Neat piles of money lay on the table in front of them.

With a flourish of smoke and flame, God appeared in His devil suit.

"Who in the hell is that?" Simon asked weakly.

"A friend of mine," Lurk told him. "Relax. He just likes to make a grand entrance."

"Actually, I'm a colleague of Niemand's," God said.

Simon jumped up and scuttled for the door. "I don't want to be mixed up in this! I know what's going on here! I've seen *Faust: The Movie!*"

"Where do you think you're going?" Lurk sneered. "What would you do without me? Fry patties for the meat vendor?"

Simon paused with his hand on the doorknob.

"You don't really want to quit, do you, Simon?" God asked. "You need Lurk. And Lurk needs you. We all need an accomplice. Even I have one. He threatens to leave too, but he always thinks better of it. You like the money you make here, don't you? And the work's easy."

"I guess," Simon admitted. He took his hand off the doorknob and walked back to the table.

"So we can be friends." God eased down His tights. "If you've read anything at all about these contracts," He said, "you know there are rituals ... traditions..." He turned and exposed

His bare behind. "Tradition is the foundation of culture," He told them encouragingly.

When He'd taken Satan's form, He'd done so only in the parts of his body not hidden by the tights and cape. Everything underneath them was His own, and Lurk, despite his previous heterosexuality and present impotence, was enchanted by the ivory perfection of God's rounded buttocks. He and Simon eagerly pressed their lips to the smooth, pale flesh.

In Heaven, Michael kicked the mirrored wall and broke it.

Chapter Twelve
Pie Goes to His Reward and Lurk Doesn't

-1-

Lurk continued to cure the world, and Pie continued to fuck it. By the year 2057 Lurk was impossibly rich, and Pie was impossibly tired and ninety-one years old. His time to die had come, provoking a crisis in Heaven. God maintained that fair was fair. Pie was one of the Elect, besides having done a very good job of saving the world, and he deserved to be in Heaven. But Pie's mother stormed around the celestial precincts, lamenting and insisting that if Pie was coming to Heaven, she wanted to go to Hell. God tried to explain that she'd suffer eternal torment, but she said it couldn't be any worse than Pie's company.

Finally, God relented and agreed to send her to Hell before Pie arrived, but He didn't put her in the corn popper. She was allowed to live in a tent on the grounds, and she and Satan became quite friendly when he found out she liked horror movies as much as he did. They'd sit for hours, watching the l7" set and munching popcorn that they tossed into the corn popper along with the Reprobate.

-2-

Pie dropped dead a few weeks after his ninety-first birthday while doing God's will. The woman crawled out from under him and rifled his pockets, finding only the scrap of parchment with Latin writing that God had given him years before. She carried it away with her, and she and small circle of friends venerated it as a relic.

When Pie entered Heaven, he wandered around forlornly, looking for his mother. He would walk up to each of the celestial beings, peer into his or her face, then turn away, shaking his head and sighing. After only a few days, he'd gotten on everyone's nerves almost as badly as he had when he was alive.

To distract him, God sat him down with a huge pile of ashes and rat shit and told him that to separate one from the other was good and true and beautiful, solving the rat shit dilemma that Pie had been pondering when he received his call so many years before. His mother was having her hair done, God told Pie, and would return by the time he'd finished his task.

As he toiled away, Pie didn't notice that the original pile never decreased in size and the separate piles of rat shit and ashes that he was making from it stopped getting larger at a certain point. To maintain heavenly aesthetic standards, God hid Pie with a large painted screen. And he's still sitting behind it, patiently working and waiting.

-3-

For men who were respectively ninety-eight and eighty-seven years old, Lurk and Simon were quite well-preserved. In fact, neither looked a day over thirty-five, and a youngish thirty-five at that. God visited them often and kept thinking up new ways for them to pledge their loyalty.

Michael was incensed. "They were both fated to die years ago!" he told God angrily. "When Pie was a cosmic sanitation hazard, fate was a very big deal, according to You. You couldn't get rid of him, You said, because he wasn't fated to go till he was ninety-one. Now, all of a sudden, fate is out of the picture."

"I made the rules, and I guess I can break them," God answered haughtily. "You go create a universe. Then maybe I'll listen to your complaints."

"But You promised Satan You'd make Lurk king of Hell, so he could come back up here."

"I didn't say when. Besides, Satan doesn't seem particularly anxious to leave Hell. I haven't heard a thing from him."

"Of course not! You got him a girlfriend, and now he's content to stay down there forever!"

"Good. Because he may just have to."

Michael walked blindly away from God, not trusting himself to speak. When he'd calmed down enough to be aware of his surroundings, he was astonished to find that he'd gone all the way to the narrow end of the room. The blinds, their hard glitter alien to the snug, dim comfort of the rest of Heaven, were only a few feet away. They were shut tightly, like overlapping knives, and it hurt his eyes to look at them.

He turned away and walked back toward the other end of Heaven, but he couldn't help wondering what was outside. As he wondered, he suddenly felt God lock onto his mind, probing it meticulously. He forced himself to stop thinking about the blinds and went to sit in front of the mirror, where he stared at his reflection in the broken glass. He felt God leave His mind and turn His attention back to the screen, which, as always, was focused on Lurk.

Part Two
The Age of Faith

Chapter One
The Apotheosis of Pie

Even before his death, Pie had been considered a saint. By 2100, a little less than fifty years later, most people believed he was the son of God. God was offended at first (even Pie's father hadn't much liked being Pie's father), but His sense of humor reasserted itself in time to keep Him from blasting Earth to rubble. After a while, He began to go along with the joke, calling Pie "sonny" when He visited him behind his screen and wearing a locket containing his picture and a few greasy strands of his hair.

For a long time, Pie's devotees used a phallus to symbolize his presence in deference to his only talent. But in 2193 a discovery was made that revolutionized the cult. The descendants of the woman who'd taken the parchment from Pie's corpse still prayed daily in front of the shrine she'd made for it. A growing number of people attended these services, and word of the parchment's existence came to the ear of one of the local warlords.

He ordered the parchment and its owners brought to his citadel and heard the story of how the relic had been taken from the pocket of blessed Pie himself. Intrigued, the warlord summoned the wise men of his court, as well as his personal physician, Niemand Lurk, and Lurk's assistant, Simon.

Although Lurk remembered enough of his medical-school Latin to translate the passage written on the ancient fragment and was old enough to recognize it for what it was, he was prudent enough to feign ignorance. His knowledge would make him suspect, since he had no plausible way of explaining how he'd come by it.

Deep in the Everglades lived a scrawny old Negro man named Honker, who was the last classical scholar in the world. Only the isolated and pestilential surroundings in which they made their home had enabled his family to pass the knowledge and languages of the ancient Greeks and Romans from generation to generation. There was nobody to harass them, since their neighbors had all succumbed to malaria many decades before. Honker's family had been spared because they were carriers of the sickle cell trait, which made them resistant to the disease. Of course, many of them died at an early age because of complications due to sickle cell anemia, but enough always survived to carry on the scholarly tradition. Since no one had known about the family's library, it hadn't been burnt during the worldwide bibliocaust that occurred at the same mad, unsettled time as the Great Deodorant Riots.

Honker spent most of his days tending his garden and leafing through his dusty old books. Inbreeding had destroyed his family, and he was the only survivor, his wife having died before she could bear any children. He was close to a hundred now. Soon, he knew, he'd be dead, and the glories of Greece and Rome would die with him. As a youth he'd ventured into the world beyond the swamp a few times and had discovered that people possessed only the most rudimentary learning, distorted by time and superstition.

The warlord's men had failed repeatedly in their quest. They'd ridden hundreds of miles, each carrying a strip of bark on which a single word from Pie's parchment had been scratched, but they'd found no one who could translate it. Murder in his voice, the warlord ordered them out once again and warned them that if they didn't succeed this time, they'd pay with their lives.

Desperation drove one of the men, who'd ridden southward, into Honker's swamp. He was quite certain that nobody lived there, but he thought it would be an ideal place for him to hide from the warlord's wrath, since everyone was terrified to enter it. Probable death by malaria, he reasoned, was at least a slightly better option than certain death by slow torture at the hands of the warlord's executioner.

For three days, he led his horse blindly over the marshy ground, not caring which direction they took, since one part of the swamp was as foul as the other. On the fourth day, to his amazement, he stumbled into a clearing and saw an ancient Negro weeding a carefully tended garden. The old man tethered his horse and helped him into a neat little house, where he had him lie down while he brewed some herb tea.

The warlord's man was strong, and after a cup of the herb tea, he'd recovered sufficiently from his ordeal to joke with Honker. "I'm sure you're a smart man," he teased, "living right here in the center of things as you do." He pulled the strip of bark out of his tunic and showed it to the old man. "If you know what this word means, you can save my life a second time."

Honker took the bark from him and held it close to his face. His eyes were weak with age and cataracts. "That means 'swine' or 'pigs'," he said finally, rather surprised that any knowledge of Latin still existed in the outside world.

The warlord's man sat bolt upright in bed and clutched Honker's wrist so hard that he winced. "You know what language that is?"

"Why of course. It's Latin. It was spoken by. . . ."

"You're coming with me!" the warlord's man said abruptly, leaping from the bed.

Honker stared at him in utter confusion. "Oh, no! My house! I don't want to leave. . . ."

"I'll bring you back myself," the warlord's man promised. "My master just wants you to read something for him." Barely giving Honker time to put on a jacket, he shoved him out the door and lifted him onto the horse.

Honker was apprehensive as he rode through the swamp. He hadn't left it in years. But along with the fear was pleasure in finally being able to share his knowledge, to connect with another human mind. And, he reminded himself, this man had said he'd bring him back. Surely, he wouldn't break a promise to the person who'd saved his life.

When at last they galloped into the courtyard of the warlord's citadel, Honker was exhausted. He'd ridden for miles and miles behind the warlord's man, clinging to his belt. Every one of his bones ached, and there was a tightness in his chest.

He was given no opportunity to rest, though, but was brought almost immediately to the warlord, who had placed the parchment on a table by a window, where the light was strong. "Read!" he ordered Honker, indicating the parchment.

Niemand Lurk, the only member of the court besides Simon who could read and write, waited with pen and paper to take down the translation.

Honker bent over the table and was disappointed to find that the passage wasn't written in classical Latin. "This is only. . . ." he began.

The warlord stopped him short with a furious look. "I don't want a speech! Just translate!"

Honker read in a faint, halting voice. He seemed to be out of breath.

"So the devils besought him, saying, If thou cast us out, suffer us to go away into the herd of swine. And he said unto them, Go. And when they were come out, they went into the herd of swine: and, behold, the whole herd of swine ran violently down a steep place into the sea and perished in the waters."

Honker sagged against the table, faint from the pain that was tearing at his chest. "That's all," he whispered.

"Did you get that down?" the warlord asked Lurk.

Lurk nodded. Then, watching Honker slide to the floor, he commented, "That guy doesn't look too good."

The warlord nudged Honker with the toe of his boot. "Hey! You!"

Honker opened his dimming eyes.

"Before you translated that thing, you were going to say something about it. What?"

"Yes," Honker gasped. "That passage . . . it's from the . . . the . . . Bi. . . ." His voice thickened into a rattle and his head fell to the side.

Lurk went over and had a look at him. "He's dead," he announced and walked away again, reading his English transcription of the parchment's contents. He was proud of his handwriting. In the old days, people had joked about doctors' handwriting, but his own had always been flawless.

The warlord had fallen to his knees and was banging his head against the floor in a clumsy gesture of reverence. "He was struck dead because he touched the sacred law! Blessed Savior Pie, be merciful to us!"

"But you touched it too, sir," Lurk reminded him, "and you're still alive."

The warlord considered this for a moment. Then he said solemnly, "It's clear to me now. The Lord Pie has chosen me to be his priest. I am the anointed one!" He stood up and reached for the parchment, but drew back his hand without touching it. "Bring me the tongs from the kitchen," he told one of his men. "Just in case."

When the tongs had been brought, the warlord used them to gingerly lift the parchment from the table and carry it to the temple of Pie on the citadel grounds. It was propped against the phallus that was Pie's symbol until the warlord could have a proper tabernacle built for it.

"What do you think those strange words on the parchment mean?" the warlord asked Lurk as they walked away from the temple.

"I'm sorry, sir, but I haven't the faintest idea," Lurk lied.

"There's only one thing to do. Bring your transcription to the meeting hall tonight after dinner. I'll call my wise men together, and they will discover the hidden meaning of these words from the Blessed One."

That night, the warlord and his wise men gathered in a circle and passed around Lurk's English transcription of the words on the parchment. Although each examined it with great care, this was a mere formality, since none of them could read a word of it. Then Lurk read it aloud to them, and they sat for an hour, eyes closed, silently rocking back and forth and pondering the contents.

"It's obvious, sir," one of them told the warlord finally. "This is a warning from our Savior Pie that pigs are unclean, devilish things, and we must not eat their flesh."

The other wise men nodded and muttered, "Yes, the meaning is clear. Pie be praised!"

Then one man stumbled to his feet, pale with horror. "Pie have mercy on us!" he wailed. "We had porkchops for dinner!"

All of them began to rock and moan and tear their hair.

"Bring water!" one cried. "We must cleanse ourselves!"

Lurk and Simon had been sitting a little apart, watching the drama unfold and trying to keep straight faces. Simon rushed off to get a basin of water while Lurk tried to calm the assembly. "We've had pig meat for dinner three times this week alone," he told them. "Tonight's porkchops will not defile you, because you ate them in a state of innocence."

Simon returned with the water, and there was a mad rush toward the basin.

"Wait!" cried one of the wise men, stopping suddenly. "What was it that our Savior Pie drove the loathsome creatures into?"

"Water!" the others gasped, backing away from the basin as if it contained poison.

"Then water too is unclean," one murmured.

Another swore fervently, "I'll never bathe again!"

"But if we don't drink water, we'll die," the warlord protested.

"We can drink wine."

"No good. There's not enough, and even if there were, we'd be drunk all the time. That may be okay for you wise men. You're about the same, drunk or sober. But my soldiers can't fight in that condition."

"Evidently, the message of Our Savior Pie needs to be reinterpreted," ventured one of the wise men.

"Evidently," the warlord agreed.

They sat for another hour, deep in thought. The warlord began to fidget, and Lurk and Simon had to bite their fingers to keep from going to sleep. The wise men held up very well, though, because thinking is what they do best.

At length, one of them broke the silence. "I have the answer," he announced portentously.

All eyes were on him.

"I believe Our Savior Pie encoded this message so it could not be read by profane eyes," he continued. "Water is the key. Since it is necessary for life, it couldn't possibly be unclean. This was Blessed Pie's clue to us that the real message is the exact opposite of what was written on the parchment. In other words, pigs are sacred."

The other wise men nodded sagely, wishing they'd thought of it.

61

"Are pork chops okay then?" one asked.

"Of course not!" the first speaker answered sternly. "They're sacred because pigs are sacred. No pig must ever be killed again, for chops or bacon or any other reason."

"I just realized something," Lurk offered helpfully. "If you rotate the last letter of our Savior Pie's name until it's upside down and then flip it around, it becomes a 'G'. Almost, anyway."

The warlord, totally illiterate as he was, didn't grasp the significance of this. "So?" he asked.

"So," Lurk explained, "'Pie' becomes 'pig'."

"Ah! Of course! Pie is pig! That confirms the truth of the message." The warlord began to chant softly, as if in a trance. "Pig, pig, pig, pig, pig. . . ."

The others, even Lurk and Simon, joined in. "Pig, pig, pig, pig, pig. . . ."

A faint smell of roast pork filled the air, and the milky, shifting figure of a pig seemed to appear in the center of the circle.

The next day, the warlord summoned his messengers. "Go throughout my realm," he commanded, "and tell the people they must never again kill a pig, on pain of death. They're to roam freely and root wherever they please, because they're the living soul of Our Savior Pie."

Because of this powerful warlord's influence, a new mode of worship soon spread across the land. The phalluses were replaced with pig statues, some of which bled and wept miraculously and cured revolting diseases. People wore silver pig snouts on chains around their necks to ward off evil. Mysterious oinks issued from certain troughs, and these were used as fonts in which people were confirmed in the new faith by being sprinkled with slops.

As the cult began to take hold, God obligingly assumed the form of a pig, and the rest of Heaven followed suit. Michael, who was still pouting in front of the broken mirror, decided that he absolutely was not going to become a pig. But struggle as he would, he watched his face flatten into a snout and his stomach distend, while his arms and legs shrank and his hands and feet hardened into trotters. His hair vanished. His skin took on a grayish-pink color and formed flaps and jowls. His eyes narrowed into slits.

Michael realized for the first time that although he'd always thought he was imitating God because he wanted to, in fact, he'd never had a choice. For a moment, he wondered if God Himself might be forced into His own transformations, but immediately dismissed this notion as ridiculous.

Chapter Two
Lurk Gets His Monsters

-1-

Slowly, the world repaired itself, and by the 2600s life wasn't too bad. The United States had a central government again, based in Potpourripolis. Most people were farmers, but they were able to read and write after a manner and do simple arithmetic. When a library was discovered, it was no longer burnt. There was a rebirth of technology, and televisions were beginning to appear again after the excavation and analysis of a few sets and badly rusted transmitting equipment. Some shops, restaurants, and even a few nightclubs had opened in the larger settlements.

Thanks to Lurk, Europe had also recovered from the devastating plagues of the late twentieth century. When he gave up his insemination business, he sold his thirty fertile men to a British colleague, and they repopulated England and the Continent. This same colleague marketed Lurk's killer-syphilis cure overseas. Lurk had hated giving up even a small part of the take, but travel was uncomfortable and time-consuming, not to mention expensive. It was easier to sell large amounts of the antibiotic wholesale to his friend than go to Europe himself and peddle it.

Lurk and Simon were living in Manhattan now. Although it was far from the capital, New York was still the largest city in the country. It even had occasional foreign tourists, who came by sailing ship. Lurk had rented a two-story house on fashionable Pink Street. It was a good mile and a half south of the Central Park garbage dump, so unless there was a strong north wind, the air was quite nice. Lurk's office and operating room were on the first floor of the house, while he and Simon had their living quarters on the second.

Since learning was no longer suspect, Lurk felt free for the first time in centuries to use the entire spectrum of his surgical expertise. At the moment, he was dabbling in plastic surgery, more for his own amusement than to make money. But despite the millions of dollars in gold and silver that he had buried all over America, he asked exorbitant fees of the government officials and their wives who came to him to have their youth restored. To have done otherwise would have been to violate his most cherished principles.

Lurk also had a hobby—designing monsters. Many feeble-minded people wandered about the slums which surrounded the wealthy center of town. Often Lurk and Simon would make a late night trip into one of these areas and lure some poor moron back to their house. Then he was anesthetized, and his face and body were sliced and stitched into something grotesque enough to horrify and human enough to make people wonder if they might wake up and find it in their mirror some morning.

Lurk cared tenderly for these new monsters until their scars had healed. Then he photographed them and hung their pictures in a secret gallery adjoining his bedroom. Finally, on some dark night, the creatures were left in an area where children played during the day or placed on the doorstep of a prominent citizen.

The monsters caused quite a stir. They were featured in newspaper articles and sometimes even shown on television. Speculation about their origin was rife. Some thought they were the result of genetic mutations caused by the ancient pestilences. The uneducated believed they were devils. By far the most disturbing theory was that they were victims of a hitherto unknown sickness that was probably contagious. People sneaked looks in every mirror they passed to see if their faces had begun to warp. The monsters couldn't put everyone's minds to rest by explaining what had happened to them because Lurk had made sure they were too retarded to speak coherently before he performed the operations.

When God visited, Lurk and Simon entertained Him on a large mattress on the floor of the secret gallery. He would look carefully at the pictures and compliment Lurk on his monsters, but always in a tone of voice that implied He could do better.

"Well, damn you, Satan, let's see what you can do then!" Lurk said finally. "Long ago you promised me monsters, and the time has come for you to deliver."

"I was only waiting for you to ask," God told him with a smile. "You'll have them tomorrow."

Lurk bristled with excitement, and God embraced him quickly, to savor it at its peak.

-2-

Long before the Mongolian people that came to be called Indians crossed the Bering land bridge, another race dwelt in North America. Even at its height, the Pusgrub nation was pretty shabby, and it only survived because of the lack of anything with a strong enough stomach to be its natural predator.

Pusgrubs had greenish, scaly skin that constantly shed in pieces measuring about a square inch. One Pusgrub in each tribe was charged with the task of gathering these skin chips and stuffing sacred pillows with them. The Pusgrubs didn't have hair as we know it. Something grew on their damp, pear-shaped heads, but it could more accurately be described as moss. Things lived in it, which the Pusgrubs picked out and ate. Young Pusgrubs pledged their love by eating each other's. These creatures had extremely weak eyes, but they had no trouble finding one another because their sensitive nostrils were able to hone in on the rancid odor of viscous, yellow Pusgrub perspiration, which they found very agreeable. Pusgrubs were vaguely human in shape, though quite short, and their four boneless arms nearly touched the ground when they stood erect.

After the Indians arrived, they launched a wholesale slaughter of the Pusgrubs, less from aggression than nausea. The remnants of the Pusgrub nation fled deep into the earth, where living conditions eventually caused them to become even more revolting. They fed on bats and eyeless fish. Their children began to be born in litters and spent the first year of their life in a transparent egg of slime, feeding on maggots which their parents introduced into a sucking opening at the bottom.

Many centuries passed, and the Pusgrubs forgot that they had ever lived on the earth's surface. Some groups burrowed so far underground that they couldn't find their way out again. In other cases, landslides and earthquakes blocked the exits. It reached a point where when one did accidentally glimpse the upper world, he cowered away in superstitious terror and scurried to some deeper place.

-3-

The day God told Lurk to expect his monsters was February 15, 2684. It was a great feast day, the anniversary of Blessed Pie's death, and people were strolling in whatever finery they could scratch together and visiting their neighborhood temples.

Although the warlord who had begun pig worship had forbidden their slaughter, the rituals had changed gradually. Now pigs were sacrificed by the high priests on even the most trivial occasions, and the priests, their relatives, and the city dignitaries gorged themselves secretly on pork after the ceremonies.

Since February 15th was the holiest day of the year, temple aisles ran with pig blood, while in the back rooms, the elite stuffed themselves. But Lurk and Simon didn't go to temple. They roamed the streets expectantly, waiting for something hideous to appear.

Around noon, the tremors began in the middle of the country. Since America was still somewhat underpopulated, God centered the geological upheavals in sparsely inhabited regions. At dozens of these points, the earth turned inside out, and after ages of darkness, millions of bewildered Pusgrubs were exposed to the light.

Lurk and Simon went to bed disappointed on February 15th. But in about two weeks the first Pusgrubs had blundered into populated areas. In another few weeks, reports of them started to reach New York. Initially, many Pusgrubs were killed by terrified people who couldn't figure out whether they were very small monsters or very large bacteria. A number managed to escape into the wilderness, while others were put in cages and displayed to a horrified yet fascinated public.

Lurk yearned to see them. From what he'd heard, Satan had indeed surpassed him.

Chapter Three
Prelude to the Age of Reason:
The Dawn of Social Conscience

-1-

The Pusgrubs were finally saved by Figg Walmsley. He was the son of a high-ranking member of Our Bunch, the twenty-four-man ruling body of the United States. Figg grew up to be benevolent, since, thanks to his father's wealth, his life had been comfortable enough and uneventful enough not to irritate him. So he nosed into the lives of the underprivileged, rooting around for dramas and turbulence, convincing everyone, even himself, that he was not a busybody, but a humanitarian.

The year the Pusgrubs came, he was a tall, thin man of forty, with gentle blue eyes and sparse, sandy hair. He'd been a vegetarian for most of his life and had recently given up eating asparagus after he fancied having heard one of the stalks on his plate scream when he pierced it with his fork. Inspired by this experience, he published a slender volume of poems called *Meditations on a Forked Asparagus,* which brought him a certain amount of fame in artistic circles and established him as a sensitive person.

In June of 2683, Figg Walmsley had received the very first MSW from the newly established Potpourripolis School of Social Work. A large collection of books dealing with this field had been unearthed by a team of Canadian archaeologists a few years before, and since they didn't think it would be worth the trouble to lug them back to Canada, they donated the entire find to the city of Potpourripolis. Figg was captivated from the beginning and spent hours a day buried in lurid case histories. He and a few like-minded friends started a school and awarded each other degrees so they could teach.

But with the coming of the Pusgrubs, Figg knew that he must abandon his teaching career to follow a higher calling. With his father's help, he maneuvered himself into the office of Grand Palliator of Our Bunch, tolerating the necessary duplicity because it was for a good cause. Once he'd seized power through guile, money, and lots of illicit pork chops from the local temple, Figg abolished Our Bunch and made himself dictator (benevolent, of course) for life. He formed a new governing body called The Social Sanctuary, which ruled using the humanitarian principle of preservation of the weak and destruction of the strong. Excellence was to be treated as a form of pathological egotism and degeneracy excused as an amusing foible, if not embraced as a positive good.

As soon as he could, Figg mobilized the Social Sanctuary to rescue the Pusgrubs. Since they were a minority, it was obvious that, in a democratic society, their rights should prevail over the rights of the majority. An elite Social Sanctuary force was established to protect the Pusgrubs from harassment. The SS slaughtered thousands of American citizens who'd expressed their distaste for Pusgrubs in one way or another, but these killings were condoned, because the victims were normal.

Sometimes people came directly to Figg Walmsley and asked him to get rid of the Pusgrubs. But when they left his office, they were surprised to find that Figg had actually talked them into liking the creatures. He was a very charming man, who had a knack for being modestly apologetic about his money, education, and position without ever referring to them directly and an ability to seem to be smiling even when he wasn't.

The Pusgrubs weren't at all sure what was going on. But they sensed dimly that it was benefitting them, so they memorized a few catchwords, like "Don't hate! Palliate!" and went along with it. They even made an attempt at Pusgrub solidarity. This was quite a feat, since each Pusgrub hated every other Pusgrub, except possibly his or her current sexual partner. Because most Pusgrubs were incapable of learning English, Figg Walmsley commanded that Pusgrubet, a system of grunts, become America's second official language. The members of the Social Sanctuary were encouraged, none too gently, to intermarry with the Pusgrubs. To everyone's surprise, children resulted from these unions—gelatinous things with human parts imbedded in them, seemingly at random. Since Pusgrubs were unable to do physical labor, they were paid vast salaries to sit in government offices and do nothing. This resulted in Potpourripolis having an especially large number of Pusgrub residents. And it's a tribute to the genius of Figg Walmsley that although he read reports about them, looked at photographs of them, and listened to and made speeches about them, he managed to reach the end of his life without seeing one in the flesh.

–2–

Lurk took a particular interest in the Pusgrubs, since he considered them his very own monsters. He and Simon even traveled to Potpourripolis to aid the integration drive by disinfecting and delousing the Pusgrubs and explaining to them about soap and water. Walmsley was so grateful he offered Lurk a job as chief medical officer for the SS. But Potpourripolis was a little too provincial for Lurk's taste, so he thanked Walmsley and returned to New York, secure in the knowledge that his monsters were in good hands.

Back in New York, Lurk found that the first floor of his house, which he'd used for an office, had been rented to someone else. He complained bitterly, but there wasn't much he could do, since he'd fallen several months behind in his rent while he was in Potpourripolis. His excitement over the monsters had driven everything else from his mind. The landlord agreed to let him and Simon continue to live on the second floor after Lurk paid the back rent. It had a separate entrance, and the downstairs tenant was willing. But Lurk would have to find office space somewhere else. Since decent buildings were scarce, he decided to share one with an acquaintance of his, a high priest named Bubby, who was about to revolutionize the entertainment industry.

While rural devotees were still often fanatics, pig worship had degenerated into a mere gesture in the big cities. Pie's redemption of mankind was treated as a myth by the educated populace. And while pork still couldn't be eaten legally, its prohibition was now considered a health measure, stemming from its high fat content.

Bubby had developed a grill that cooked every bit of fat out of his spareribs and was about to open the country's first legal rib joint, called Pie in the Sty, in honor of the mythical savior of mankind. An ancient law library had been excavated a few decades before and a law school founded, so there were now plenty of rich lawyers in the city who could afford the outrageous prices Bubby planned to charge. Also New York was beginning to get more and more foreign visitors. Bubby had a vision of his sparerib joint becoming a magnet for the newly emerging elite not only of America, but of the world.

On the day Lurk and Bubby made their deal, a government permit had arrived. Bubby hung a sign in the window announcing the opening of Pie in the Sty for the middle of the next week, Wednesday, June 8th, 2691.

Part Three
The Age of Reason

Chapter One
Defective Affinities

It was a hot July night in the year 2700. The mob had assumed a nearly triangular formation, because the efficiency of the bouncers standing on either side of the entrance to Pie in the Sty had eliminated enough people at the front to create an apex of the most determined. One woman, all sweat and feathers, clung to the door handles. Muncie, the larger of the two bouncers, smashed one of his big feet down on her instep. Although her face twisted with pain, she didn't let go. Then he plunged his fleshy hand between her legs and mauled her crotch as best he could through the intervening layers of feathers and sleazy material. Astonished, she lost her grip on the handles for a moment. That was all Muncie needed. He grabbed her by the waist, lifted her, and flung her several yards away from the door. Immediately someone new attached himself to the handles. Muncie decided to let his partner deal with this one while he took a breather and watched the crowd.

The feathered woman had been way out of style, he realized. Most of the nut cases were wearing the new "cow look." The women had on flesh-colored rubber bra tops with multiple teats, which were supposed to resemble cows' udders. The men had miniature bulls' horns attached to the crotches of their leather pants. Weirdos, Muncie thought as he looked at them. Loons.

He forced himself to start swinging at the crowd again, even though his arms were still tired. He wished Bubby would come out so the maniacs would quiet down for a few minutes. Glancing across the street, he spotted a dumpy couple watching the melee. He knew they'd never cross the street. The wrong kind of people sensed they mustn't come too close to Pie in the Sty. It made Muncie's job easier. He didn't mind insulting the manicured shits that tried to claw their way in, but it would have hurt him to turn away normal people. Like most Americans, his father had been a farmer. And Muncie knew that if he didn't have his job, he wouldn't be able to get into Pie in the Sty himself.

Actually, only Shirley Lee Wittigrew was looking at Pie in

the Sty, mesmerized by the gigantic sparerib suspended from a flagpole over the door. She stared at it in wide-eyed fascination, clutching a tiny pink bundle to her bosom.

Her husband Wilbur was more interested in a pothole. "Lord, that's a big one!" he exclaimed. "Folks up here are crazy. If they can't keep the road up, they ought to make it into a dirt one, like we got back home. This is downright perilous."

"This street is Park Avenue, Wilbur. It used to be a real fancy place back in the ancient times. I guess they're preserving it as some kind of landmark."

"They're not preserving it very damn good. A person could kill himself!" Heat and aggravation were getting to Wilbur. He unbuttoned his suit jacket and shirt collar and loosened his tie, wishing he could take off his shoes as well. He and Shirley Lee were wearing clothes that had been popular hundreds of years ago, in the 1950s. About forty years earlier, a Canadian archaeological dig in New Mexico had yielded a trove of fashion magazines from the '50s that had been preserved in metal boxes buried in the dry, sandy soil. Careful drawings of the clothes were made before the magazines disintegrated, since they were considered relics from America's Golden Age. These drawings were circulated all over the country, and people sewed themselves copies of the ancient garments to replace the draped pieces of cloth and skins they had been wearing. Now everyone dressed '50s with the exception of ultra chic, like the mob outside Pie in the Sty.

"Why do they call this 'Park Avenue'?" Wilbur asked Shirley Lee. "I don't see any park."

"That must be it," she said, pointing at a line of detritus that ran along the middle of the crumbling street. "It's probably somewhere under all that stuff."

Wilbur was skeptical. "Looks like garbage to me."

"Now, maybe. I guess it was a park once, though." She squinted at it through her thick eyeglasses. "I think I see a vine working its way up through some broken crockery."

Across the street, Bubby emerged from Pie in the Sty and stood imperiously on the top step, flanked by the two bodyguards. He was wearing a chef's hat and an apron with the picture of a smiling pig on it. The hat was grayish, and the apron was filthy with barbecue sauce and drippings.

Bubby was successful because he loved his work, and his work was pigs. He loved them alive, but he loved them even better dead and in pieces on the end of his fork. As a result, he was as plump and sleek and oily as a broiled pork butt. Although he was a fastidious man who bathed daily, his sweat was mixed with enough pig fat to grease the soft, jowl-length curls of his dark hair and make his olive skin glisten. His brown eyes were as sleepy and gentle as those of a castrated bull. His nose was longish, and the tip drooped toward his swollen wet lips. Such mild features could have seemed weak in a smaller man, but Bubby's size lent authority to his rather insipid face. He was well over six feet tall and weighed close to three hundred pounds.

Though in his mid-thirties, Bubby still was unmarried. He could have had his pick of the women who clustered around Pie in the Sty, but he was really only interested in pigs.

When Bubby appeared, the frenzied men and women on the sidewalk became quiet for a moment, pleading with their eyes. Then they began to shriek more loudly than before.

"Me, Bubby!"

"Please pick me!"

Bubby scanned the crowd languidly and jabbed a negligent finger at one section of it. "You, there. You're in."

The entire mob rushed the door.

Bubby shrank back and looked coldly at the wriggling mass of people. "Not you, jerks. Go back to the Jersey wetlands." He signaled to the bodyguards. "Get those fools back!"

The bodyguards bludgeoned the rejects while Bubby politely ushered in three giggling young women.

Shirley Lee watched the turmoil from across the street, absently rocking the tiny blanketed form in her arms. Part of the blanket moved and a miniature snout poked through the opening. She looked down, pulled the blanket aside, and revealed the rosy little face of a newborn piglet.

Leaning over it, she kissed its snout gently. "Don't you get nervous, now, honey," she crooned. Rearranging the blanket, she covered the piglet's face again and looked back across the street at the rib hanging over Bubby's door. "My sakes!" she breathed to her husband. "I'd like to see the pig that came off of. It looks like some old monster bone."

Wilbur snorted. "Don't be so dumb, Shirley Lee. You know the fool thing's carved out of wood."

"Well, sure I know," she told him indignantly, "but I'd like to see a pig that size anyhow. And give him a kiss on his nice big snout."

"Hell, woman, we're supposed to be on vacation! I never did see how a pig farmer's wife could get so romantic about the creatures. Especially since you know what happens to them."

Shirley Lee spun away from him and clutched the piglet to her breast. "You be quiet! I don't want to hear about that!"

"Where do you think spareribs come from?" Wilbur persisted. "Do you think the pig farts them out like a chicken with an egg?"

"They wait till they die naturally," Shirley Lee replied, her face stony. "They don't. . . do anything. Our government people are decent. They wouldn't do anything."

"You're right, honey," Wilbur told her sarcastically. "They don't do anything. They wait till the animal gets heart failure, or takes a fit, or commits suicide."

"Of course they do." She bent over the piglet. "Don't they, woodgie-lambie-pussy-pie? Nobody would hurt the sweet little angelkins! No, no, no!" She opened its blanket and tickled its snout fondly.

Wilbur wrinkled his nose with disgust. "Lord, woman, the way you carry on, a person would think you'd given birth to the thing! There was no reason to take him with us. Daughter-in-law would have nursed him for you."

"Daughter-in-law isn't worth a tinker's dam around pigs," Shirley Lee snorted. "And even if she did have the feel for it, I wouldn't trust anybody but myself to look after one this tiny. It's a good thing I had the sense to wrap a blanket around him. I don't think we could've got him into the hotel otherwise. City folks get all peculiar about animals."

Shirley Lee opened the piglet's blanket wide so she could kiss his tummy. Just as she was bending over him, making smacking noises with her lips, he squirmed out of her arms and shot across the street toward the luncheonette.

She let out a horrified shriek. "Good merciful heavens! You come right on back here!" She waddled desperately after him. "I said you come back here, baby pie!"

"You just go ahead and catch him yourself!" Wilbur hollered after her. "I'm not working up my asthma over any pig!" As he watched her, he shook his heady sadly. "Damn fool woman," he thought. "No wonder she gets along with the animals. She's every bit as dumb as they are."

At that moment, Bubby stepped out of Pie in the Sty and descended into the crowd to choose five or six people worthy of being admitted. The piglet ran squealing through the maze of legs and rooted affectionately around his feet, as if they were old friends.

He looked down, and his arrogant face softened. Stooping, he gathered the piglet up in his arms. "Aw, ickle piggy-poo-poo," he whispered. He'd never seen a baby pig before. They were shipped to him alive, but fully grown and ready for slaughter.

Shirley Lee trotted breathlessly over to him and clutched his arm. "My baby! You've saved my baby!"

Her fleshy-lidded, porcine eyes, blurred by the thick lenses of her glasses, met Bubby's eager gaze. He was afraid to look away from her, terrified she might disappear. She couldn't be real, he thought miserably. She must be some goddess or angel, who would stay long enough to tantalize him and then vanish forever. He ached to touch her skin, which was the enticing rosy gray of a raw pork loin. He was faint with the desire to embrace her, to clutch her tightly against his body. She wasn't sleek and hard, like the women who frequented his luncheonette, but flaccid and yielding, like a pile of wet, moldy leaves.

It was several moments before he was sufficiently under control to say a few choked words to her. "I'm glad I was able to do something for you," he mumbled shyly. "If you ever need me . . . at any time. . . ."

The crowd looked on silently, stunned by Bubby's transformation. One unfeeling man tried to take advantage of the situation and sneak into Pie in the Sty, but Muncie grabbed him.

"Haven't you got any reverence?" he asked sternly, pointing to Bubby and Shirley Lee. Normally, Muncie would have clouted the man, but he'd been influenced by the profound hush that had spread over the street. So he only tossed the offender aside and told him to go to the back of the mob.

Finally, Bubby handed the piglet to Shirley Lee. She took it almost absently, her eyes still locked with his.

Across the street, Wilbur was becoming impatient. He wanted to see the Radio City National Monument and get back to the hotel. He was tired. Down home, they'd have been in bed hours ago. "Come on, sugar!" he bellowed. "It's getting late. The guidebook says they turn off the spotlight on the monument at midnight."

Shirley Lee drew gently away from Bubby. "I guess I'd better go. My husband's getting ants in his pants over there."

Bubby flinched. "Your husband?"

"Yep." Shirley Lee looked back across the street, where Wilbur was impatiently shifting his weight from one foot to another. "That's my Wilbur over there. He's always in a hurry."

"Oh. Well, I guess you'd better go then," Bubby said hoarsely.

"I guess so," she answered. "Thanks again for catching the little one for me."

Bubby stared at her dumbly.

"Bye, now," she said with false cheer.

Wilbur waited irritably on one side of Park Avenue while Bubby stood motionless on the other, watching Shirley Lee. She walked away from him with obvious reluctance, turning frequently to meet his anguished gaze. When she reached the center of Park Avenue, her distraction made her stumble continually as she picked her way through the garbage.

Wilbur was puzzled by her clumsiness and dazed expression. When she reached the sidewalk, he grabbed her by the shoulders and stared into her face. "What's wrong with you? You look all funny."

Shirley Lee sighed rapturously. "Oh, Wilbur!"

"What? 'Oh, Wilbur' what?"

"There's a man over there," she told him, her face glowing.

"A man who looks like a pig. And not just any pig, Wilbur. He's the spittin' image of Old Prune."

"That big old daddy pig you wouldn't let me send away with the others?" Wilbur asked. "The one you got buried in the family plot?"

"Yes. It must be that carmel thing daughter-in-law's always talking about."

Wilbur was confused. "What carmel? Pigs is pork."

"Not the candy type carmel," Shirley Lee explained. "This is getting even carmel. Each one of your lives gets back at you for the one you lived before it."

"That doesn't sound like anything Preacher Reeves would say," Wilbur told her suspiciously. "Is it in *The Sacred Revelations of Our Savior Pie?*"

"No. It's in stuff like laundry tubs. Don't you remember how daughter-in-law said she couldn't help me do the wash, because that little foreign peddler told her it was her carmel to drown in a washtub? She won't go near one, and sonny has to do both their clothes."

"What's all that got to do with some piggy man across the street?"

"That ain't no piggy man!" Shirley Lee declared passionately. "That's pure pig! That's Old Prune himself, born again in a human body!"

"Nonsense!" Wilbur snorted. "Old Prune only died about five, six years ago. Are you saying he rose from the dead, came all the way up here, kicked this fella's regular soul out, and moved on in?"

"I can't tell you how the dickens it happened, Wilbur, but I know what I know, and that's Old Prune!" Shirley Lee clamped her lips together in a thin, stubborn line.

Bubby was still mooning over her across the street. The crowd stared too, wondering who she was and what she'd done to Bubby.

Wilbur squinted sourly at his rival. "Well, if that's Old Prune, he's sure come down in the world. That fella ain't no better than a dope pusher."

"Don't you say that!" Shirley Lee snapped.

"What do you think that rib's doing over the door?" Wilbur asked, smirking.

"He has it there because it's pretty. He loves pigs. Just like I do."

"He sells spareribs, you damn fool!" Wilbur exploded.

"He couldn't," Shirley Lee protested weakly. "That ain't even legal."

"There's some ain't worried about legal."

"But selling spareribs is against that fat law. To save our blood from fat clots. 'Keep America's arteries empty!' That's what the teevee is saying all the time."

"It's more than that, and you know it," Wilbur said darkly. "All that talk about fat is just a notion the city folk have. They don't believe in God or Pie or any damn thing. The truth is, Pie saved us all by driving the syphilis and the killer fleas into a herd of pigs and running them off the sacred Staten Island Ferry slip. Ever since then all pigs are full of syphilis and flea parts. You couldn't pay me to eat one of the filthy things."

"Pigs are not filthy, Wilbur. You don't even know your *Revelations*. We're not supposed to eat pigs because they're holy. They saved us by taking our afflictions onto themselves. But I don't want to talk religion with you. And that man isn't selling spareribs. I think you're jealous because he was nice to me."

"I am not!" Wilbur told her indignantly. "If you'd be fool enough to go for that piggy thing over there, he could damn well have you, for all I care!"

Shirley Lee turned pink with hurt. "Wilbur! Do you mean that?"

"No, sugar, of course not," Wilbur said hastily. "You know I love you like crazy. But all the same, that man is selling spareribs, and that's the honest-to-God truth. I'm not fooling with you."

"He couldn't if he wanted to," Shirley Lee insisted. "It's against the law. He'd get himself arrested and sentenced to twenty years of therapy."

"There's places the law don't apply," Wilbur said smugly, proud to be in the know. "There's places you can get spareribs and even pork sausage, if you're willing to pay the price."

Shirley Lee was unconvinced. "But where would he get the

pig meat? All our pigs go straight to the capital. It's government policy."

Wilbur adopted a preachy, almost scholarly tone. One of his greatest pleasures was playing teacher with his wife, whom he'd married because she was even dumber than he. "Some of these folk have special ovens," he explained, "ovens that're supposed to cook out every bit of the fat. You need a license from the government to operate a sparerib joint, and I guess this fella's one of the handful of people in the country that has one."

"But he looks so . . . noble." Shirley Lee glanced back over at Bubby and let out a squeal of horror.

"What now?" Wilbur sighed, looking in the same direction. Instantly he stiffened, a shocked expression on his face. "Will you look at that!" he said softly.

Several people whose faces were heavily bandaged had staggered out of Pie in the Sty and were weaving down the street, supported by friends.

"You see, Wilbur?" Shirley Lee quavered. "Something awful's happening in that place. Those poor folks have been mutilated."

"Oh, be still!" Wilbur told her. "Anybody who'd mutilate them wouldn't bother to bandage them up afterwards, would he?"

"I tell you, something's going on! Look! Here come some more!"

As she spoke, another group of bandaged people emerged from Pie in the Sty, stumbling around in circles, as if they were sick or drugged. Finally, one by one, they succeeded in staggering off into the night.

Bubby ignored them completely. He had himself back under control and had managed to take his eyes off Shirley Lee long enough to escort a few more people into the luncheonette.

A tear trickled down Shirley Lee's face as she watched him. "Poor Old Prune," she said anxiously. "He doesn't seem to know what's happening. Oh, Pie help us! I hope whatever it is doesn't get him."

"This whole business is peculiar," Wilbur conceded. "You may be right for once." He looked up the street and spotted a small, beat-up car making its way uncertainly toward them. "Here comes a cop car. I'm going to flag it down and tell 'em about this."

Chapter Two
The Executives of Anarchy

Neither of the two men in the police car was in uniform, since the SS policy board had decided long ago that uniforms were intimidating and tended to encourage aggressive behavior in those that wore them. Frank, who was driving, had on a shabby blue suit with a service revolver strapped grotesquely on the outside of the jacket. There had been much discussion of this matter at the SS policy board. It was pointed out that, like a uniform, a gun tended to intimidate and provoke. Some suggested that the police go unarmed, but traditionalist elements argued that they might be killed. Finally it was decided by a very close vote to allow them to keep the guns.

Then the board turned to the problem of where the guns should be worn. If they were visible, they might scare someone. If they were hidden, the police would be violating the law against concealed weapons, and that would never do. In the end it was decided that they should wear them on the outside of their jackets, but that the holsters should be decorated with something cheery to put people at ease. Some of the men had songbirds or daisies painted on the leather. Frank had seen a picture of an ancient smile face in *History for the People: Interpreted* and had copied it onto his holster. This would have been completely appropriate, except that he'd drawn it upside down, turning the smile into a scowl. Due note of this was made by the area's Social Sanctuary representative, who thought it might indicate a negative attitude. It was hotly debated at SS headquarters in Potpourripolis for a couple of months. Then everyone went on vacation, and when they came back, they'd forgotten about it.

Frank's father had been a cop, and since they were very close, Frank came to share his interest in police work. Still, when he wanted to join the force at the age of twenty, his father did his best to dissuade him. It was 2688, and Figg Walmsley had just decreed that a psychiatric social worker trained at SS headquarters was to accompany every police officer while he was on duty.

Frank's father was having difficulty adjusting to this, as well as the other restrictions police had been subjected to following Walmsley's rise to power. But Frank's new wife had just died giving birth to their son, and he needed a challenge to take his mind off his loss. He sold his small farm and moved back in with his parents so his mother could care for his son while he worked. Then, despite his father's protests, he joined the force.

Now he began to experience for himself all the petty humiliations the older man was suffering, and this brought them even closer together. When they were at home, trying to forget their jobs over steaming cups of hot milk and his mother's homemade raisin bread, Frank would listen raptly as his father told stories of faraway times when cops had pitted their strength against The Boys, that conglomerate of evil that once threatened to grasp the entire ancient world in its tentacles.

His father also showed him reprints of old books, smuggled in from Canada, which told about those days in the remote past when it was permissible to loathe and fear hideous things. Frank particularly enjoyed Edgar Allan Poe's work. He was certain that if a Pusgrub had appeared to one of Poe's characters, he would have known how to deal with it.

The Pusgrubs had surfaced when Frank was fifteen. He'd hated them on sight and continued to hate them, although to admit it publicly would have branded him as antisocial and let him in for years of punitive psychotherapy.

Frank's father never complained about his SS partner or any of the other things he was forced to endure. To do so would have cost him his job. But when he died in 2693 of heart failure, he was only forty-seven years old. Frank was certain that the degrading conditions under which he'd been compelled to work had shortened his life. His mother died a year later, and Frank had to put his son, then six, in an SS day-care center while he was on the job. He supposed that was when the boy started to go wrong.

Frank was forty now and wished with all his heart that he'd stuck to farming. He was paunchy. His brown hair was rapidly thinning. His muscles were turning to flab. At this point in his life he'd never have the physical strength to build a farm from scratch. His son could be no help to him either. They seldom saw one another, even when they were both in New York. And now he was far away in Potpourripolis, attending the SS Academy.

His son's choice of profession deepened Frank's customary gloom, depressing the man who'd been his partner for five years so much that he asked for a transfer. The past year this same man had been certain he'd seen Frank grin broadly when Figg Walmsley's death had been announced on their patrol car radio. This was inappropriate behavior and certainly should have been reported. The trouble was, he liked Frank. He couldn't turn him in, even though he knew he was shirking his duty as a social worker and a police official. He was relieved when his transfer came through.

Hilly was Frank's new partner. A slender, freckled man, he was Frank's junior by at least fifteen years. His perpetual optimism was abrasive, even to people with similar dispositions, and Frank found him nearly intolerable. He never stopped smiling, not even when they visited the morgue or were told they were getting a pay cut.

His well-kept appearance made it clear that he felt good about himself. He wore carefully tailored suits, usually made of a light solid-colored fabric or a tasteful plaid. His light brown hair was frequently and expertly trimmed. He never passed a sink without washing his hands, and he never held anything without cleaning his fingernails with it, if at all possible.

Like most of the Social Sanctuary people, Hilly was married to a Pusgrub, and the two of them had already had a litter. Marriage to a Pusgrub wasn't required by the SS leaders, but it definitely enhanced one's potential for advancement, since it was seen as a healthy acceptance of minority cultural deviance.

Being a psychiatric social worker, Hilly didn't carry a weapon. It was his job to handle all their calls, unless something explicitly violent was happening. That's why patrol cars were always driven by the regular police officers. It kept them out of trouble, since they needed to stop the car before they had both hands free to do something rash.

During the year and a half they'd been driving around together, Hilly had tried diligently to make friends with Frank.

The time they spent with each other would be so much nicer if they had a caring relationship, and Hilly loved it when things were nice.

"Aw, Frank," he pleaded as they drove down Park Avenue. "Come to our Strange Fruits party. I promise you'll have a great time."

"No," Frank told him firmly. "After I went to your Strange Cheeses party, I was up all night."

"So what's wrong with that? It's nice to be up."

"We're not talking about the same kind of up. My kind would make even you stop smiling."

"Why do you have to be such a down person?" Hilly chided. "I'm so up ever since they caught that Guido Mocha, and I want all my friends to be up with me. That's why I'm having this party. So we can all be up together. It's really nice when everyone's tuned in to each other, feeling the same thing at the same time. It's unity. We can hardly tell one another apart when we get like that."

"That's all the more reason for me not to come. My downness would spoil everyone else's upness, and your party would be a flop."

"I don't believe you're as down as you say you are. How could you be down at a time like this? Doesn't it make you feel good to know that Guido Mocha is off the streets?"

"Why should it?" Frank answered with a shrug. "He was never on our streets. As far as anyone knows, he never left the Potpourripolis area."

"But he attacked the Social Sanctuary! And an attack on the Social Sanctuary is an attack on us all! Personally, I feel great about their catching him, and I'll feel even better after he's executed. They're going to televise it, you know. I think I'll have another party then so I can have my friends around me while I watch it. Will you come to that one?"

"No. The execution is supposed to take place at 10:00 P.M., and I try to get to bed early when I don't have night duty. I'm not as young as I used to be."

"You're just depressed because you spend too much time alone," Hilly insisted. "Please, for your own sake, come to my

Strange Fruits party. It'll do you good. Besides, Yog and the kids haven't seen you for ages."

Frank shuddered inwardly as he thought of Yog. Hilly's wife had done an ethnic Pusgrub dance at the Strange Cheeses party while he was eating a slice of Gorgonzola, and he believed that was the real reason he'd been up all night. That particular combination was enough to unsettle anybody's stomach. The kids were pretty bad too, but not nearly as bad as their mother. After all, kids were kids, even when they looked like dirty mayonnaise.

"You mean you're going to let your kids wander around while you're having a Strange Fruits party?" he asked Hilly. "They're awful young for something like that."

"It's not like you think," Hilly assured him. "We're going to send them right upstairs if anyone brings a fruit that's beginning to ferment. And by the way, we're having some of the finest white organic grape juice in the world." He lowered his voice conspiratorially. "Imported from Saskatchewan. SS connections come in handy once in a while, whether you believe it or not. So please say you'll come."

"I'm sorry. I just don't want to go to a party where everyone goes around being introduced to everyone else's fruit."

"Come on," Hilly prodded. "The truth. You don't want to go because you can't think of a fruit. Right?"

Frank shrugged. He decided to let Hilly believe this.

"I'll tell you what's coming already," Hilly continued. "Maybe it'll give you some ideas. Pomegranates, kiwis, uglis . . ."

"It's no use," Frank told him. "I'm the kind of guy that thinks apples and oranges."

"So bring apples. But try to get the green ones at least."

"Your friends will laugh at me. They always do. And they'll force all those weird things on me. 'Have a little of this, Frank.' 'Try just a bite, Frank.' And before you know it, I'll be sick, just like the last time."

"You're wrong about my friends," Hilly insisted. "They think you're very interesting. Just the other day one of them called you a 'learning experience.'" He looked out the patrol car window and saw Wilbur waving frantically at them. "We'd better back up," he told Frank. "That man seems to want to speak with us."

Frank backed up to where Wilbur was standing and pulled over to what remained of the curb.

Hilly got out and flashed his best smile. "Yes, sir? Is something the matter?"

Wilbur looked dubiously from Hilly to the patrol car, which was pink and had "Hi! We're Frank and Hilly!" painted on the doors, hood, and rear end. Then he spotted Frank. "I want to talk to the real cop," he told Hilly. "With the gun. This is serious."

"You know the law, mister," Frank called to him, trying not to look too pleased. "The mental hygienist handles all initial, nonviolent contacts with the public."

"Oh, all right," Wilbur said. "Maybe the mental whatsis is what we need. There's some loony in that place over there who can't decide whether he wants to be a butcher or a nurse."

Hilly chuckled indulgently. "Oh, my! That does sound highly unusual. Why don't we talk about it?"

"It's just terrible, officer!" Shirley Lee piped in. "People are coming out of that place all tore up!"

"What place is that, ma'am?" Hilly asked gently.

She pointed at Pie in the Sty just as more bandaged, disoriented people wobbled out the door. "Look! There come some more right now!" she gasped.

Hilly looked over his shoulder at the luncheonette and turned back to Shirley Lee and Wilbur with a reassuring smile. "Oh. So that's what you meant. I bet you're strangers here, aren't you?"

"Yes, sir," Wilbur told him. "We're visiting from Tennebama."

"Welcome to our city!" Hilly gushed. "I hope you have a wonderful trip. Now, as for those people with the bandages, they're patients of the eminent plastic surgeon, Dr. Niemand Lurk. Pie in the Sty is the hottest luncheonette in town. Some of the richest and most famous people in the world eat there. Dr. Lurk had the terrific idea of setting up an operating room in the basement so the luncheonette's patrons can dine, socialize, and have twenty years lopped off their faces, or whatever, all in the same building."

"Now ain't that something!" Wilbur remarked.

"So there's nothing to worry about," Hilly assured him. "Enjoy your visit." For the first time he noticed the blanket-swathed form that Shirley Lee held. "Aw, let me see him," he coaxed. "I have four myself."

Shirley Lee opened the blanket.

Hilly leaned over, got a glimpse of the piglet's snout, and recoiled. Although he'd rather die than admit it, he'd had trouble getting used to his and Yog's children. But this one made them look like cherubs. He hurriedly climbed back into the patrol car. "I wouldn't be too concerned about that if I were you," he stammered through the window. "Those things can be corrected nowadays." He kept smiling nervously at them as Frank started the patrol car and drove off.

"Well, you smiled your way to victory again," Frank commented sarcastically.

Hilly sighed. "Don't be hostile, Frank. I'm no threat to you. You're just as necessary as I am. If someone had to be shot, I'd be all thumbs." He smiled reflectively. "Of course, in situations like this, where the human touch is needed, I think I'm quite effective. They responded pretty well to my approach, didn't they?"

"Doesn't everybody? But you sure made a quick getaway this time. Usually, you take a good fifteen minutes to bow and scrape your way back into the car."

Hilly shuddered. "I was just so startled. That woman had the ugliest baby I've ever seen."

He's a fine one to talk, Frank thought, but kept tactfully silent. He had the feeling that Hilly was less than satisfied with his Pusgrub wife and hybrid children, especially since his wife's younger sister had come to live with them about a year ago. Ever since her arrival, Hilly's tirades about equality for Pusgrubs had become less frequent and he'd developed a slight twitch in the corner of his mouth. The sister, whose name was Elphlegm, had already moved in when he went to Hilly's Strange Cheeses party, but she'd kept out of sight. He'd heard she was tall for a Pusgrub and not as slimy as most. Also, she was one of the few who'd been able to master English. But Hilly's face wore a strained look every time he mentioned her, and Frank was pretty sure she was giving him some kind of a hard time.

"You must admit," Hilly continued, apparently determined that Frank should appreciate him, "since they added us social hygienists to the department, mortality among perpetrators has declined significantly."

"Sure. But among police officers, it's increased significantly."

"Are you implying that some lives are more valuable than others?"

"God forbid," Frank said. "It's just that it takes longer to train a police officer than a perpetrator."

Chapter Three
The Forbidden Vegetable

-1-

Yog looked in on her children and was happy to find all four of them asleep. Now she could watch television. Last night she'd caught one of the females making a cradle for her pet waterbug after midnight. If Pusgrub children didn't get at least twelve hours of sleep a night, their feelers wouldn't develop properly. And she felt she had to be especially careful, since hers were the product of a mixed marriage.

She settled herself in front of the television set that was in her and Hilly's bedroom. Her favorite program was on, a situation comedy about a Pusgrub who designed clothes for humans and kept putting in too many sleeves. The dialogue was in Pusgrubet, but there were English subtitles.

Yog sat in a cozy slime hammock she'd exuded between the arms of a chair. She would have had to sit on the seat or lie on the bed, like a human, if Hilly were at home. The sight of her hammock made him sick, she knew, though he was too polite to say so. As much as she loved him, she was only able to relax when he wasn't around.

As she rocked contentedly, she played a string game with her two pairs of hands and hoped Elphlegm wouldn't spoil her night. If only she'd be asleep when Hilly came home! She never ceased tormenting him, and he was too kind to defend himself. This resulted in Yog having to scream at her sister until she was exhausted. And since Elphlegm insulted Hilly in English, which Yog didn't understand very well, most of the time she didn't even know exactly what to yell at her for.

She supposed the girl's plain appearance had helped spoil her disposition, but there was still no excuse for the way she treated Hilly. If it continued, she'd have to go, Yog decided. Then she forgot about her sister and concentrated on the television program, which was particularly funny that night.

Although to fellow Pusgrubs she was a complete washout, by human standards Elphlegm was considerably more appealing than her sister. Besides being larger and more intelligent than the average Pusgrub, she had been born without the second set of arms that usually grew from the armpits. Her skin was firm and her hair thick and not very fungus-like. And because she imitated the human practice of bathing daily, she lacked the characteristic Pusgrub stink.

Despite her resemblance to people, Elphlegm hated them bitterly, because she was enough like them to realize they were far superior to her own race. She wished that if she had to be a Pusgrub at all, she could have been a stupid one. It seemed to her that being inferior wasn't as bad as knowing that you are.

Humans like Hilly, who were so scrupulously tolerant, enraged her more than the bigots. By not acknowledging, even to themselves, the disgust they felt for her and her kind, they attempted to deprive her of the pleasure of hating them. That was why she persecuted Hilly so relentlessly. One day, she hoped, his guard would drop, and he would reveal openly the contempt that lay behind his patronizing affection for her sister and their odious children.

Elphlegm recognized the irony in the fact that she, who had been born after the Pusgrubs were cast back up on the earth's surface and who was not really accepted by her own people, was the only one who seemed to treasure the old ways. Nine years ago, when she was eleven, she'd discovered a way into one of the tunnels. Since then she'd spent a good part of her time beneath the earth, exploring the ancestral passages, which were relatively intact in the New York area. She loved the damp, fragrant earth and the way her instinct and keen sense of smell led her unerringly along mazelike paths and over subterranean rivers. The darkness felt so good on her eyes, which always ached in the sunny upper world. In the entire nine years that she'd traveled along these buried roads, she'd never met another Pusgrub. They'd abandoned their heritage and attached themselves to the human community like parasitic growths. She realized that she hated Pusgrubs even more fervently than she hated humans.

When she heard Yog turn on the television, she knew it would be safe to leave. Her sister loved the late night programs and would be too engrossed to bother checking on her. She put on a dress and shoes, and slipped out of her room. Tonight the moon was full. She couldn't remain at home, even though she was tired and would have preferred to. A year ago she'd done something that had made her a slave to the moon for the rest of her life.

-3-

That night the moon had been full too. Elphlegm had fought violently with her sister, as usual, over Hilly. She'd stormed out of the house and hurried to the refuge of the ancient tunnels, where everything was simple and there were no Hilly and Yog to tempt her malice.

In the floor of an abandoned building near their home was a hole which led into New York's ancient subway system. She dropped down it and raced along the old track bed until she reached the tiny opening to the Pusgrub tunnels. The location of this opening intrigued her, because it meant there probably had been some contact between the Pusgrub and the human populations in ancient times. She wondered about the nature of that contact and whether her alien ways could be due to some long-buried human gene.

Once inside the tunnels, she dropped to her hands and scurried swiftly on all fours along the dirt floor. She could move almost as quickly as the other Pusgrubs, even though she lacked their extra set of arms. That night, with her anger to give her strength, she ran farther than ever before. The rivulets that cut across her path became more frequent and took on a cold, clean smell that told her she was far from the city.

Finally, she turned off into a peculiar narrow tunnel that looked as if it hadn't been used much by the local Pusgrubs. When she spotted a silvery glow in the distance, she knew why. Up ahead was one of those places which the Pusgrubs called by a name only translatable as "interface"—an open grotto where the underground and the surface world met, where dank subterranean air mixed with wind and light. These interfaces were viewed with superstitious horror by most Pusgrubs and scrupulously avoided, since such places were known to breed disease and weaken the nerves. Still, there was a path, however narrow, so some Pusgrubs had visited the spot.

As she made her way toward the glow, she became aware of a rushing sound. Drawing closer, she saw a waterfall tumbling down from the surface world into a black pool, which was girded by a ledge about a foot and a half wide. A willow grew above, near the place where the river spilled over the edge of the human world. Through the drooping branches of the tree shone a full moon, which danced on the cascading waters.

A ray of moonlight fell on an odd plant that had thrust itself up from the darkness in a quiet part of the pool. It was an ugly, knotted, fleshy thing that looked like the withered hand of an old woman. Elphlegm approached it warily, staring at it in disbelief. She couldn't get a really good look at it without venturing onto the narrow ledge, but even from a distance she was certain of its identity. She'd thought it existed only in legends. Now that she saw it before her, recognizable from the descriptions she'd heard in old wives' tales as a child, she wondered if the legends could be true. If they were, that plant could help her revenge herself on the despised humans. Of course, there would be consequences, but at that point she was still too angry to care.

Elphlegm crept along the ledge until she was as close as she could get to the plant. But when she stretched out her hand, she couldn't bring herself to touch it. She had the uncomfortable feeling it would clutch her and drag her beneath the inky water. Finally, she clasped her hands behind her back to steady herself and leaned over to it, just barely reaching it with her mouth. She tore off one of the fingers and flung herself back against the wall of the cave with it between her teeth. Taking a deep breath, she bit into the flesh of the plant, and a brackish, oddly warm liquid coursed down her throat.

Feeling terribly sick, she crawled back along the ledge. For a long time she lay shuddering on the floor of the tunnel, convinced that she had poisoned herself and was going to die. Excruciating pains tore at the center of her body. They weren't in her stomach, and they weren't the kind that came every month during her menstrual period. She had a peculiar sense of their being orchestrated. Each pain was discrete, starting as a faint twinge, rising gradually to a crescendo (during which she nearly lost consciousness), and slowly receding. They came closer and closer together, and in the end, she fainted.

When she awoke, far from feeling sick, she was stronger than she'd ever been before. Her clothes lay in shreds around her, torn by her body's transformation. She'd lengthened into a cylinder, which had swallowed her neck and most of her arms and legs. Her skin was gray now and as slimy as that of any Pusgrub. And her face was all mouth and fangs. Elphlegm had become a wereworm, doomed to lust for human blood and meat whenever the moon was full.

Suddenly ravenous, Elphlegm skimmed along the tunnels toward New York. By coiling and stretching her body, she could move twice as fast as she'd been able to when she was in her Pusgrub form. And her sense of smell, normally very acute in Pusgrubs, was now astonishing. She could identify tiny insects by scent alone as she sped past them.

When she reached the city, she made her way to the surface and slithered through the deserted streets, looking for a human, any human. Finally she encountered a late-night reveler, staggering home from Pie in the Sty. Instinct guided her. She leapt at his neck and killed him instantly by severing his carotid artery. After she'd quenched her thirst with his hot, pumping blood, she licked her way down his body to his thigh.

With her fangs, she neatly tore away his trouser leg, exposing the white, hairy skin. The hairs tickled her mouth, and while his skin was salty, it hadn't the clean salt taste of the arterial blood she'd just swallowed. But still, it satisfied her teeth to plunge them into the heavy, meaty flesh. Her jaw quivered with pleasure as she bit away a chunk, and gouts of fresh blood oozed from it, washing over her tongue.

She crouched there on the sidewalk over her meal, gnawing and lapping, until her hunger receded with the coming of dawn. Looking anxiously at the brightening sky, she hurried home, barely making it to her room before she began to be wracked by the pains of metamorphosis.

Her sister came to her room around 1:00 P.M. the next day to see why she was sleeping so late and was shocked to find her sprawled across the bed, naked and smeared with blood. When she shook her, Elphlegm woke long enough to mutter something about cutting herself and then sank back into a state of near catalepsy. Yog stared at her for a long time, maybe remembering legends she'd heard as a child. Then she shook her head as if to clear it, covered her sister with a blanket, and left the room to return to her chores.

When Elphlegm finally woke up, she startled the entire family by not only being civil to Hilly but helping Yog prepare dinner. From that point, her mood slowly deteriorated, until it became particularly foul around the time of the next full moon. Then, suddenly, she was almost pleasant again. After several months of this, Yog and Hilly decided it all had something to do with her menstrual cycle.

Meanwhile, reports of strange murders had begun to appear in the newspaper. Approximately once a month, several people were found dead, horribly mangled and nearly drained of blood.

Chapter Four
Frank Has a Hunch

Wilbur waved after the departing patrol car. "Those police were nice fellas," he told Shirley Lee. "A little peculiar, though. That one boy said he had four pigs of his own, but when he looked at ours, he got an expression on his face like he'd never seen one before."

Shirley Lee didn't answer. She was admiring the full moon that was just rising above the jagged skyline.

Wilbur looked up at it too. "It is real pretty. But it's nicer back home, because you don't have all these buildings. If you can see the moon on the horizon, it's enormous. It looks strong. This little city moon doesn't seem like it could do much of anything."

"Well, what should a moon do?" Shirley Lee asked, faintly amused.

"I don't know." He shrugged. "Pull the tides back and forth, I guess."

A short distance from them, underground, a large worm was making its way toward the heart of the city.

The moon went behind a cloud, and Shirley Lee turned her attention back to Pie in the Sty. "Will you look at that!" she exclaimed. "Now something else is happening over there!"

A car of any kind was a rare sight, either in the city or the country. But now a chauffeured limousine was driving up to the entrance of the luncheonette, accompanied by four smaller cars filled with men. As the limousine drew over to the curb, two of the other cars swung around to block the path of Frank and Hilly's patrol car, which was making another circuit of the block.

Frank slammed on the brakes, and both men were thrown violently forward. As soon as he'd recovered enough to be angry, Frank flung open the door. "Sonofabitch! I'll get those goddammed fools!"

Hilly laid a restraining hand on his shoulder. "Wait, Frank. Don't overreact. Remember, I have to make the initial contact, since, at the moment, this is a simple traffic violation."

"What are you talking about?" Frank asked him

incredulously. "They could have got us killed! We're lucky our heads didn't go through the windshield!"

"It would have been our own fault. Neither one of us was wearing his seat belt."

"Don't make excuses for them!" Frank snapped. "They tried to kill us!"

"Now, now, that's paranoid thinking," Hilly said calmly. "Let's be rational about this. They just stopped a little too fast, and they didn't park correctly."

"They didn't park at all. They're spread all over the road."

Hilly opened the door on his side and climbed out of the patrol car. "Please. Let me handle it. You might get nervous and use your bullet, and then you won't be able to get another one until next month."

"You have a point," Frank conceded. "It's only the 3rd. I'm not going to take the chance of being unarmed for twenty-nine days because of these jerks. Go ahead and see what you can do."

Hilly smiled confidently and headed for the group of cars. Very large men, wearing tee shirts with "DPL" stenciled on the fronts and backs, were pouring out of the smaller ones. He approached the man who seemed to be in charge. "How do you do, sir," he said pleasantly. "I'm a New York City police officer." He pulled out his wallet and showed him some identification.

The man looked down at the wallet and back at Hilly with silent contempt.

"The badge number's 13642, if you want to make a note of it."

The man remained silent.

"You don't? Okay," Hilly told him cheerfully. "I don't blame you. I'm sure we'll get along just fine." He returned his wallet to his pocket. "Now, if you don't mind, I'd like to say a few words to you about your cars . . ."

The man grabbed Hilly by the shoulders, spun him around, and kicked him to one of the other men. He in turn kicked him to another, and soon they were all playing an impromptu game of football with Hilly, who managed to retain at least the trace of a smile throughout the entire ordeal.

Across the street Wilbur and Shirley Lee cheered and

applauded, thinking it was some kind of acrobatic display.

"It's that young policeman," Shirley Lee said. "He sure is talented. I swear, he just bounced."

Finally the men tired of their game, and one of them gave Hilly a particularly energetic kick. He sailed several feet and wound up draped over the hood of the patrol car.

Frank looked at him with disgust as he crawled limply back into the car. "Why didn't you defend yourself?"

"It would have been illegal," Hilly gasped, wiping his face with his handkerchief. "They were wearing DPL tee shirts. That means they have complete immunity from everything."

"Not as far as I'm concerned," Frank told him. "We tried it your way. Now I'm going to go kick some ass!"

"Wait!" Hilly begged. "Don't be mean-spirited about this thing. It's not entirely their fault. I may have been a little too abrupt with them. Or maybe they don't speak English."

Frank sank back and buried his head in his hands. "I give up," he sighed wearily. "You can't fight militant masochism."

The men from the cars formed two human chains, making an aisle from the limousine to the door of the luncheonette. A heavily veiled woman, accompanied by four more bodyguards, climbed out of the limousine and hurried into Pie in the Sty. The crowd howled and shoved, trying to get a closer look at the woman.

"Well, well! Now that was someone!" Wilbur announced.

"Do you think it was 'S'?" Shirley Lee asked excitedly.

"Could be. Why don't we go over there and ask one of those people. Maybe we could get her autograph." Wilbur took Shirley Lee's arm, and they strolled across the street.

The bodyguards had gotten back in their cars and parked them at the curb, directly in front of the luncheonette.

"Now they've parked in a 'No Standing' zone," Frank complained.

"That isn't very serious," Hilly told him. "Let's just ignore it. We don't want to be inflammatory. Besides, traffic regulations are more traditions than actual laws. They're a throwback to the days when people had cars. They don't mean much now."

Frank started the patrol car, and they drove slowly down the uneven street. "I bet those guys were The Boys," he said darkly.

"Oh, please," Hilly groaned. "Not The Boys again. Pie preserve me from mythology freaks! The Boys haven't been around for centuries, if they ever existed at all."

"The Boys will always exist! You can't smile them away!"

Hilly stifled a yawn. "You know, you really should think of going into therapy. Whenever you don't have an opportunity to go charging around with your gun for a few days, you get totally paranoid. I admit those men weren't the most pleasant people in the world, but I'm sure they weren't The Boys. There just isn't enough crime around anymore for people to bother organizing. The Social Sanctuary takes wonderful care of us. Everyone's coming from a center of inner peace, and most of us . . ." He looked significantly at Frank. ". . . don't need violence."

"Ha!" Frank snorted. "That's what you think! I have a gut feeling about Pie in the Sty. Those two hicks may have been making more sense than we realized. We'd better keep an eye on that place. I bet there's something going on there tonight."

"I'm sure there're a lot of things going on at Pie in the Sty," Hilly replied, "but they'd be of more interest to a voyeur than a police officer." He wanted to change the subject, because he knew from experience that once Frank started talking about The Boys, he could rant for hours. "There's a lovely full moon tonight, isn't there?" he commented.

Frank refused to be distracted. "Have you noticed that those weird mutilation murders always happen when the moon is full?"

"Oh, for goodness' sake! Don't tell me The Boys are doing that too?"

"I thought so at first . . ."

Hilly sighed with inexpressible ennui.

"But now," Frank continued, "I think the murders are being committed by a Pusgrub."

Hilly turned on him furiously. "May I remind you my wife is a Pusgrub!"

"I know, I know. You remind me at least once a week. And you talk about me and The Boys!"

"Well, I hope you also know that the Social Sanctuary

doesn't want a racial element introduced into criminal investigations. And they're perfectly right. Whether you admit it or not, the SS is nearly always right."

"Look, don't be so touchy, okay? Just hear me out."

"I'll listen," Hilly agreed reluctantly, "but please don't be offensive."

"Did you ever think that maybe the two races, Pusgrub and human, had some contact with one another even before the geological upheavals?"

"What do you mean?"

"Have you read any of the Pusgrub mythology in the ethnic-appreciation pamphlets the SS distributed?"

"Of course," Hilly replied, "but I'm rather surprised that you have."

"I'm not the complete idiot you take me for," Frank told him. "Anyway, there's a certain legend that deals with the ability of Pusgrubs who eat a certain herb to transform themselves into wereworms when the moon is full."

"That's absurd! You're not suggesting those ghastly murders were committed by a worm? Why, the victims were torn to shreds! Worms don't have teeth!"

"Worms don't, but wereworms do. If you'd read your ethnology carefully, you'd remember the Pusgrub myth says that wereworms have fangs. And what's more, I think they've been preying on humankind for centuries. I've found evidence."

"That's difficult to believe."

Frank pointed at the glove compartment. "There's a book in there. Take it out."

Hilly opened the glove compartment and removed a tattered, yellowing Canadian paperback. Its title was *The Selected Poems of Edgar Allan Poe*. Hilly looked at it curiously. "Edgar Allan Poe? Wasn't he one of the writers of the early classical period?"

"Right. Turn to the page I marked, and read the part I underlined."

Hilly opened the book to the place where a piece of paper was inserted and read: "'But see, amid the mimic rout a crawling shape intrude! A blood-red thing that writhes from out the scenic solitude!' You know, Frank, this isn't a very up poem."

"Keep reading," Frank said impatiently.

"'It writhes! It writhes! with mortal pangs the mimes become its food.' Yecchh! 'And seraphs sob at vermin fangs in human gore imbued.' Is that all?"

"No. I underlined another part. At the bottom."

Hilly sighed. "'. . . the play is the tragedy, *Man,* and its hero the Conqueror Worm.' So what?"

"Don't you see? Poe could only have been talking about a wereworm. Pusgrubs have been stalking us practically from the beginning of time."

"You're a bigot, Frank."

"I'm not saying that all Pusgrubs are wereworms. Just a very few. An occasional truly malevolent one." He looked thoughtfully into the darkness outside the patrol car. "Like the one that's probably out there at this moment, looking for human blood to slake its fiendish thirst."

Chapter Five
Innocence Besieged

Wilbur and Shirley Lee tried to get someone's attention to ask if the veiled woman had been "S", but they were ignored by the frantic mob. In an age when hardly anyone even had a bicycle, people would kill for the chance to eat in a place that had been sanctified by the patronage of an actual limousine owner. All the noise and movement woke the piglet, and it squealed with terror.

There was a sudden stillness as everyone turned to gape at the tacky-looking couple who'd had the audacity to come into their midst.

"That was a terrific noise," someone told Shirley Lee nastily. "How did you do it? Do you sing professionally?"

Intimidated, Wilbur and Shirley Lee backed nervously away. The blanket fell from the piglet's face, and it squealed again.

A thrill of excitement ran through the crowd when they realized who Shirley Lee was. They jabbered and speculated feverishly.

"It's the woman with the pig again!"

"Bubby was talking to her before! She must be somebody!"

"Who's that with her?"

"This is Wilbur, my husband," Shirley Lee told them helpfully.

The crowd tittered.

"No, really! Who is he?"

"I wonder if one of them is 'S'!"

"I wouldn't be surprised. Those clothes are quintessential wit."

"It is 'S''s sort of thing."

"I love that blouse!" somebody gushed at Shirley Lee. "Where on earth did you buy it?"

"At a mold sale in the dress store back home," she answered truthfully. "We had a damp spring, and stuff began to grow on some of the fabric. There was a little on the collar of this, but I scraped it off."

The crowd shrieked with laughter.

"Only 'S' would say that!"

"Fantastic!"

Just then Bubby stepped out of the luncheonette. When he spotted Shirley Lee, his eyes glowed with damp lust. "You've come back!" he breathed moistly.

"Yes. Me and Piggy." She remembered her husband. "And Wilbur here too."

"Don't leave again," Bubby pleaded. "Come inside and have a bite to eat with me."

Wilbur answered for her. "Thank you kindly, sir, but if we don't get going, we won't see the Radio City National Monument all lit up."

The crowd chuckled with delight, which puzzled Wilbur. He took the Radio City National Monument very seriously.

"I'll have the lights turned on especially for you," Bubby assured him. "I have friends who can get things done."

"We couldn't put you to all that trouble," Shirley Lee protested.

"It's no trouble at all." Bubby made a sign to the bouncers, and they expertly swept Shirley Lee and Wilbur through the door while he followed. Then Muncie and his partner hurried out again, to beat back the people who tried to surge in after them.

Chapter Six
Lurk Takes Care of Business

Lurk's basement operating room was almost entirely red. The walls and ceiling were coated with red lacquer. The floor was made of red tile. The furniture had been painted red. Even the operating table, which was cluttered with instruments and debris, was covered with a red sheet. There were large posters of celebrities, pigs, and spareribs on the wall. These were splattered with blood, as was a small white refrigerator in one corner.

Lurk and Simon, clad in red surgical gowns, were in the midst of stuffing a naked corpse through an opening in the wall.

"Holy shit!" Simon panted. "I'm glad this doesn't happen too often, boss. This guy's heavy."

"This is the first time it happened since we moved down here," Lurk said petulantly. "You'd think anyone would be entitled to one lousy mistake, wouldn't you, Simon?"

"Sure, boss. We're all human."

"Oh, no, we're not! A doctor isn't! Didn't you know? A doctor's supposed to be a god. Everybody's hand gets a little shaky now and then. But is my hand allowed to get a little shaky? Hell, no! They'd blame me for this. They'd pull my damned license, that's what they'd do."

"Where's His Satanic Majesty?" Simon grumbled as he struggled with the corpse. "He's never here when we need him."

"He'll be around. Remember, last time we saw him, he said he'd be away for a while because he had a lot of tempting to catch up on. Even devils get behind in their work, I guess."

Simon looked at the corpse's face and shook his head with disbelief. "What a mess! I don't suppose you could say he got an uncontrollable nosebleed?"

"Be serious! His nose looks like it exploded."

They gave a final shove, and the body disappeared through the hole.

"Ah! That's done!" Lurk said, smiling with relief.

"But won't someone miss him?" Simon asked.

"That bunch upstairs is too far gone to notice anything.

They'll just think he's gone on to someplace else. Which he has." Lurk went to his desk and pushed a button hidden underneath it. A panel slid shut over the opening in the wall. Not the slightest trace of a seam was visible. "Naturally, if anyone should ask about him. . . ."

"I've never heard of the gentleman."

"Exactly."

"What about his clothes?"

"Put them in my desk," Lurk said. "I know a place where I can sell them."

Simon lifted the man's things off a clothes hook and shoved them into the bottom drawer of the desk under a pile of clean red sheets. "Where does the chute lead, boss?"

"A basement room on the other side of the block. I'll pick him up later. I have to drive upstate anyway tonight to do a job for Bubby. So I'll just take the corpse along and dump it into some quicksand I know about up there."

Simon examined the part of the wall where the opening had been, trying unsuccessfully to find the seams. "This is a terrific job. Who built it for you? It's kind of a weird thing to ask a contractor to do."

"Some dumb foreign kid. Probably in the country illegally. He had his name and address hanging on the bulletin board in the grocery. Said he did cheap repairs and carpentry. I told him I needed a way to sneak girlfriends out if the wife showed up unexpectedly."

"He believed that?"

"Why not? He was getting paid."

"Yeah. I know what you mean, boss. Money gives things credibility." Simon stretched, yawned, and scratched his stomach. "I'm going upstairs for some ribs. Do you want an order? You must be hungry. You've been hacking away for hours."

Lurk looked around the operating room with distaste. "Don't you think you should clean up after the nose job first? Or, rather, the nose job manqué." He giggled.

"Clean, clean, clean! Scrub, scrub, scrub!" Simon whined. "What do you have? Some kind of fetish? I thought we did this place in red so we could avoid all that eternal mopping up."

"At least wipe off the posters and the refrigerator," Lurk insisted. "We don't want to disgust people."

"Oh, all right!" Simon went irritably into the bathroom and returned with a wet, dirty rag. He took a few hasty swipes at the posters and refrigerator, smearing and diluting the blood rather than removing it.

Lurk grimaced but didn't protest. Most of his clients were lucky if they were seeing double instead of triple or quadruple. They didn't notice petty details like blood and mangled tissue.

Simon tossed the rag back into the bathroom, where it landed on the edge of the sink. Pinkish water dripped from it onto the tile floor, which, in contrast to that of the operating room, was the usual white. Patients didn't normally go into the bathroom, so there was no need for camouflage.

"I suppose not much can be done about the posters, but you could have some consideration for me and paint the refrigerator red at least," Simon told Lurk indignantly. He rubbed his dirty hands on his smock and headed for the door. "Now do you want some ribs, or don't you?"

"No thanks," Lurk said. "I have a diet supper in the fridge. I've been putting on a little too much weight."

"Suit yourself," Simon told him as he left. "I'll be right back."

Lurk opened the refrigerator and removed an emesis basin that had been used for a jello mold. He poked the quivering orange mass with his finger and said out loud, "Good. It's set." He often spoke aloud when he was by himself. Ever since his first encounter with Satan, he'd had the feeling he was being watched and should at all times play to his audience.

He put the jello on his desk and went back to get a platter with a whole roast chicken on it. Taking a spoon from his top desk drawer, he sampled the jello, rolling it around in his mouth until it melted and letting the sweet fluid trickle down his throat. Then he took a bloody scalpel off the operating table, wiped it on his surgical gown, and used it to carve thick slabs of white meat from the chicken's breast. He was about to put a slice in his mouth when Simon reentered, chewing on a sparerib.

"Finish up quickly, boss," he said. "There's a stomach on the way down. None other than Basile St. Just-l'Espalier of Paris, London, and so forth."

Lurk dropped the chicken back onto the platter and leapt up, trembling with exitement. "Mlle. St. Just-l'Espalier? The richest woman in the world? Right here? In my little operating room? What an honor! You say she wants her abdomen tightened?"

Simon was a good deal less impressed than Lurk. "Yeah," he replied casually. "She'll be right down. She just stopped to look at some weird couple with a baby pig. Nobody can figure out who they are. Bubby's fawning all over them, so a lot of people think one of them may be 'S'."

There was a knock at the door.

"That must be Mlle. St. Just-l'Espalier now," Simon said. "I'll get it."

"No! Not yet!" Lurk gibbered frantically. He shoved his interrupted dinner back into the refrigerator. Then he grasped the four corners of the operating-table sheet, gathering up the detritus from the last operation in it. He threw the bundle on the floor and kicked it under his desk. "Quick!" he whispered to Simon. "Put a clean sheet on the table!"

Simon took a clean red sheet out of the bottom desk drawer and spread it over the table while Lurk trotted into the bathroom and smoothed his hair in front of the mirror.

He came back out and looked nervously around the room, wondering if he'd forgotten anything. "My God!" he said suddenly. "The richest woman in the world! I'd better sterilize my instruments!" He opened the bundle under his desk and pulled out a handful of surgical instruments. Then he dropped them into a sterilizer along with the scalpel he'd used to cut his chicken.

"Why are you going through all that, boss?" Simon asked. "The antibiotics you give them after the operation knock out any germs."

"Simon," Lurk replied patiently, "you just do not take a chance with several billion dollars worth of flesh. That much money imparts something of the sacred to its possessor, and you do not use a greasy scalpel on God. You may let her in now."

Simon opened the door.

Basile St. Just-l'Espalier, a thirtyish brunette who sagged a bit all over, entered with twelve bodyguards.

Lurk bustled solicitously around her. "This is a great pleasure and honor for me, mademoiselle."

"For me too," she said politely. "Your skill is world renowned, Dr. Lurk."

The bodyguards milled around the room, peering under things and tapping the walls. One of them frisked Simon and pulled a sparerib out of his pocket.

"I hope your hands are clean," Simon chided. He took back the sparerib and began to eat it.

Lurk watched the bodyguards anxiously. They were poking around in the vicinity of the chute. "Is it necessary that all these people remain during the operation?" he asked Basile. "It would be somewhat unhygienic."

"Of course not," she said graciously. She turned to the bodyguards and clapped her hands together. Instantly, they stopped their search and stood at attention. "That will do," she told them. "The man is a doctor, not an assassin."

Their leader bowed to Basile. "We'll be in the hall, mademoiselle."

They opened the door and marched out. Lurk hastened to lock it after them.

"I apologize, Dr. Lurk," Basile said. "But you realize a woman in my position is extremely vulnerable."

"Of course. I understand completely," Lurk assured her. "My assistant told me you wanted something done about your abdomen. Is that correct?"

"Oh, yes." Her chin began to tremble. "I have a terrible problem. A tragic problem. One that has been with me since adolescence."

Lurk led her gently to a chair. "Please sit down, mademoiselle, and tell me about it," he urged.

She took a handkerchief out of her purse and wiped her eyes as she struggled to compose herself. "When I was around fourteen," she told him tremulously, "instead of discovering sex, like most young girls, I became involved with . . . with. . . ." She started to sob.

Lurk hovered over her, clucking and patting her on the head. "You poor darling! Are you all right? Would you like me to get you some smelling salts? A glass of water? A sparerib?"

She shook her head. "No. I must be like a soldier. I must be strong—strong enough to tell the truth, no matter how sordid. When I was a young, innocent girl, I became horribly involved with . . . chili dogs."

"You poor girl." Lurk said compassionately. "And to look at you, one would never guess that your life had been marred by such a terrible thing. I believe some corner of your soul remained untouched."

"And yet I suffered the anguish of the damned," Basile moaned. "I became insatiable. Ten, twelve a day were nothing to me. Then Mother noticed my expanding waistline and guessed my terrible secret."

"I know," Lurk told her. "Some brute had taken advantage of your distraught condition. You were pregnant."

"No. Fat. One thing about chili dogs, they can't make you pregnant. Anyway, my mother was horrified. She feared I would become a social leper and insisted I undergo intensive psychotherapy."

"A wise decision! I assume the treatment was successful?"

"Not for a long time," Basile admitted sadly. "I was too confirmed in my depravity. But then my therapist hit upon a sensitivity training technique using parts of his body and a hot dog bun. It worked. I lost a hundred pounds, and now I'm ready to try men. But first something must be done about my hideous abdomen."

Lurk looked at her closely, somewhat puzzled. "But you seem to have a lovely figure."

"No. I have a corset that was designed by one of the top engineering firms of Europe. I'll get undressed and show you what I mean."

Lurk unzipped her filmy lavender dress and helped her slip it over her head. Then she removed her lacy slip and stood naked except for a formidably boned corset. "I'd better lie down for the rest," she told him. "I tend to lose my balance." Simon and Lurk helped her onto the operating table and covered her with a red sheet. She struggled mightily beneath it, panting and gasping as she forced open the hooks. "Here it comes!" she said breathlessly. "This is it!" She gave one final heave, and the sheet rose suddenly as her abdomen burst free of the corset. "Now do you see what I mean?" she asked.

"Uh, yes, there is a little problem," Lurk acknowledged. "But don't worry. You'll leave here a new woman." He handed her a mimeographed sheet and a pencil. "Now if you'll just put an X next to the drugs that are currently in your system. So we know how to adjust the anesthetic."

She made several marks on the paper.

Lurk took it from her and examined it. "Very good," he told her approvingly. "That's at least five less than most of my patients. I like a clean-cut girl." He beckoned to his assistant. "Come, Simon. Administer the anesthetic. Number Three Blend."

Simon inserted a needle in Basile's arm and set up an intravenous.

Chapter Seven
Frank, God, and Bubby
Close In On
The Boys, Michael, and Shirley Lee

-1-

Frank and Hilly were cruising slowly through the deserted midnight streets. They'd had dinner and answered a few calls, but Frank couldn't stop thinking about Pie in the Sty. "I still have a funny feeling right in my gut," he said, half to himself.

"Nervous tension," Hilly pronounced. "Close your eyes and concentrate on experiencing a luminous glow at a point directly between and slightly above them."

"I'm driving. Besides, it's not that kind of funny feeling."

"Well, then, maybe the soybean curd in those tofu twirls we had for dinner was a bit off. My earlobes feel odd, and that's always a sign that my system has been deranged by something impure."

"It's not that kind of funny feeling either. I just know those guys back there were The Boys."

"Frank," Hilly said patiently, "you must accept the fact that The Boys probably never existed at all. And if they did, according to the legends, they were disbanded in 1990 for refusing to comply with affirmative-action guidelines."

"No!"

"Yes! The book I read said that they were able to hold their own with the FBI, the CIA, and even the IRS, but the BSPU and F double OLS finally did them in."

"What were all those? Terrorist organizations?"

"No one knows anymore. In fact, supposedly that's how they broke up. Even the members forgot what the initials stood for."

"Whoever they were, they couldn't have gotten rid of The Boys," Frank insisted. "They just pretended to disband. The Boys would never give up so easily." An edge of hysteria crept into his voice. "I know The Boys exist! No matter what you say! They're really there! I believe they're really there! I believe!" He punctuated this credo by hammering on the steering wheel, which caused the car to swerve dangerously near some very ugly potholes.

Hilly's finely honed psychological radar sensed the approach of a psychotic episode, and he took evasive action. "Hey, don't get excited," he soothed. "You may be right."

Frank slammed on the brakes and turned to Hilly, his face twisted by the intensity of his passion. "You know I am, don't you? Deep down in your heart, you believe! I know you do!"

Hilly slid closer to the window, smiling nervously. "I'm willing to entertain the possibility that some sort of organized crime may...."

"Yes. They're out there." Frank said quietly. "I've always believed. I've always kept my faith. And it's been worth it, because now they've come." His eyes blazed suddenly with ardor, and he started the car again, dragging it around in a screeching U-turn. "We're going back to Pie in the Sty! You can put your fingers into the barrels of their guns! Then you'll believe!"

"Oh, what the heck," Hilly said as they sped through the night. "I've always wanted to see that place anyway. But what if they won't let us in?"

"They have to let us in. We're police officers. Besides, I've known Bubby for years. I've been in Pie in the Sty lots of times to grab an order of ribs after I go off duty."

Hilly was impressed. "Gosh! You mean you go there all the time?"

"Two or three times a week," Frank told him with a shrug. "If I eat ribs more often, my gallbladder starts acting up."

"But if Bubby's such a good friend of yours, won't he take offense if you accuse him of harboring The Boys?"

"I'm not going to tell him what we're looking for," Frank explained. "If The Boys are working out of Pie in the Sty, I'm sure Bubby's not aware of it. Besides, I don't think they'd want to have anything to do with him. They've got standards."

Hilly looked at him doubtfully. "Are you sure this isn't just your hemorrhoids talking, Frank? Pain can do funny things to a man."

"My hemorrhoids always hurt like the devil," Frank said. "They're no worse tonight than they ever are. Quit patronizing me. I know something's going on in that place, and I'm going to prove it to you right now."

-2-

"That's what I like," God announced. "Pure, dumb belief. Pigheaded, unreasonable stupidity. There's no greater source of energy. If only humans could harness their stupidity, they could forget about their windmills and petroleum."

Michael tried to kiss Him, but God pushed him away.

"Careful," He warned. "You're blocking My view."

Michael got up and stalked away in a huff. When he looked back to see if God was upset, he realized that He hadn't even noticed he'd gone. Or was pretending He hadn't.

Michael left the area around the screen, where all Heaven was gathered, and went to sulk next to the Venetian blinds. As he stared sullenly at them, it occurred to him that what lay outside might not be as horrible as everyone feared. Maybe there was freedom. Another universe. Another God. One who knew how to appreciate devotion, Michael thought resentfully.

He touched the blinds, but dared go no further. His anger still wasn't as strong as his fear. He glanced over at the group around the screen and was surprised to find that although the attention of the others was focused on the drama unfolding on earth, God was looking at him. Of course, Michael thought. He'd been so upset, he'd forgotten that the rat bastard was omniscient.

He had a queer expression on His face, though. Expectant rather than angry. And there was a trace of the same fear that was visible whenever He warned newcomers to Heaven to stay away from the blinds.

Out of spite Michael formed mental pictures of how he'd open the blinds and escape. He tried to project his delight at leaving this claustrophobic, wearisome paradise. But the love he still felt for God crept in and undermined his lies.

God read this, smiled slightly, and turned back to the screen, which showed a close-up of Frank and Hilly pulling up in front of Pie in the Sty.

Michael struggled not to cry, because he felt God's attention still on him, though it was weakened by His interest in the doings on earth. He rested his face against the cool metal of the blinds and tried to ignore the mocking laughter that forced its way into his head.

-3-

As Frank and Hilly got out of the patrol car, Hilly looked at the crowd and self-consciously adjusted his clothes. All at once he felt extremely shabby.

"Hey, Frank!" Muncie called. "You're early. Don't tell me this is an official call."

"Sort of, but I'm sure I can find time for a plate of ribs. Nothing's that official. Is Bubby around?"

"Inside with 'S' and her date. What's the problem?"

"I'm not even sure there is one," Frank said casually. "We got a tip that there's going to be a robbery here tonight, and I wanted to talk to Bubby about maybe putting on more security. To tell you the truth, the person who gave us the tip is sort of unreliable. Probably nothing will come of it."

"We didn't. . . ." Hilly began indignantly.

"This is my partner Hilly," Frank cut in. "Come on, Hilly. Let's go inside." He dragged him through the door.

"Bubbie's probably in back, in the Sausage Bower," Muncie called after them.

The dimly lit interior of Pie in the Sty was crowded with people who were hunched busily over plates of spareribs. You could see at a glance they took their pork seriously. There wasn't an amateur in the place. Even the musicians working out on their electric oboes and tambourines and the singer wailing garbled lyrics into her bullhorn couldn't compete with the charred piles of meat on the oily plates.

Frank and Hilly picked their way through the maze of tables.

"You shouldn't have told that lie about a robbery," Hilly scolded. "That isn't the way to build a relationship of trust with the public."

"If the public wants to trust me, that's its problem," Frank said. "Because I sure as hell don't trust the public. Now stop your moralizing, and let me do the talking for once."

They approached a nook, which was enclosed by a white wicker fence and hung with garlands of sausages.

Inside the Sausage Bower Bubby was seated very close to Shirley Lee, staring hungrily into her eyes and playing with her piglet.

Wilbur, who was making his way through a double order of spareribs, didn't seem particularly concerned. "Come on, honey, try some of the ribs," he urged Shirley Lee. "They're real tasty."

"Wilbur! Not half an hour ago you told me you'd never eat a pig!"

"There weren't any around half an hour ago, except that runt of yours," he chuckled.

Shirley Lee gave him a baleful look and hugged the piglet closer.

"I appreciate this, sir," Wilbur told Bubby. "I raise the damn things, and I can't even get a plate of ribs. The government inspector comes every month to make a count of the stock. And if so much as one pig is missing, you'd better be able to show him the carcass. With the ribs still on it."

Bubby looked at Shirley Lee's untouched plate. "Please. Won't you have just one?"

Shirley Lee's eyes filled with tears. "How could I ever? When I know that black old piece of meat was once a little pink squealy thing." She began to sob and turned her wet, accusing eyes on Bubby. "I can't believe a wonderful man like you is a murderer. Old Prune never harmed a living soul."

Bubby looked puzzled. "Old Prune?"

"Don't mind her crazy talk," Wilbur told him. He jabbed Shirley Lee with his elbow. "You be still! He don't kill the pigs. I told you before, but you don't want to hear it. The people in Potpourripolis do all that messy stuff. Ain't that right, Bubby?"

"Well, not exactly," Bubby hedged. "The customers like fresh meat. And, besides, the slaughterhouses in Potpourripolis leave a lot to be desired. They're run by Pusgrubs, and you couldn't imagine a dirtier bunch."

Shirley Lee shoved her plate of ribs away. "Then you do kill them!" She glared at him with savage contempt.

"Look, I don't do it myself," Bubby said defensively. "That would make me really nauseous. I pay this plastic surgeon, Lurk, to do it. He's a good man with a knife."

Shirley Lee blanched, her rage replaced by horror.

Bubby blundered on. "And if he can't get up to Earwig—that's where I have the holding pen—he gets some friend of his there to do it. I would never, never do it myself. I'm a very sensitive guy."

"I don't believe you!" Shirley Lee sobbed wretchedly. "I bet you do it with your own hands!"

"I swear I don't. Lurk does it all. You can ask him. He's going upstate to kill a bunch for me tonight after he finishes work."

"Oh, no! Oh, my Blessed Pie, no!" Shirley Lee moaned.

Frank and Hilly, who were just entering the Sausage Bower, froze.

Frank unsnapped his holster. "What's the trouble, ma'am?" he asked Shirley Lee.

"Murder!" she howled.

Frank drew his gun and looked eagerly around for someone to point it at.

Hilly grabbed his arm. "Put it away. There's no blood or anything. It must have happened someplace else."

Frank complied, obviously disappointed.

"It's all right, Frank," Bubby said. "Nobody's been murdered. The lady's just a little upset."

Shirley Lee smiled tremulously through her tears. "He's right. I'm just being silly, I guess."

Bubby gave her a fond look. "With everything else, she's sensitive too. Beautiful women are usually bitches."

Shirley Lee beamed at him, and he shyly squeezed her hand. Wilbur, still busy with his spareribs, didn't seem to notice.

Bubby tore his eyes away from Shirley Lee and looked curiously at Hilly. "Who's your friend?" he asked Frank.

"This is my partner Hilly. He comes along to keep me from hurting any of the perpetrators' feelings."

"Oh, one of the Social Sanctuary boys," Bubby said affably. "Pie bless them! They've made crime so much healthier." He shook Hilly's hand. "Happy to meet you."

"The pleasure is mine," Hilly said, trotting out his best smile. None of his friends had been able to get into Pie in the Sty, and he was very proud of himself for succeeding where they'd failed. He'd tell them all about it at his Strange Fruits party.

"What brings you here so early tonight?" Bubby asked Frank. "Couldn't wait to get a plate of my ribs?"

"Maybe a little later," Frank said. "After we check some things out. We got a tip this place is going to be hit, and we just want to make sure your security's up to par." He motioned to Hilly. "Come on. We'll start in the basement."

Bubby seemed shaken. "The basement?"

"Take it easy," Frank told him. "We're friends, aren't we? We understand each other."

Bubby looked significantly at Hilly. "What about. . . .?"

"I told you, it's okay," Frank said. "Relax and finish eating." He walked toward the back of the luncheonette, followed by Hilly.

-4-

God glided over to the Venetian blinds, where Michael was still sitting. "You're missing a good show," He said.

Michael grabbed hold of His sleeve. "Stay with me for a while."

God sat down next to him, positioning Himself so that their bodies were just barely touching. His radiance made Michael tingle. He drew God's face down so they could kiss, but His lips stayed hard and tightly sealed. Michael tried to read His eyes and saw only contempt and, beneath that, illegible turmoil. He wished he were strong enough to do something horrible to God—maybe tear those sick eyes out so they'd stop laughing.

As God heard Michael's thought, contempt faded from the eyes and was replaced by a starved glitter.

Suddenly furious beyond reason, Michael grasped a handful of God's fragrant golden hair and pulled with all his strength. But God turned it into fire, and Michael dropped it, wincing with pain. "Why don't You want me anymore?" he asked miserably, cradling his wounded hand.

"You've become too predictable," God told him, His face

119

politely bland now. "But I want us to be friends. Come watch the show. You can still sit next to Me."

"Fuck You!" Michael told Him.

Something kindled briefly in God's eyes again, but He turned away and went back to the screen.

Michael remained where he was. He took the cord of the Venetian blinds in his good hand and toyed with it as he stared at God's back.

Chapter Eight
Elphlegm Lends Her Talents to a Noble Cause

-1-

Beneath the ground a crazed wereworm was burrowing her way into a part of the city where she knew she could find enough fresh, hot blood to quench her thirst.

As she tunneled through the darkness, Elphlegm was surprised to feel vibrations coming from off to the side. Something or someone was down there in the earth with her. Curiosity got the better of her, and she decided to investigate. Perhaps there were others, she told herself, who'd transformed themselves into wereworms in order to wreak vengeance on humankind. Or perhaps some ordinary Pusgrubs had become nostalgic for their subterranean life and had returned to their ancient homes.

But as she came closer, she picked up the characteristic smell of people. She followed it to an abandoned subway tunnel and peered out at the two men who were standing in the circle of light cast by an electric torch.

Heinri and Klausiere were wetbacks from Alsace-Lorraine and members of that dread terrorist band, the Lorratian Liberation Organization. They were dressed in the uniform of their group, berets and lederhosen, and had guns strapped to their sides. A pile of tools lay at their feet. They each held a pick and were getting ready to start hacking their way through the ceiling of the tunnel.

"Are you sure this is the place?" Klausiere asked.

"Certainly," Heinri assured him. "I planned this all very carefully. We are directly below the operating room in the basement of Pie in the Sty."

Elphlegm was amused. Both her superior Pusgrub sense of direction and her superior Pusgrub sense of smell told her they were directly below the Central Park city dump. She concluded from their guns and furtive manner that the two were planning some mischief, and this put her in a double bind. They were nice healthy specimens. The odor of their blood was making her painfully hungry, and she wanted to jump them. But she was restrained by her hatred of their race, which inclined her to wait until they'd done whatever evil thing they'd planned. That way, not only would someone suffer, which was always fun to watch, but she would have the opportunity of eating the whole lot of them at once after they'd provided her with entertainment. Not only would these two become her victims, but their victims would be hers as well.

But the fools were so hopelessly disoriented that it looked like they wouldn't be able to get anything done without her help. Most of her victims were people who'd staggered out of Pie in the Sty in the wee hours of the morning, so she'd be able to find it easily.

Once she'd decided to help them, Elphlegm was faced with the task of dealing with their probable fear of her. She wasn't worried about them shooting her, since only a bullet made of anthracite coal could kill a wereworm. But she had to put them at ease so they'd let her help them get where they were trying to go.

She could tell by their accents that they were foreigners. There were no Pusgrubs outside of America, so the two men weren't apt to know about wereworms. Even American humans didn't know about them, apparently, or there would have been speculation along those lines when clusters of dead people were found every month on the night of the full moon. For that matter, most of the younger Pusgrubs had never heard of them either. So she'd only have to worry about how the two men would react to a large talking worm.

Suddenly, she had an idea. She crawled along the ceiling until she was right over their heads. Then she dropped to the ground, directly in front of them, and smiled cordially. "Hi!" she said. "I'm a quadruple amputee!"

Heinri and Klausiere stared mutely, too astonished to even think of going for their guns.

"Don't be embarrassed," Elphlegm told them. "Most people find my appearance startling at first. I guess it's as much the skin disease as the fact that my arms and legs are missing."

"You get around pretty well," Klausiere said in a shaky voice.

"I was in a good rehab program." Elphlegm made her voice spiteful. "It was the least they could do after turning me into a monster!"

"The least who could do?" Heinri asked.

"The government. They confiscated my farm and resettled me right over one of the ancient nuclear waste dumps. By the time I realized what was happening, it was too late. I had such bad gangrene that my arms and legs needed to be amputated. My skin peeled off and was replaced by scar tissue, leaving me the hideous thing I am now."

"What are you doing down here?" Klausiere asked suspiciously.

Elphlegm gave a bitter laugh. "Do you think I can walk the streets? People shrink from me with horror."

"I see your point," Klausiere said. "You do look a bit peculiar."

"So do you," Elphlegm countered. "Why are you two wearing those funny short pants? And those idiotic caps?"

"These are our uniforms!" Heinri replied indignantly. "We are members of the glorious Lorratian Liberation Organization."

"I never heard of that one."

"You will soon. After tonight the entire world will know us. We are going to bring this country to its knees."

"Good!" Elphlegm said shortly. This was even better than she'd anticipated.

"You're not very patriotic," Klausiere commented.

"Would you be, in my position?"

"I guess not."

"So I hope your plans, whatever they are, will succeed. If you'd let me, I could make sure they succeed."

Heinri and Klausiere exchanged wary looks.

"Why should we trust you?" Klausiere asked her. "We met you all of about five minutes ago."

"Yeah," Heinri added. "We ought to shoot you or at least tie you up until our mission is accomplished. We're desperate men."

Elphlegm stifled an urge to go for their throats. "Why don't you give me a chance to prove my good will?" she asked them calmly.

"Like how?" Heinri sneered.

"Well, for one thing, you're nowhere near Pie in the Sty. I've saved you a lot of futile labor just by telling you that. Doesn't that prove I'm on your side?"

"How did you know we were trying to get into Pie in the Sty?" he asked her. "We didn't mention that after you showed up."

"I overheard you."

"You were spying on us!"

Elphlegm's patience had reached an end. She licked her fangs and prepared to attack.

Then Klausiere unwittingly saved his and Heinri's lives. "Our group should welcome new soldiers from the ranks of the oppressed," he said, "even if they're not Lorratians. It already knows half of what we're up to anyway. Why don't we give it a chance?"

"It!" Elphlegm said indignantly, uncoiling from her attack position. "What do you mean by that?"

Klausiere blushed. "I'm sorry," he stammered, "but it's kind of hard to tell what sex you are. Your accident seems to have wiped out your secondary sex characteristics." He looked at her more closely. "And your primary ones too," he added.

"You've got some nerve!"

"So, what are you then?" Heinri asked impatiently. "Male or female?"

"If I have to tell you, you don't deserve to know. But I will tell you this, stupid. Dig where you plan to, and you'll end up buried under a pile of shit. You're directly beneath the town dump."

"That's impossible!" Heinri snapped. "My calculations were flawless. You're trying to thwart us!"

Elphlegm spotted a place on the ceiling where the concrete was entirely gone and only dirt lay between them and tons of garbage. "Come here," she told Heinri and Klausiere. "Stand right under that spot." She indicated the bare place with a jerk of her head. "I'll show you I'm telling the truth." She leapt up to the ceiling. Using her fangs and twisting her body rapidly so it acted as a drill, she cut through the dirt.

Klausiere and Heinri walked over and looked up into the rapidly deepening hole. All at once, Elphlegm dove out and rolled to the side, and the two men were struck with a barrage of garbage. They jumped out of the way, cursing and brushing no longer identifiable decayed things off themselves.

"For what it's worth, you've convinced us," Heinri said when he'd recovered from the shock. "But there's no hope now. Even if we could find the right place, we'd never be able to dig our way to the chute in time."

"Chute? I thought you wanted to get into Pie in the Sty," Elphlegm said.

"We do. The chute leads to its basement from the sub-basement room of a building on the other side of the block."

"Wouldn't it be easier to break into the subbasement room and climb up the chute?"

"We can't. The man I made the chute for had me install a burglar alarm which can only be deactivated from inside the room or by using a special key on the outside of the door."

"Well, why didn't you have a duplicate key made?" Klausiere asked. "It would have saved us a lot of trouble."

"Don't you think the idea occurred to me? That bastard Lurk watched me every moment when I was putting in the alarm. He even came to the locksmith with me. There was no way I could have gotten an extra key. Besides, at the time I didn't know what a big deal he was. The only thing I'd have wanted a key for would have been to rob his office. And it didn't seem worth the trouble."

"Don't worry," Elphlegm told them. "I'll get you where you want to go. Just follow me." She led them down the subway tunnel until they came to a bare earthen wall. Then she drilled into it, taking care to make the opening large enough for the two humans. The gluey sweat she exuded glazed the walls of the tunnel as she dug it, making them as firm as cement. They continued for some distance, weaving around rock and ancient pipes. Finally, Elphlegm struck a length of new metal. "This must be your chute," she told Heinri and Klausiere.

They climbed around her and shone the electric torch on the metal.

"That's it," Heinri confirmed. "We'll take over now." Using a portable drill, he cut through the wall of the chute.

"I'd better go first," Elphlegm said as they crawled inside.

"Oh, no, you don't," Heinri told her peevishly. "This is my mission, and I'm going first. You come after me so Klausiere can watch you from behind. I'm not at all certain you can be trusted."

"Whatever you say." She fell in compliantly between Heinri and Klausiere. They hadn't much power to annoy her, since she'd gotten hungrier and now looked on them as her dinner-to-be. She couldn't be angry at them any more than a human could be angry at a veal cutlet.

"What a break this chute was," Klausiere remarked as they made their way slowly through the metal tube.

"Yes," Heinri agreed. "Who would have guessed what excellent use we'd make of it when I build it for that character?"

"Luck was with us. If it hadn't been for a newspaper article about him, we wouldn't even have known who he is."

"We have more than luck going for us," Heinri told him. "We have the best intelligence network of all of the smaller groups. Any day of the week we can put our hands on a dozen valuable hostages."

"But this is the biggie!"

"Yes! The richest woman in the world!" Heinri said with awe. "And thanks to our informants, we knew she was coming to Lurk for surgery even before he did."

Elphlegm had realized from the beginning that their mighty leader was leading them in the wrong direction. The pungent odor of Bubby's spareribs, which she would have thought even a human could smell, was fading in back of them. And they were crawling downward instead of up as they should have been. Since Heinri had been so anxious to take the lead, she decided to let him discover his mistake for himself. He did a few moments later when, utterly blinded by rapturous dreams of Basile's money, he dropped over the ledge at the end of the chute. The electric torch broke as he fell, plunging them into darkness.

Elphlegm let herself down next to him. "What an odd place to find the richest woman in the world," she giggled.

"Have the decency to shut up!" Heinri moaned. "Get the

flashlight out of the sack," he called to Klausiere. "I can't see a damned thing."

"Neither can I," Klausiere answered. "That's why I'm having trouble finding the flashlight. In fact, I can't find the sack."

Elphlegm's stomach contracted with pleasure as she smelled dead, bloody human flesh. She slithered over to Lurk's discarded corpse and licked it ecstatically.

"I've got it! I found the flashlight!" Klausiere shouted to them. He flicked it on, and Elphlegm wriggled swiftly away from the corpse, hoping there was no blood on her mouth. Leaning over the edge of the chute, Klausiere shone the flashlight around the room. "Where are we?" he asked. "And who's that?" he gasped as the light hit the corpse.

"We went in the wrong direction," Heinri told him. He pushed himself into a sitting position and experimentally moved his arms and legs. "I don't think I broke anything. Let me have the flashlight."

Klausiere handed it down to him. "There's something in back of you that I think you should have a look at."

Heinri stood up and moved the flashlight beam over the floor. When he saw the corpse, he recoiled with a little squeak of terror.

"What's the matter?" Klausiere asked contemptuously. "Don't tell me a soldier of the Lorratian Liberation Organization is afraid to look into the face of death!"

"It's just that I never saw a guy with a shredded nose before," Heinri told him. "I was startled. There's a difference between being startled and being afraid."

Elphlegm crawled back over to the body on the pretext of examining it and was able to sneak a few more gulps of blood. She wiped her mouth covertly on the dead man's arm. "Who do you think he is?" she asked Heinri.

"He must be one of Lurk's former patients. So that's what he wanted the chute for! To get rid of his mistakes!" He kicked at the ground. "This room has a dirt floor."

"So? What does that have to do with anything?" Klausiere asked.

"So we're going to bury this guy." Heinri looked at

Elphlegm. "With our new friend's help. This makes Lurk a murderer, and it'll give us one more thing to hold over him. We know where the body is, and he doesn't. Bury him!" he ordered Elphlegm.

"Glad to oblige," she replied. And she was, because during the burial, she had ample opportunity to feed unobserved. Heinri, who was more squeamish than he cared to admit, had climbed back into the chute with Klausiere. He sat there, dangling his legs, and just turned the flashlight on her often enough to see how her work was progressing. When she'd finished, Elphlegm swept the loose dirt over the body and slimed it down with her sticky sweat. No one would guess that the earth had been disturbed. "Finished," she told Heinri.

"Good," he said. "Now, I'll disarm the burglar alarm from in here. That way, Lurk will think we took the body away." He climbed out of the chute and went over to the door, widely skirting the place where the grave had been dug. There was an alarm box down near the ground. He carefully opened it and disconnected the bell. Then he unlocked the door and left it slightly ajar. "If we'd discovered the body when we were making our escape, we wouldn't have had time to bury it. Even our mistake has worked out in our favor."

"Your mistake," Klausiere reminded him.

"Anyone can get turned around. Especially when they're thinking about billions of dollars. Try to look at the positive side of this. Now that the body is securely hidden, Lurk's completely at our mercy. Wouldn't you rather use this as a threat than the other?"

Klausiere shuddered. "That's for sure!"

"Do you still have the thing in your pocket?"

"Yes. It's here."

"Then let's get going. I have the ice pack in my shirt, and it's starting to give me a chill. Come on," he said to Elphlegm.

She climbed back into the chute with them.

"We have to move fast," Heinri said. "Klausiere, check your watch. What time is it?"

"Four."

"What? That's impossible! We entered the subway tunnel at

about eleven o'clock. Are you trying to tell me five hours have passed?"

"You're going by American time," Klausiere explained. "I keep my watch set at the time in our great mother country, Alsace-Lorraine."

"You jackass!" Heinri groaned. "Let me see. That's six hours difference. No. Five hours difference. Oh, hell! I can't figure it out now. Let's just hope we're in time. Come on." He began to scurry up the chute with Klausiere and Elphlegm right behind.

They reached the point where they'd drilled through the wall of the chute very quickly, considering that they had to travel up a rather steep incline.

"Speak in a whisper from now on," Heinri warned them after they'd gone a little farther. "We're getting very close."

In another few minutes they saw the panel up ahead.

Heinri approached it and looked at it silently. Then he slumped against the wall and buried his head in his hands. "Oh, no! I forgot! It only opens from his side!"

"So let's use the drill," Klausiere suggested.

"We can't. The panel is right near his operating table. He'd hear us before we even got started."

"Maybe we should knock. He'd be surprised, anyway, and he might be curious enough to open the panel."

"He also might be pointing a gun at us when he does." Heinri looked around desperately. "There has to be some way!" Suddenly his face brightened. "I have an idea. Now that I remember, the chute was about six feet from the bathroom door. We'd be taking a big chance, but we just might be able to come up through a hole in the bathroom floor."

"But we'll still need to use the drill to break through the tiles," Klausiere objected.

"It won't be as audible if it's coming from the next room. And don't forget, he's performing surgery on the richest woman in the world. He's bound to be preoccupied."

"But he's going to hear something."

"He'll think it's the band playing upstairs. Or the pipes knocking." Heinri motioned them back. "Let's go down the chute a way before we cut an opening."

When they'd moved back far enough, Heinri pressed the drill to the wall of the chute.

"Wait," Elphlegm told him. "You're drilling in the wrong place. The bathroom is on the other side."

"How do you know?" Heinri asked. "You've never been in Lurk's operating room, have you?"

"No. Of course not. But when you lose most of your body, whatever's left becomes extremely sensitive. And my acute sense of smell tells me the bathroom's on the other side."

"I'll take your word for it, I guess," Heinri said. "You were right the last time." As quickly and silently as possible, he drilled a hole in the side of the chute Elphlegm had indicated. This time she took the lead when they went through the hole. Without hesitation she slithered through dirt and around pipes, bringing them to a point directly below the bathroom.

-2-

"Is Elphlegm Your instrument?" one of the Elect asked God. "Did You send her to guide Heinri and Klausiere?"

"No," God answered. "If I wanted to guide them, I'd do it telepathically. What do I need with a middleman?"

"How about Pie?"

"Pie was a doer. He never told anyone anything."

"Don't You ever speak through the mouths of certain special people?"

"Very rarely. I have a mouth of My own, after all."

"But what about the prophets?"

"What about magicians? What about traveling salesmen? They make life interesting, but anyone who believes them is mad. I repeat, if I want something told to someone, I do it Myself. Do you really think that God can't make Himself understandable to whatever He created? You ought to know Me better than...." God broke off and cast an annoyed glance over His shoulder at Gabriel, who was cursing loudly and yanking at a strange young man's clothes. "Why are you making that dreadful racket?" He asked coldly.

Gabriel released the young man and prostrated himself before God's throne. "I'm sorry about the noise, Lord, but I just don't know what to do!" he complained. "One of the group of Elect that passed over today is giving me so much trouble! My nerves are shot!"

"What's the matter?"

"He won't put on his robe."

"He has to. If he's allowed to wear civilian clothes, they all will want to. And Elect or not, some of them have pretty vile taste. The robes I've provided are lovely. Why doesn't he like them?"

"I don't know," Gabriel said helplessly.

"Bring him to Me. I'll talk to him."

"That might work. He's been clamoring to meet You ever since he got here."

God was delighted. He appreciated enthusiasm. Some of the Elect had developed a ho-hum attitude about the divine presence that He found extremely offensive.

Gabriel led a young man with a bland, goony expression over to God. He wasn't wearing the usual earth clothes, God noted, but was wrapped in a confusing, intricately draped length of white material. It was held in place by dozens of colored strings, which were tied in complex knots. The young man's shaven head was painted with odd designs and symbols and circled by a macrame fillet. Although he was barefoot, strings and rings adorned his feet decoratively and with perfect uselessness.

God tried to read his mind, but was unable to, because he didn't seem to have one. "What's his name?" He asked Gabriel.

"Horace."

The young man held up his hand in a mild gesture of protest. "That was only my profane name, which I bore before I entered onto the path of the spirit. My true name is Bal-wak Frngess Yam."

"That's a name?" God asked.

"More than a name," the young man replied. "It's a description of my soul's essence."

God was speechless. People had bored Him before, but never so intensely in so little time. When He'd recovered a bit, He stretched out His lovely hand to the young man. "Welcome to Heaven, Yam," He said politely. "I'm God."

Yam stared at Him without taking His hand. "You have a face! You're not supposed to have a face!"

"I can be anything I want," God told him. "But I would have thought you'd prefer Me to have a face, since that's what you're used to."

"I didn't come to Heaven to find what I'm used to." Yam looked crestfallen and sulky.

"Maybe I'll be a golden cloud for you later," God said. "But first things first. Gabriel tells Me you're making trouble. You have to put on one of our regulation robes."

Yam shook his head firmly. "It would be impossible for me to remove my clothing. I even bathe fully dressed. The only time I change is at the vernal equinox, and then only after observing certain ritual purifications. Everything I have on is a symbol of some aspect of my quest for God."

"But you can stop questing. You have the real thing now. You don't need symbols anymore."

"I'm not so sure of that," Yam said.

Heaven quaked at the wrath in God's voice. "What? You don't believe I am what I am?" He bellowed.

"Frankly, I don't," Yam told Him. "You're supposed to be incorporeal."

"If I were incorporeal, I wouldn't exist, you fool! Just because you can't see someone's body most of the time doesn't give you the right to call Him incorporeal!" God turned Himself into a cloud. "Now do you believe?" the cloud asked. "Is this incorporeal enough for you?"

Yam reached out to poke at the cloud, but his finger went right through it. "I believe!" he exclaimed. He began to tear at his strings and draperies.

God resumed His humanoid form. "I'm glad you decided to put on the robe," He said. "You'll find it a lot more comfortable than all that stuff you were wearing."

"What do I need with a robe?" Yam asked. "Now that I'm sure who You are, I want to join with You."

"Okay," God agreed, taking off His robe. "Usually I give people a couple of hours to get used to the place, but since you're so anxious. . . ." He approached Yam and prepared to join with him.

Yam shrank back. "What are you doing?"

"You said you wanted to join with Me," God said, reaching for him.

Yam slapped Him smartly on the face. "Not like this!"

Heaven was paralyzed with horror. Even God was genuinely shocked. "You hit God!" He murmured in disbelief. "You must be insane!"

"Not at all. I want to become one with You. In my earthly existence I overcame all my passions, and now I demand the right to lose myself in Your infinite essence."

"Why would you want to lose your self?" God asked.

"That's the only way to true peace. I've cleansed myself of anger, lust, greed, and now I want to be rid of life as well."

"But you are. You're dead now."

"Death isn't enough. It's too much like life. I demand annihilation."

"You ninny! You've cleansed yourself, all right!" God said angrily. "Of everything that I find amusing! What did you have besides your passions? What can you offer Me? Your mind, which is only fit to compile grocery lists? Passion was the only language we had in common! I spew you out! Take him to hell, Gabriel!"

"But this is highly irregular," Gabriel protested. "He's one of the Elect."

"He just lost the election. Get rid of him."

Gabriel left hurriedly with the naked young man.

Yam's strings and draperies lay in the middle of the floor, where he'd thrown them as he took them off. God pointed His finger and dissolved them into a vapor. "So he wanted to be one with Me!" He muttered. "Next thing they'll all want to be one with Me. Why not? What could be easier than nonexistence? Then they wouldn't have to be bothered anymore with selves or anything else. But what about Me? Nobody ever considers My feelings. If I let everybody be one with Me, I wouldn't have anybody to talk to!" He glared at the angels and the Elect, who were watching him with frightened expressions. "If I'd wanted to be one, I would've stayed one!" He snarled.

Chapter Nine
Into the Trough

-1-

Frank and Hilly made their way through the crowd, toward the door which led to the cellar of Pie in the Sty.

"Why was Bubby so nervous about us going downstairs?" Hilly asked.

Frank shook his head sadly. "All sorts of nightmarish things go on down there. Things that most of us don't even know exist."

"I understand," Hilly told him. "I have terrible eye bags, but I'll probably never do anything about them, because I'm frightened to death of doctors. The thought of anyone going near my eyes with a knife just makes me swoon."

"I didn't mean Lurk and his plastic surgery," Frank said. "There are other things, that people don't talk about."

Hilly was puzzled. He talked about everything. "I don't know what you mean."

Frank nudged him and pointed at a seedy little man who was peering furtively out from the cellar door. As they watched, the man beckoned to a young couple seated at a nearby table. They got up and disappeared through the basement door with him.

"There!" Frank said. "Do you know where they're going?"

"To the restroom?" Hilly ventured.

"No!" Frank glanced around to see if anyone were close enough to overhear them. Then he lowered his voice and spoke directly into Hilly's ear. "They're going to lard up!"

Hilly started and turned deathly pale. "I don't believe it!" he protested, shuddering with revulsion. "You can't tell me that those two fresh-faced kids are going to lard up! Why, that's a federal offense!"

Frank laughed. "In more ways than one, since most of our federal officials come here to commit it when they're in town."

Hilly was appalled. "You've known about it all along, and you haven't done anything to stop it! How can you dare call yourself an American!"

"Take it easy," Frank said. "It's a victimless crime. Believe me, we're dealing with something much worse. I admit, larding up is ugly. You'll have to be strong to walk down into that cellar with me. You'll find that you never knew what degradation was before tonight. Are you ready?"

"I guess so," Hilly said miserably. "Good grief! No wonder Bubby was so worried about me seeing the basement. Animal fat is at the top of the list of controlled substances. It's only legal when used externally to treat skin diseases. He could do a lot of time for this."

"Not really," Frank said. "He took the precaution of having himself registered as a Type Nine eczema patient. That's the kind with the oozing water blisters. He could make a good case for any animal fat found on the premises being medicinal. We'd only make trouble for ourselves if we tried to bust him for that. But I'm worried about something else."

"What could be worse than an animal-fat violation?"

"That conversation about a murder that we overheard is bothering me," Frank said thoughtfully. "I'm afraid Bubby might be commissioning hits for The Boys."

"But there aren't any...." Hilly broke off and shrugged. "Oh, have it your way. I swear, you almost have me believing in them myself."

-2-

Inside the Sausage Bower Wilbur had fallen asleep with a half-eaten sparerib dangling from his mouth. Bubby and Shirley Lee were in earnest conversation.

"But dearest," Bubby pleaded. "You're asking me to give up everything I've worked for. There's going to be the biggest party of the year here tomorrow night, and I'm almost out of ribs."

"That's all right," Shirley Lee said. "I'll make them a nice carrot salad."

Bubby smiled wryly. "When that bunch comes here tomorrow night and sees a carrot salad instead of ribs, they'll laugh, because they'll think I'm putting them on. When they find out I'm not, they'll stop laughing and kill me."

"Then let's just get on out of here, honey."

"Darling, you're not just asking me to leave a business. Pie in the Sty is a lifestyle."

"It's a choice you got to make." Shirley Lee told Bubby firmly. "I can't stay with any man who'd kill a pig."

"But it would be irresponsible to turn all those pigs loose. They've led a sheltered life. Where would they go?"

"We can take them with us."

"What?"

Shirley Lee's round face glowed. "We'll go off into the woods with them, like we're shepherds. We'll build ourselves a little cabin, and we'll make a shelter right next to it for them to winter in. And the baby ones, like my angel here," she looked down at the piglet tenderly, "can stay in the house with us."

Bubby embraced her and the piglet with tears in his eyes. "It's madness! But I'll do it! I love you, Shirley Lee. You'll be more than my woman. You'll be my salvation. We'll go to the woods together and begin a clean, new life. Oh, darling, darling!" he sobbed, burying his face in his hands. "I've seen things that it'll take me a whole lifetime to forget."

"Don't you worry, lambchop. I'll be there to help you," Shirley Lee vowed fervently. "We'll make our own little world, where no one will ever hurt us or our piggies again."

-3-

In the basement of Pie in the Sty Frank and Hilly watched from the shadows while the sinister man who had brought the young couple downstairs handed them and several other people greasy slices of bread. More slices lay on a metal sheet, fat dripping down on them from a hole where the ceiling should have been.

"See?" Frank whispered to Hilly. "That bread's right under the rotisserie that grills the spareribs upstairs, the one that's supposed to burn off all the fat."

The people who were waiting to lard up stood on a line. When someone's turn came, he handed the pusher a thick wad of cash and was given a slice of bread reeking with fat. Sometimes the addicts would lose control and thrust their faces into the bread while it was still in the pusher's hand. Then he'd kick them away and fling the bread after them. It didn't matter to the lard freaks if it fell on the dirty cellar floor. They'd pick it up and devour it in a frenzy. One fix was usually not enough. The addicts almost invariably returned to the end of the line for more.

Hilly was barely able to look at them. "To think this is happening on my beat! And young innocents are being lured into this filthy habit! They say it takes only one slice, and you're hooked for life."

"Yeah, and the tragic thing is, they all think they can stop any time they want," Frank added.

A newcomer walked down the stairs.

"Hey," Frank said to Hilly, "look who just got on line!"

"I don't believe it! Our precinct captain! And he has a doctorate in sociology!"

"Now are you beginning to see why we can't bust Bubby for an animal-fat violation?" Frank asked. "But never mind that. Like I said before, I'm afraid he's into something a lot worse."

Chapter Ten
Assault

-1-

Lurk was diligently slashing away with his scalpel. "You'd better bring me some baggies," he told Simon. "All this stuff I'm lopping off her is starting to get in my way."

Simon went over to the desk to get some out of one of the drawers.

Underneath the bathroom Heinri was getting ready to break through the tile.

"I wouldn't drill in precisely that spot," Elphlegm warned him. "Try a foot or so to your right."

Heinri turned on her furiously. "Listen, you know-it-all," he said in an angry whisper. "I happen to be in charge here, and I'm sick of you butting in all the time. We're under the bathroom, aren't we?"

"Yes, but. . . ."

"Then shut up and let me drill!"

Elphlegm moved back a ways. "Suit yourself."

Heinri switched the drill on.

Simon heard the noise as he was giving the baggies to Lurk. "What's that awful sound?" he asked. "It seems to be coming from the bathroom."

"No," Lurk said absently, "it's coming from upstairs. I think it's that new group Bubby hired. Those electric oboes sound like clogged pipes, don't they?"

As Heinri drilled, Klausiere leaned eagerly over his shoulder. All at once they were drenched by a torrent of water that poured out of the hole Heinri had made.

"What the hell was that?" Klausiere sputtered, diving back.

Heinri peered cautiously upward after the water had subsided. "Damn! We're coming up through the toilet bowl."

"Weren't you able to tell from the way the pipes are connected?" Klausiere asked.

"I'm a carpenter, not a plumber." Heinri shot Elphlegm a nasty look. "Why didn't you warn me?"

"I tried, but you wouldn't listen," she said innocently. "I thought maybe you had some kind of strategic reason for wanting to make your entrance that way."

Lurk had filled most of the baggies. "Refrigerate these," he told Simon. "I know a cosmetics firm that pays top dollar for this stuff."

Simon grabbed an armful of the bulging baggies and carried them to the refrigerator. "I'm sorry, boss," he said when he returned to the operating table. "One burst all over your organic jello."

"You clumsy oaf!" Lurk snapped. "Now I'll end up getting a soyburger or a frozen fruit fluff. I'll never lose weight if you keep on sabotaging me like this." He dropped something into Simon's hand. "Put her bellybutton over on my desk on a piece of tissue so it doesn't get lost in this mess. I'm going to begin stitching her up now."

Simon brought the bellybutton to Lurk's desk. "Cute little bugger," he said as he laid it on a moderately clean tissue.

-2-

In the hallway outside Lurk's operating room the bodyguards were lounging around and chatting while they munched on fruit and nut mix.

Bubby and Shirley Lee approached them hesitantly, observed by Frank and Hilly, who were peeking around a corner.

Bubby went up to one of the bodyguards. "Is Lurk still operating?" he asked. "I have to talk to him. It's very important."

"Sorry," the bodyguard told him, calmly chewing his cashews. "We can't let anybody in."

Dejected, Bubby returned to where Shirley Lee was standing a way down the hall.

She tried to console him. "Well, at least if he's operating, he's not killing. Not piggies, anyway. We can stop him on his way out and tell him you changed your mind."

Bubby didn't answer her.

"Isn't that right, honey pie?" she persisted.

"It's a hit, all right," Frank whispered to Hilly. "Bubby must be a middleman. He gets contracts from The Boys and hires Lurk to carry them out." He strained to hear what Bubby and his girlfriend were saying to each other, but their voices were too low.

"Why do you look so funny?" Shirley Lee asked Bubby.

"Remember, I told you that sometimes when Lurk can't make it, he gets a friend of his upstate to do the job?"

"Oh, Pie help us!" Shirley Lee gasped. She waddled over to the bodyguards, wailing and wringing her hands. "You've got to let us in!"

"Sorry, lady," one of the guards told her indifferently. "We have our orders."

"Something's wrong," Frank said. "Maybe The Boys ordered a hit and then changed their minds."

"I thought they were The Boys," Hilly protested, indicating the bodyguards.

"No, no. Those are just The Little Boys. Policy decisions are made by The Big Boys."

Shirley Lee had recovered her composure. "You know, baby doll," she said, "we're silly to get all excited. The doctor can't call his friend anyway until he's finished."

"I'm afraid he can," Bubby told her unhappily. "He has a phone in there."

"His own private phone! Back in Tennebama we just have one for each town." She thought a moment and then smiled with relief. "Why that's even better! Let's us just call Dr. Lurk."

"We can't," Bubby sighed. "He has an unlisted number."

-3-

Lurk was nearly finished with the operation. "Bring me the compass," he told Simon. "I'm ready to reposition the bellybutton."

Lurk took the enormous compass that Simon brought to him and climbed onto the operating table with it, assuming a position that Simon had seen once in a copy of an old print by an artist named Blake. He thought the print had been called *The Ancient of Days*. Usually, Simon didn't pay much attention to art. But he remembered this print, because it looked so much like Lurk doing a bellybutton. This part of the operation always took the most time, so Simon knew he'd have a few free moments. "I'll be right back. I have to take a leak," he told Lurk.

"Wash your hands afterwards," Lurk said. "Remember whom we have here."

In the bathroom Simon unzipped his pants and stood over the toilet, staring absently into space. There was a grating noise, and Heinri's head and shoulders emerged suddenly from the bowl.

"Hold your fire!" he ordered. "And get that thing out of my face!"

Simon backed hurriedly away, zipping up his pants. This wasn't really happening, he told himself. Someone had drugged his spareribs.

But Heinri climbed out of the toilet and leveled a very real gun at him. Klausiere followed and then Elphlegm, who stood on her tail, staring into Simon's face and baring her fangs.

"What is that?" Simon asked faintly, looking at Elphlegm.

"One of your victims," Heinri sneered.

"Look, obviously whatever was done didn't turn out very well. But Dr. Lurk is happy to give refunds. All this unpleasantness isn't necessary."

"I didn't mean your victim specifically, stupid," Heinri said. "It was destroyed by your facist government."

"Oh. Well, go to Potpourripolis and sue them. What are you doing here?"

"You'll find out soon enough," Heinri told him. "Move it! Into the other room!"

Simon backed through the bathroom door, followed by Elphlegm and the two terrorists.

Spotting them, Lurk jumped off the operating table, still holding his compass. "Who are you? What do you want? How did you get in here?"

"You're not going to believe the answer to that last question, boss," Simon said.

"Shut up! And you drop that thing!" Heinri ordered Lurk.

Lurk let the compass fall to the floor.

Klausiere bent down to examine it. "So that's what he operates with. No wonder that guy in the cellar looked so bad."

"What guy?" Lurk asked nervously.

Klausiere grinned and pointed to his nose.

Lurk blanched. "How did you know about that?"

"We have our ways," Heinri told him. "We're a class outfit."

"I know you," Lurk said, looking at Heinri intently. "You're the kid who built the chute for me. This is the thanks I get for helping someone earn a living."

"Oh, stuff it!" Heinri snorted. "You weren't being charitable. You figured an illegal alien who had to advertise on a grocery store bulletin board to get work would be too desperate to ask any questions about your chute."

"How did you get into the basement room? The alarm and the locks I have on the door are the best available."

"Nothing can withstand the expertise of our organization."

"That's right," Elphlegm added with amusement. "These men are wizards."

Lurk took a good look at Elphlegm for the first time and recoiled. "Good God! Who did you?" he asked. "You should have come to me. Never look for bargains when you're dealing with your appearance. Cheap is cheap."

"You didn't do much for the fellow in the basement," Klausiere giggled. "At least our friend here is still breathing, which is more than can be said for him."

"I suppose you're here to blackmail me," Lurk said with resignation.

"We are not common blackmailers!" Heinri bristled.

"Although we do accept contributions," Klausiere said.

"Shut up, Klausiere!" Heinri told him angrily. "You cheapen our cause!" He turned to Lurk and announced with great solemnity, "We are the Lorratian Liberation Organization. We demand that Alsace-Lorraine be given the status of a republic, free of both French and German tyranny."

"And we want our native language, Freutsch, taught in all the schools," Klausiere piped in.

"Freutsch? I never heard of it," Lurk said.

"Of course you haven't. The French and German imperialists have banned it. They spread a filthy slander that speaking it injures the lips."

"And," Heinri continued, "furthermore, we want the writings of Freutsch statesmen, philosophers, poets, novelists, and historians published and placed on the shelves of bookstores and libraries all over the world."

"But, Heinri," Klausiere said, "there's only one, and he hasn't written anything yet. Just a manifesto, and he brushed his teeth with it the other day."

"Never mind. He'll start producing as soon as they lower his dosage of Thorazine."

"All that intellectual stuff's okay, but don't forget the food," Klausiere reminded him. "Tell them about our wonderful gourmet delights."

"That's right." Heinri pointed an accusing finger at Lurk. "I'll bet you've never even heard of our Lorratian national dishes, like Wienerschnitzel à l'Orange and Champignons mit Knackwurst."

"You're right," Lurk conceded. "Those are two taste thrills I've missed."

"Our national identity has been obliterated," Heinri said mournfully.

"That's a shame," Lurk told him, "but I don't see what I can do about it."

Suddenly, Klausiere spotted the bellybutton lying on Lurk's desk. "There it is!" he cried, diving across the room to grab it.

Heinri took the ice pack out of his shirt and tossed it to him. "Put it in there."

Lurk watched them with horror. "Stop! What are you doing? This is infamous! Do you know whose bellybutton that is?"

"Of course," Heinri replied. "It belongs to the lady on your table, who happens to be the richest woman in the world. Her money can purchase a great deal of influence. Enough to get autonomy for Alsace-Lorraine."

With their guns still pointed at Simon and Lurk, Heinri and Klausiere backed toward the chute.

Elphlegm didn't know what to do next. Now would be a good time to eat someone, and she certainly was in the mood. But she wasn't quite sure whom to choose. Lurk, plump and sleek, was by far the most tempting, but there was something peculiar about him. Even in his present agitated state, he seemed oddly invulnerable. She had the unnerving feeling that he just might eat her instead. His assistant was totally unappealing. He looked like he'd taste of rat meat. The woman on the operating table was out of the question, since she smelled strongly of chili peppers, a sovereign charm against wereworms. Heinri and Klausiere would be tasty morsels, but she didn't like to disturb them while they were doing something rotten. Besides, she didn't really care to eat in that room. Lurk made her nervous, and she wanted to get away from him.

She decided to accompany the terrorists and watch their antics for a while. She had a little time to spare. It was only about midnight, and she wouldn't return to her Pusgrub form until dawn.

"We want publicity. Lots and lots of media," Heinri told Lurk. "We'll be waiting by a radio. So if that lady wants her bellybutton back, she'd better be on the 8:00 A.M. news, offering to help our cause."

"You'll never get away with this!" Lurk said defiantly. "I'll construct an artificial bellybutton."

"Do you think Basile St. Just-l'Espalier would be satisfied with an artificial bellybutton?" Heinri asked. "You'd be ruined."

"If you do this to me, I'll be ruined anyway. No one will ever feel secure on my operating table again."

"Anyone who ever did had to be crazy. And don't forget, there are various degrees of ruination. I'm thinking of how the police will react to the discovery of a certain noseless person," Klausiere said.

"That's right," Heinri added. "You'd better persuade the lady to cooperate with us, or we just might call homicide. We buried the dead guy for you, Lurk, but we won't bother you with petty details, like where. The cops might be interested in knowing, though. Now open the panel for us."

Lurk pushed the button under his desk, and Heinri climbed through the opening, followed by Klausiere and Elphlegm.

"Should I call the bodyguards?" Simon asked. "Maybe they can catch them."

Lurk stood indecisively by his desk, looking from the door

144

to the opening in the wall. "I don't know. If they find out what happened, they just might kill me."

"Do you think they'd be able to? I mean. . . ." Simon trailed off, embarrassed. They'd never felt comfortable discussing the fact that they seemed to be immortal.

"Even if we only get arrested," Lurk said, "what if we were sentenced to life imprisonment? Imagine the implications. We'd sit there and sit there and sit there, until the jail rotted. Or what if those bodyguards wounded us, mortally, and we had to walk around that way. We can still feel pain, and maybe we'd be hideously deformed. What if we looked as bad as that mess the two terrorists had with them?"

"It looked like a worm to me," Simon observed.

"Worms aren't that big. And they don't have teeth. Did you see that guy's snaggle teeth? He really ought to have them capped."

"Maybe I should call the police," Simon suggested. "They don't know about the dead guy yet, and they could protect us from the bodyguards."

"Don't be so sure. Now that they have those Social Sanctuary idiots going around with them, we could be in a thousand pieces before they got through taking notes about everyone's toilet training. Besides, if this ever gets out, I might lose my license."

That would be tragic, he told himself. He'd have to wait years, until everyone who knew him was dead, before he could get a new one. Unless he was willing to go abroad, and he didn't want to do that. New York was his kind of town. He had to solve this problem somehow on his own, he knew, or face years of inactivity and boredom. Medicine was his life. He was convinced that in the whole world there was nothing as exquisite as a scalpel.

"I must try to catch them," he told Simon. "I have to get that bellybutton back and find out where they buried our corpse." He took off his surgical smock and put a suit on, sticking a gun in the pocket. "Keep Basile under," he said. "She mustn't wake up until I've gotten her bellybutton back in place."

"But if I keep her under too long, she'll get brain damage," Simon objected.

"That's okay," Lurk told him. "Nobody will notice. Close the panel after me." He stepped into the opening and slid out of sight.

-4-

In the hall outside, Bubby and Shirley Lee whispered nervously together.

"On my keychain, I have keys to all the rooms in the luncheonette, including Lurk's," Bubby told her. "I don't think he ever bothered to have an additional lock installed." He looked helplessly at the bodyguards. "Damn them! If only something would distract them for a few minutes, just long enough for me to get in and lock the door behind me."

"I think I can get their attention long enough for you to make it through the door," Shirley Lee said.

"How?"

"With my body."

"No! Never! I couldn't bear to have even one other man look at your lovely body. And you want to expose yourself to a dozen? That would kill me!"

"But it's our only chance," Shirley Lee pleaded. "I could do a striptease. Get them so worked up they wouldn't notice you at all. When I do it for Wilbur, he just goes all to pieces."

"I forbid it!" Bubby whispered harshly. "Do you think they'd be content to stand there and look? They'd become like mad things! They'd all fling themselves on you and . . . and. . ." Bubby fell silent, unable to put into words the elaborate and gruesome pictures forming in his mind.

"All of them?" Shirley Lee breathed, eyeing the well-built bodyguards, whose muscles rippled enticingly beneath their tee shirts. "Oh, dear me! Well, we don't have any choice. It has to be done. But while I'm doing it, I'll try not to notice." She handed him the piglet. "You hold baby. Have the right key in your hand, and be ready to run for the door." She licked her lips. "Now here I go!"

Swinging her generous hips, she wriggled toward the puzzled bodyguards. She removed her eyeglasses and twirled them around by the ear piece, now and then rubbing the lenses suggestively over her lips. She folded them and stuffed them in and out of the pocket of her sweater while undoing the decorative chain that held it shut at the neck. Putting her glasses back on, she slowly shrugged her way out of the sweater, her meaty bosom jiggling with every movement of her shoulders. The bodyguards were riveted by the spectacle. They had totally forgotten their fruit and nut mix.

As Bubby watched, a single tear trickled down his flushed cheek. Her blouse was beautiful, he noted. Its tasteful print of bumblebees and daisies told him that the woman he adored possessed a highly developed aesthetic sense. Finally, she tore off the blouse, revealing a sturdy white cotton brassiere.

The bodyguards drew closer, as if unwilling to believe their eyes.

Seizing the opportunity, Bubby cast a final anguished glance at Shirley Lee's gyrating body and slipped unnoticed through Lurk's door.

-5-

Inside the operating room, Bubby swiftly locked the door behind him.

Simon, who was monitoring Basile's vital signs, looked up with surprise. "Hey, Bubby, how did you manage to get past the guards?"

"Where's Lurk?" Bubby demanded. His eyes swept the room frantically.

"Are you all right?" Simon asked, alarmed by his wild look and by the fact that he was carrying a baby pig wrapped in a blanket. He recognized it as the one he'd seen upstairs earlier and wondered if Bubby were smuggling something inside it.

"Where did Lurk go?" Bubby asked hysterically. "How did he get out of this room? Tell me, for Pie's sake! I have to catch him before it's too late!"

Simon looked at him warily. "I don't know where Lurk went. Uh, why do you have the pig?"

Bubby grabbed Lurk's bloody scalpel off the table and menaced Simon with it. "There's only one way out of this room, and it's guarded! Now, tell me where Lurk is, or I'll cut your face off! I warn you, I'm a desperate man!"

Simon backed away, trembling. "I swear I don't know where he is. He went through there." He pointed at the invisible panel.

"You bastard!" Bubby hissed. "A woman . . . no . . . an angel is out there sacrificing her precious virtue, while you try to tell me that Lurk walked through a wall! I swear, I'll kill you!" He advanced on Simon with the scalpel.

Simon hurried over to the desk and pushed the button that opened the panel.

Bubby threw the scalpel back onto the operating table and, clutching the piglet to his breast, leapt through the opening in the wall.

-6-

Shirley Lee had stripped down to her support stockings and white cotton underpants. The bodyguards stared fixedly, their eyes glazed more with shock than passion. Most of them had never seen white cotton underpants before.

Frank and Hilly watched with increasing interest from around the corner of the hallway.

"Well, Bubby got in," Frank said. "I wonder if he was in time to cancel the contract."

"Now you're beginning to get me all excited," Hilly told him. "I never saw such real crime before. I'll be able to present a whizbang paper about it at the next Social Sanctuary convention." He tugged at Frank's arm. "Come on! We've got to get in there! There may be evidence, and I'll need it for my footnotes."

"There's evidence in there, all right. I wouldn't be surprised if Lurk had files linking him and Bubby with every hired killing in the metropolitan area. We're onto something big. Let's kick the door down!"

Hilly's fervor diminished when something as physical as door-kicking was mentioned. "If we try that, those bodyguards will take us apart."

"No they won't, because I'm going to arrest them."

"What about their DPL status?"

"I'll take the chance that those tee shirts are phony. A lot of them are smuggled in from Canada and sold on the black market. You can get anything, if you know your way around the underbelly of the city."

Hilly was unconvinced. "But what if the tee shirts aren't phony? Those guys will be able to kill us and not spend so much as an hour in jail."

"With the criminal justice system as it is now, anybody can kill us and get away with it. We're going to give it a try. Are you ready?"

"Well . . ."

"You'd look great up there on the podium at the Social Sanctuary Center in Potpourripolis, delivering a psychological profile of The Boys."

"I'm ready," Hilly said. "What are we going to arrest them for? The traffic violation?"

"No. Public lewdness. Can't you see they're having a stag party?" Frank drew his gun. "Run out to the patrol car and get a bunch of handcuffs while I make the arrest."

"Shall I bring the audio-visual stuff too?"

"Yes. We won't need it for the lewdness charge. It doesn't matter if we can't make that one stick. But we'll want a record of everything that happens once we get inside Lurk's door."

Hilly bustled off, and Frank crept forward with his gun leveled at Shirley Lee and the bodyguards.

-7-

Lurk had tumbled down the chute headfirst and lay unconscious on the basement floor. The room was dim, the only light being what spilled in through the slightly open door.

Just as Lurk was starting to come around, Bubby shot through the opening of the chute, pig in arms, and fell heavily next to him. Since he landed on his well-cushioned behind rather than on his head, he remained conscious. But the piglet was knocked from his grasp and ran squealing into the darkness.

"Huh? What's that?" Lurk asked. He raised himself on his elbow and stared blearily around.

Bubby embraced him. "Lurk! Pie be praised! Is it really you?"

"It's me," Lurk said, disengaging himself. "Who are you?"

"Bubby. Don't you recognize my voice? It's me and my pig."

The piglet trotted back over to him and nestled in his arms.

"I'm so dizzy," Lurk moaned. "What are you and that animal doing down here?"

"I'm in love, Niemand!" Bubby said ecstatically.

"To each his own," Lurk shrugged. "I'll leave you two by yourselves as soon as my head clears."

"What do you think I am?" Bubby asked in a shocked voice. "The pig just came along for the ride. I'm in love, I tell you!"

Lurk edged away from him. "You know I respect you and value your friendship, Bubby, but. . ."

"Not with you!" Bubby told him indignantly. "With a goddess, who at this very moment is sacrificing her dear, chaste body for me!"

"Well, why aren't you officiating at the sacrifice, instead of sitting here with me in this dank basement?" Lurk asked.

"I had to talk to you about the pigs you're supposed to kill tonight."

"Oh. I see now. You're worried about the party you're giving. After all these years, don't you know that you can trust me to do a job? When my last patient showed up, I realized I wouldn't have time to do it myself, so I called my friend. He's going to take care of it for me. Have I ever let you down?"

"You've got to stop him!" Bubby cried.

"Don't worry. He's helped me out many times, and he does a nice clean job."

"But I don't want him to kill them!"

"Why? Has the party been canceled?"

"Yes!" Bubby said. "Forever! I'm giving it all up, Niemand. I don't want to kill anymore."

Lurk smiled coldly and ran his hand over the bulge the gun made in his jacket pocket. "Right now I can't really sympathize with your feelings, Bubby. There are a couple of guys that I'd like to kill as painfully as possible."

"That's only because you haven't been touched by love. If you've any humanity at all, you must help me stop your friend before he kills those pigs."

"Listen, I have some very serious problems."

"Please! I'll give you a ten percent reduction in your rent!"

"You must be desperate," Lurk said. "Oh, all right. I'll call him as soon as we leave."

Bubby looked around curiously. "Where are we anyway? And why did you and Simon have that weird chute installed?"

"Garbage disposal," Lurk told him. "We can't bring surgical refuse through an area where food is served because of the danger of contamination."

"But I see Simon carrying out garbage every night."

"Oh. Well, uh, that's normal garbage. Old magazines and so forth."

Bubby pulled the door all the way open so that the light from the hall illuminated the room. "You medical people are so efficient. This is the cleanest garbage receptacle I've ever seen. The only thing on the floor is that matchbook over there."

"Matchbook? Where?"

"In the corner."

Lurk went over and picked up the thing. "This isn't a book of matches!" he exclaimed. "It's a condom! And not just any condom!" He shoved it in Bubby's face. "Look at that brand! Uncle Chuck's Saving Grace!"

Bubby turned away. "I don't want to hear about sex while the woman I love is probably being raped."

"You don't understand. This comes from the town near where you keep your pigs. An old guy up in Earwig makes them as a hobby. They're only sold in his pharmacy. He puts a little hand-carved sex toy in with each one of them." Lurk slipped the condom into his pocket. "This can mean only one thing. Those bastards must have been in Earwig. Maybe they even live there. At least it's something to go on."

"I don't understand."

"There're some people I have to find, and thanks to your discovery, I have an idea where to start looking."

"I'm happy for you," Bubby said. "Now please let's get to a phone."

"Okay. Would you like to leave your friend in here· for the time being?" Lurk asked, looking at the piglet.

Bubby clutched the animal so tightly it let out a shrill squeal. "No! He stays. with me! He's all I have left of my darling!"

"Whatever you say." Lurk ushered Bubby out of the room and locked the door after them. "Are you sure you want me to make this call?" he asked as they climbed up the cellar stairs. "You'll regret it tomorrow night, after you've gotten what you want and a restaurant full of hungry celebrities hasn't. I hope this woman is worth blowing a million-dollar business for."

"She's worth it," Bubby told him rapturously. "We're going to live a clean, new life, shepherding pigs in the mountains."

Lurk sighed and shook his head. He was glad that he was never victimized by such aberrations as love. "There's a phone booth on the corner," he said as they stepped out onto the street.

"Let's hurry," Bubby urged.

The two men rushed down the deserted street to the telephone booth. Lurk stepped inside, put a twenty-dollar gold piece in the slot, and dialed. He held the receiver to his ear and turned away from Bubby to avoid his desperate, questioning eyes. Also, Bubby was holding the piglet close to his face, and it was disconcerting to Lurk to see how much alike they looked. "Sorry," he said finally. "No answer. He must have left already." He hung up and retrieved his gold piece.

"We've got to get up there and stop him!" Bubby insisted. "Maybe we can at least save some of them."

"I have to get to Earwig too," Lurk told him, "but there's a problem. Since I didn't think I'd be going upstate tonight, I canceled the appointment I'd made with my gas connection. I only have enough to get us part of the way. I sure wish you had a car."

"I never felt the need for one. Where would I go? Once you're in Pie in the Sty, where else is there to go?"

Lurk dropped the twenty-dollar gold piece back into the phone and dialed another number. "I'll have Simon call my gas connection and arrange for him to meet us. He can get the number from my card file. I don't have it with me."

Simon jumped when the phone rang. Even though he knew the room was soundproof, the jangling bell seemed so loud that it was difficult for him to believe the bodyguards couldn't hear it. He hurried to answer it. "Is that you, boss?" he asked in a low voice.

"It's me," Lurk said. "Is everything all right?"

"I don't know. Bubby came charging in here with a pig. . ."

"Yeah. It's okay. He's with me now. Listen, I have to go up to Earwig."

"Did you find the three guys?"

"No, but I think I have a lead. Max's number is in that card file I keep in my bottom desk drawer. Call him and tell him to meet me in front of the Soyburger Shack outside Crab Corner with some gas. I'm leaving now."

"I'll do that," Simon told him. "But, boss, I really have to bring Basile around. She doesn't look too good."

"Don't you dare!" Lurk exploded. "She stays under until I get back with the you-know-what!"

"All right," Simon agreed reluctantly, "but try to make it fast."

-8-

All the bodyguards had been handcuffed and were seated on the hallway floor, leaning against the wall. Their pants had been removed and used to bind their ankles.

Shirley Lee stood near them, trembling and confused. She was still wearing her white cotton pants and support hose and was trying to cover her breasts with her hands.

"What're we going to do about her?" Hilly asked. "We don't have another pair of cuffs."

"Leave her," Frank said indifferently. "She can't get the cuffs off them, so what harm can she do? We have The Boys to worry about."

He beckoned to Hilly, and they started heaving their shoulders against Lurk's door.

Blushing, Shirley Lee began to put her clothes back on. But she was interrupted by the animal-fat pusher, who sidled up to her, carrying a piece of bread that was sodden with lard.

"I bet you could use some of this," he said in a soft, reptilian voice.

"What is it?" she asked him, looking curiously at the dripping bread.

"Don't be coy with me, lady," he sneered. "If you don't want it, there're plenty who do."

"So go on and give it to them. I just want to get my clothes on and find my Wilbur." Shirley Lee was close to tears.

153

The pusher realized he was dealing with a genuine innocent. "You really don't know what this is, do you?" he asked with amusement.

"I don't know, and I don't care!" she said emphatically. "It's nasty-looking stuff."

"Oh, it's not nasty at all," the pusher wheedled. "It's a special kind of white peanut butter. Usually, I sell it, but I'll give you this for nothing. Then maybe later you'll want to buy some more." He held it out to her with an encouraging smile.

"Okay," she agreed. "I'll try some, but I don't think I'll want more. I don't like peanut butter that much." She took the bread from him and bit into it. Instantly, she underwent a profound transformation. Her eyelids drooped, and her mouth twisted into a lascivious smile. While the pusher egged her on, she devoured the rest of the bread, slavering and grunting.

When she'd finished, she turned on the immobilized bodyguards with an evil grin. She peeled off her underpants and support hose and advanced on them as they squirmed with terror. Some tried to roll away, but she fell on them like a starved animal.

-9-

Lurk's door lay in splinters. Frank had the muzzle of his gun pressed against Simon's head while Hilly set up the audio-visual equipment that he'd taken from a large black case.

"Are you Lurk?" Frank demanded after they'd tested the microphone.

"No," Simon said tremulously. "I'm just his assistant. He stepped out for an hour or two."

"Who's that on the table?"

"A patient of Dr. Lurk's."

"Bring her around!" Frank ordered. "I want to question her."

"I can't. She hasn't a bellybutton."

Frank took his gun away from Simon's head. "Keep an eye on him," he told Hilly.

Hilly filmed Simon from different angles while Frank wandered around the room, as if he were looking for something. Then he opened the refrigerator and took out a bottle of water.

He removed the cork, tossing it to Simon. "Plug her up with this. I want her awake."

"But she really doesn't know anything. She was already out when. . ." Simon broke off in confusion.

"When what? You'd better talk, or you're in a lot of trouble," Frank warned him harshly.

He remained silent, so Frank continued to hammer away at him. "Lurk and Bubby are in with The Boys, right? And Bubby passed a contract on to Lurk to make a hit, right? And then The Boys called the whole thing off, and Bubby has to try to stop Lurk, right?"

Simon was too shocked to speak.

"I knew he'd talk," Frank told Hilly smugly. "I can make anybody talk. You just have to let them know you're onto them, and they spill their guts. Where did Lurk go?" He asked Simon in a stern voice.

"Earwig," Simon said, pale with terror.

"Is that a place? Where is it?"

"Upstate."

"Where in Earwig was Lurk going? Do you have an address?"

"No. He just said Earwig. He goes there once in a while. But honest, I didn't know what for."

"Don't worry," Frank said. "We'll tell the federal prosecutor you were cooperative. Come on, Hilly, let's get up there."

"But that's out of our jurisdiction," Hilly said uncertainly.

"Don't worry about petty details. Think of your footnotes. Hundreds and hundreds of footnotes."

Hilly smiled blissfully and repacked his equipment. "Yes! Oh, yes!"

He and Frank hurried out. In the hall, they found the bound and handcuffed bodyguards in various stages of disarray. Shirley Lee was energetically molesting one as Frank and Hilly ran by.

"Please," the bodyguards begged. "Don't leave us defenseless. At least untie our ankles so we can kick."

"Sorry. We don't have time," Frank apologized. "Try to have a sense of decency, lady," he told Shirley Lee.

She merely looked at him mindlessly and drooled.

-10-

Simon paced nervously around the operating room. Lurk one of The Boys! He'd thought they were a myth. Who would have dreamed that they actually existed!

He walked over to look at Basile, who was starting to turn blue. If he didn't bring her around soon, he might have a murder rap to contend with. Lurk had finished the surgery, except for replacing the bellybutton. Simon decided he'd just sew her up, make sure she was conscious, and then get the hell out of town. He didn't want anything to do with The Boys. Not even secondhand.

Chapter Eleven
On the Road

-1-

Heinri, Klausiere, and Elphlegm were driving along the nearly empty and very badly maintained road that led north to Earwig. The radio was tuned to an all-news station, but not a word had been mentioned about Basile's bellybutton.

"Not a damned thing!" Heinri muttered peevishly. "The media should have gotten the story by now."

"Is it possible Lurk didn't call the police?" Klausiere asked. "Maybe he's going to try to come after us."

"How could he? He doesn't know where we're going. He may do his best to keep the thing quiet, but when that woman wakes up without her bellybutton, she's going to make plenty of noise. Don't worry. Lurk's smart enough to realize he could never find us in time."

"Right," Klausiere agreed. "That bellybutton has to be reattached within twelve hours. And he'd never think to look for us in a dumpy little town like Earwig. How did you ever find the place?"

"I had a date with a girl who lives up there. When we were parked in the woods, I noticed this deserted shack. We'll hole up in it. No one will even notice us. The nearest house is a couple of miles away."

Elphlegm was coiled comfortably on the back seat, trying to reach a decision. She was extremely hungry, and the backs of Heinri and Klausiere's necks, glowing white in the darkness, were nearly driving her mad. As much as she wanted to watch them bring a little more chaos into the world, she knew she hadn't much time. Dawn would come before anything interesting happened, and both her appetite and her curiosity would be left unsatisfied. She would have to leave them as soon as the sun began to rise so she could metamorphose in privacy. But despite all this, she decided to wait just a bit longer.

157

-2-

Many miles behind, another car traveled the same highway. Lurk was driving while Bubby fidgeted nervously in the seat next to him.

"Please, Niemand," he begged. "You have to drop me at the holding pen as soon as we get to Earwig."

"I have more important things to worry about," Lurk said shortly. "You'll have to take a cab from town."

"Earwig doesn't have cabs," Bubby protested. "And what could be more important than love?"

"A bellybutton."

Bubby gave him a startled look and then clucked sympathetically. "Listen, I understand fetishes," he said. "I never told anyone this before, but I used to get a funny feeling every time I saw a callus on a woman's big toe. But you have to move beyond that. You have to learn to love the whole person. Do you want to know what worked for me?"

"I'll make a deal with you," Lurk offered. "If you promise not to tell me, I promise to take you directly to the holding pen. To be honest, I don't even know for sure where I'm going, so it won't matter if I'm late getting there."

He supposed he should talk to Uncle Chuck, since the old boy was just enough of a busybody to remember all his condom customers for the past year. But his drugstore wouldn't be open at this hour, and Lurk didn't know his full name or where he lived.

-3-

Yet a third car was speeding toward Earwig.

"What'd The Boys be doing in such a nothing little town?" Hilly asked.

"They all have summer places in upstate New York," Frank explained. "We just have to drive around the richest section of Earwig until we find a mansion with an aura of evil."

Hilly looked puzzled. "An aura of what?"

"You wouldn't understand about evil, so I won't try to explain. When we're near whatever lair The Boys are holed up in, even you'll be able to sense its foul miasma."

"What do you mean I 'wouldn't understand about evil'?" Hilly said indignantly. "Don't forget, I was in training at Potpourripolis when he pulled his first raid!"

"Who? Oh, you mean Guido Mocha. Did you ever see him?"

Hilly shuddered at the memory. "I got a glimpse of him once."

"What did he look like?"

"Sort of like nothing," Hilly said after thinking for a moment. "Blank."

"What do you mean?" Frank challenged. "He had a face, didn't he?"

"Not that I can remember. That is, he had a face, of course. But I can't remember it."

"Potpourripolis sent us a description of him once, before they caught him," Frank remarked thoughtfully. "They said he wore a black leather jacket and rode a motorcycle. But while they gave the color and make of the motorcycle, they didn't say a blessed thing about him. No height, weight, age, hair color—nothing. And now that they have him in custody, they haven't even released a photo of him to the media. That's odd."

"I'm sure there's a rational explanation. Why are you so interested?" Hilly giggled. "I suppose you think he's with The Boys."

"I don't know. The black leather jacket made me wonder, but I'd have to see it. The Boys don't wear just any old kind of black leather jacket. They're faithful to a certain look. It's funny, though, isn't it? That description from Potpourripolis being so sketchy, I mean. And then you looking right into his face and not seeing him."

"Well, don't forget, I was under a strain," Hilly said. "My roommate had just been skinned right before my eyes. Believe me, it was a pretty unattractive thing to watch! Guido Mocha was alone that first time. That was before so many sick, twisted people started to join him. He seemed to come out of nowhere. One minute my roommate and I were eating bananas and discussing Pusgrub solidarity, and the next minute he'd been reduced to a bleeding pulp." Hilly's voice broke slightly, but he forced his quivering mouth into a brave smile and continued.

159

"I'll never forget the sight of him, or rather, what was left of him—lying there next to a banana peel, the lovely inflammatory poster he'd just designed drenched with his blood. And you say I've never seen evil!"

-4-

Heinri turned into a dirt road and slowed to a crawl. "I'm going to pull off into the woods," he told Klausiere and Elphlegm. "We'll walk the rest of the way. There might not be anyplace to hide the car near the shack."

After he'd parked behind some thick brush, the three of them crept along the dirt road, keeping near to the wooded margin.

"We're almost there," Heinri said in a low voice after they'd gone about half a mile. "It's behind those trees up ahead."

They moved cautiously into the grove of trees and peered at the clearing on the other side. As Heinri had promised, there was a shack. But it was inside a large pen, which was filled to capacity with rooting, snorting, wallowing pigs. A man with a shotgun stood guard at the gate.

"Is this your idea of a safe hide-out?" Klausiere whispered angrily.

"I don't know what happened! When I was up here last week, the place was deserted."

"What are we going to do now?"

"Get rid of the guard," Heinri said.

"He has a gun!"

"So have we."

"But I'm not used to other people having them too. It makes me nervous."

Elphlegm was tempted to offer her services. Her mouth watered and her fangs itched as she contemplated a very enjoyable way of getting rid of the guard. But if Heinri and Klausiere saw her in action, they'd be so terrified that they'd forget all about the rotten things they were planning to do. She hated to discourage man's inhumanity to man. It made her own workload lighter. She decided to keep a low profile for a while longer.

"We have to lure him over here," Heinri was saying. "Then we can knock him out and disarm him. Can you make a noise like a pig?" he asked Klausiere.

"I don't know. No one ever asked me to before."

"Try. The guard will think one got loose and come to investigate."

"Why don't you do it?"

"I recognize your greater aptitude," Heinri told him. "A leader has to be able to pick the right man for a job, and this particular job is you."

"Okay," Klausiere agreed. "I'll oink. But give me a few moments to prepare myself. I have to feel it." He buried his face in his hands and tried to think as swinishly as possible. After a bit, he raised his head. "I'm ready," he announced. He took a deep breath and started to make remarkably genuine pig sounds.

Meanwhile, Elphlegm slithered out of sight into a hollow log, and Heinri crouched behind some bushes with the butt of his gun raised.

The guard walked toward them, calling, "Here pig, pig, pig!" as he poked the muzzle of his shotgun into the bushes. "That sounded like a sick one," he muttered to himself.

When he'd come close enough, Heinri sprung on him and knocked him unconscious. He and Klausiere grabbed the man's gun and bound his hands and feet with the suspenders of their lederhosen.

"Let's bring him into the shed with us so no one will stumble on him," Heinri said. "He can be a hostage if the bellybutton and the noseless corpse don't do the trick. I really want to avoid the other thing."

"So do I. It makes my skin crawl, thinking of it."

"Do you still have the apparatus?"

Klausiere touched the pocket of his lederhosen. "Yes. It's right here."

They picked up the unconscious guard and carried him toward the pen while Elphlegm snaked along after them.

-5-

Lurk and Bubby were parked outside Soyburger Shack, an

all-night fast-food joint about a hundred miles from the city. The gas connection was late.

"Where the hell is he?" Lurk complained. "We've been waiting here an hour already."

Bubby was chewing on his fingernails, destroying what had been an expensive manicure. "He has to come soon, or we'll be too late. Those pigs will be dead by the time we get there. And Shirley Lee will never forgive me." He kissed the piglet tenderly as he thought of his beloved.

"I'm going to call Simon from that pay phone over there," Lurk said finally. "Maybe he wasn't able to connect with my gas man. I find that hard to believe, though. A black market gasoline dealer can't afford to be undependable. We have the government for that, and they charge a lot less to screw up." He got out of the car and walked over to a phone booth next to Soyburger Shack.

When Simon heard the phone ring, he knew it was Lurk and considered not answering it. But then he began to wonder if Lurk might not call The Boys and have them come by to take care of him in some unspeakable way. He grabbed the phone. "Hello?" he quavered.

"Simon, were you able to reach Max?" Lurk asked.

"Yes. I called him right after I hung up with you, and he said he'd leave immediately."

As preoccupied as he was, Lurk realized from the sound of Simon's voice that something had happened. "What's wrong?" he asked suspiciously. "Is anybody there with you? Did those bodyguards break in?"

"No."

"Well, then, what's the matter?"

"I know everything!" Simon blurted out.

"Know what?"

"You should have told me! I thought you'd done something with a little class, like sell your soul to the Devil! I didn't know you're one of The Boys!"

"Who? What?" At first Lurk was totally bewildered. Then he remembered newspaper stories from his childhood and understood whom Simon was talking about. Despite his problems, he had to laugh. "You idiot! The Boys are extinct. They were an endangered species way back when we were medical students. I'll tell you what. You find The Boys for me, and I'll be glad to join forces with them. Then at least I'd be working with people who have a brain or two in their heads. Where did you ever get such a crazy idea?"

Simon was uncertain now. "Some cops broke in here," he said hesitantly. "They told me you and Bubby were on your way to carry out a contract for The Boys. I . . . uh. . . . I told them you were going to Earwig. I'm sorry, boss."

"Oh, no!" Lurk groaned. "Why didn't you keep your damned mouth shut? What could they do to you? They were only cops. They don't have a license to kill, like the Legal League."

"I'm sorry, boss," Simon repeated miserably. "I just wasn't thinking. It was such a shock."

"Never mind. I'll keep an eye out for them. As long as those bodyguards didn't get in too, everything may still work out. Are Basile's vital signs stable?"

Simon didn't answer.

"What is it?" Lurk asked. "Don't tell me she's dead!"

"No. She's starting to come around nicely."

"What do you mean 'she's starting to come around'?" Lurk screeched. "You can't let her regain consciousness with a hole in her abdomen, you fool!"

"That won't be a problem, boss, because I kind of sewed her up."

Lurk thought he was going to faint. "Without a belly-button?"

"It really looks quite nice, sort of like a very narrow slit in a piggy bank. Boss? Boss?" Simon was alarmed by the choking sounds on the other end of the line.

"You've ruined me for at least fifty years," Lurk said feebly. "When I get back, I'm going to tie you in a knot. I'll see to it that you spend the rest of eternity as a very large paperweight." He slammed the phone down and walked back to his car with the unnatural calm of the shellshocked or the catatonic. Without speaking, he opened the car door and slid behind the wheel.

Bubby looked at him expectantly. "Well?"

"Some cops broke into my operating room and intimidated that idiot Simon," Lurk said. "He told them I was on my way to Earwig. Then, just for the hell of it, he proceeded to destroy my career."

Bubby was too selfishly lovesick to be concerned about Lurk's career, but the news that they were being pursued worried him. "What if the cops get there before we do?" he asked.

"I don't think it'll make any difference to you. They won't be looking for The Boys in a pigpen. I don't think it'll make any difference to me either, since I'm utterly ruined. Oh. He did reach the gas connection, so Max should be here any minute."

-6-

Frank and Hilly pulled up in front of a mansion.

"This is really quite elegant," Hilly said with awe. "Are you sure The Boys live here?"

"You heard that old guy at the Soyburger Shack. He said the only crook he knew of in these parts lived at this address. I think we ought to rush the place." Frank caressed his gun eagerly.

"No, no, no!" Hilly scolded. "Regulations say we have to knock."

They got out of the patrol car and walked up to the front door of the mansion.

Frank stood to the side with his hand on his gun. "Okay," he said. "Go ahead and knock."

"You are so paranoid," Hilly told him as he rapped on the door. "Will you please take your hand off that gun? You're going to give me an anxiety attack."

"For your information, we're going to need the gun. Just wait till you see what opens that door."

Hilly rapped again, and the door was flung open by a middle-aged woman in a robe and bedroom slippers.

"Yes?" she asked irritably. "What is it, for goodness' sake?"

Hilly threw Frank a smug look. "We'd like to speak to the owner of this house, please," he requested politely.

The woman stared at him as if he were mad. "It's three o'clock in the morning! I can't wake the mayor at this hour!"

"The mayor?" Frank asked, in shock.

"You'll have to go to his office after 11:00 if you want to see him!" she snapped, slamming the door in their faces.

As they walked back to the patrol car, Hilly could barely contain his amusement. "Now I suppose you're going to tell me that the mayor is one of The Boys."

"No," Frank replied seriously. "Like I said before, The Boys have standards. A politician would have about as much chance of getting into their organization as Bubby would. That old guy at Soyburger Shack was just trying to be funny."

Hilly was amazed that Frank recognized this. His partner had absolutely no sense of humor, and Hilly believed that anybody with this deficiency wasn't quite human. He was writing a paper on Frank, but he intended to make sure he never found out. "What will we do now?" he asked.

"We'll drive around until we find someone who knows something," Frank said. "There must be a couple of people in this town who're still awake or just getting up. A milkman, maybe."

They got back into the patrol car and rattled out of Earwig. The darkened houses became farther apart, and the brush by the side of the road grew thicker. As he drove, Frank rested his left arm on the open window and listened to the night sounds. Suddenly, he pulled over to the side of the road and stopped.

"What's the matter?" Hilly asked.

"I heard a giggle." Frank backed the car up to a particularly thick stand of bushes. "It came from in there," he said. He drew his gun and climbed out of the car. "Okay!" he told the bushes sternly. "This is the police! Come out with your hands up!"

The bushes trembled, and a very angry, seminude teen-age couple emerged.

"I don't think those are The Boys," Hilly called from the car.

"We're police officers," Frank informed the two, who didn't seem terribly interested. "How would you like to help us in a criminal investigation?"

"We'd be delighted," the boy said sarcastically.

"Are you local residents?" Frank asked.

"This isn't the kind of place that attracts tourists," the boy answered. "Yeah, we're locals."

"Then maybe you could tell me whether there's anything

going on in this town that might be considered unsavory."

The boy seemed astonished by the suggestion. "Here? In Earwig?" Then a sly smile played over his mouth. "Yeah," he said. "As a matter of fact there is. Funny you should mention it. If you keep on the way you were going, about two miles from here there's a little road that branches off on your right. You go up that road, and you'll find something at the end of it that definitely doesn't smell right."

"That sounds like what we're looking for," Frank told Hilly.

"Yeah," the boy continued. "Everyone in town says something about that place stinks."

"Thanks for your help," Frank told him as he climbed back into the patrol car. "We're going to clean up this town for you."

"Good luck!" the boy called, waving as they drove off.

"What was that all about?" the girl asked.

"Who the hell knows? But I fixed that guy's ass for interrupting us. I sent him to a pigpen someone's got hidden away in the woods. When it's not full of pigs, a lot of kids go there to make out. Now let's get our clothes on and find another bush, in case those jerks come back."

Frank and Hilly parked in the woods, some distance closer to the main road than the terrorists had hidden their car.

"We'll walk the rest of the way so we can take them by surprise," Frank said. "Bring the audio-visual stuff. We'll probably be making several arrests, and we want these to stick."

Hilly dragged the large black case out of the back seat of the patrol car, and they started up the road. After they'd walked quite a ways, Hilly's arms began to hurt. "Why don't you carry this thing for a while?" he asked Frank.

"I'd love to help you," Frank said regretfully, "but I have to keep my hands free in case I need to go for my gun in a hurry."

They trudged along in silence. Finally, they came to the end of the road, where a fringe of trees prevented them from seeing what was beyond.

"It should be right through there," Frank said under his breath. "I hear some kind of weird animal noises. Maybe we're going to get lucky and catch The Boys in the midst of one of their bizarre initiation rituals. Think of how that'll look in your paper."

"That would make Potpourripolis sit up and take notice," Hilly admitted. "Let's go!"

"Careful," Frank warned. "Take it slow. This is going to be extremely dangerous." He led the way, slipping through the trees, with Hilly and his suitcase close behind. They stepped cautiously into the clearing, and Frank found himself pointing his gun at a pen full of pigs.

"I think we've been had again," Hilly sighed.

"Hush!" Frank whispered. "I hear someone coming! Get back!"

As they ducked behind the trees, a man emerged from another part of the forest. The long knife he was carrying glittered in the moonlight. He walked to the pigpen, unlatched the gate, and stepped inside.

"Of course!' Frank muttered. "The pigs are just a front. That's where Bubby comes in. This must be where The Boys make their hits. They probably have the victims locked in that big shed over there."

"Are we going to arrest that fellow now?" Hilly asked. "We don't really have any evidence."

"What kind of evidence do you want? A dead body?"

"You're right," Hilly agreed. "We'd better grab him."

Frank hesitated. "Uh, listen, since this arrest is in earnest and all, is it okay if I have my gun drawn? You know the law better than I do, and I don't want something this big thrown out of court."

"Yes, in this case, I do believe you're permitted to draw your gun," Hilly told him. "He does have a knife. That makes it even-steven."

Frank waved his gun in the air and charged the pigpen with a savage whoop, leaping over the fence like a boy of twelve. Hilly trailed after him, lugging the heavy case. By the time he managed to lift it over the fence and crawl over himself, Frank was some distance ahead of him. Jostled by the pigs, Hilly made his way unsteadily toward his partner, who was already pointing his gun at the man with the knife.

"Drop that weapon!" Frank ordered. "You're under arrest!"

The man let the knife fall to the ground, staring at Frank with disbelief.

Hilly came puffing up to them. "Wait!" he pleaded. "This'll all be wasted effort if I don't get the audio-visuals. We won't have a chance in court. And I won't be able to present my paper."

"You're right," Frank conceded, "but you can't set up the equipment with all these pigs milling around. Why don't we go outside the pen?"

Hilly sighed with frustration at Frank's obtuseness. "Don't you understand? I have to get the knife in the picture, or you could be up on charges for drawing your gun."

"You can testify that he had a knife," Frank said impatiently.

"They won't believe me. I'm a cop."

"So we'll take the knife outside the pen and film everything out there, like I said before."

"No good. We aren't allowed to touch it until after the arrest is filmed."

Frank looked at the prisoner. "Maybe he could pick it up again and carry it outside."

"If we tell him to do that, we can be tried as his accomplices," Hilly explained. "Just shoo the pigs away so I can set up the equipment."

Still holding his gun, Frank awkwardly tried to chase the pigs out of Hilly's way.

"Do you want me to help you?" the prisoner asked.

"Don't you move," Frank told him. "You're still under arrest."

After the pigs had knocked everything over a few times, Hilly finally succeeded in setting up the lights, cameras, and microphones. He took a thick booklet out of the suitcase and cleared his throat. "Okay, Frank," he said rather self-consciously. "You keep the camera on both of us while I read him his rights. And try to get the knife in the picture during the whole thing." He walked over to the prisoner and gingerly clipped a mike to the neck of his sweatshirt. "That's in case you want to say something," he explained. "Of course, you don't have to. Most people don't. But just in case."

Hilly cleared his throat again and began to read from the booklet: "You have the right to remain silent. You have the right to the presence of your lawyer, psychiatrist, internist, and parents during interrogation. If you do not have any or all of these, any or all will be provided, free of charge, by the city of New York. You have the right to demand that the foods served to you during interrogation do not cause an allergic reaction or violate the tenets of your religion."

The prisoner interrupted him. "Wait a minute. What's a tenet?"

"Oh, darn!" Hilly said. "I've written letter after letter to Potpourripolis, begging them to change that word. Nobody knows what it means. If they can prove in court that they have a below-standard vocabulary, there goes the case."

"Quit ranting," Frank told him. "Remember, you're on tape."

Hilly blanched. "Oh my God!" He gave Frank a pleading look. "Could you erase that part maybe?"

Frank feigned shock. "What? You're asking me to break the law?"

"Oh, no!" Hilly gasped with horror. "I'd never do such a thing! Please believe me!"

"Relax," Frank said. He put the tape on reverse, then stopped it. "Go ahead. I took that part out." He started the tape again. "What religion do you belong to?" he asked the prisoner.

"None."

"Then you don't have to know what tenets are," he told him. "Keep reading him his rights, Hilly."

Hilly continued the long list in a shaky voice.

-7-

Inside the shack, the bound guard was propped in a corner. Heinri and Klausiere were listening intently to a small portable radio. It was turned down very low, but its sound and their avid concentration were enough to keep them from hearing the noise outside.

"Still nothing," Heinri complained. "What kind of game is Lurk playing?"

Elphlegm had been aware from the beginning that something was going on outside. She listened closely and was surprised to recognize her brother-in-law's voice. There were only a few hours left till dawn, and she knew she ought to make a quick meal of Heinri, Klausiere, and the guard and leave. If she stayed in Earwig until she made her transformation back to Pusgrub form, it would take her days to get back to the city. A wereworm could move about five times more rapidly than a Pusgrub. But on the other hand, the only inconvenience would be having to field a lot of questions from Yog and Hilly. She really didn't mind spending a couple of days in her beloved tunnels, and she wanted to find out what Hilly was up to. Although she'd never been this far north before, she was certain there were Pusgrub tunnels beneath her feet. No part of the country was free of them. She decided to stay just a while longer.

Abruptly, Heinri became aware of the sounds outside. "Be quiet!" he hissed. "Turn the radio off. I think I hear something."

Klausiere switched off the radio, and they were able to hear the barely audible drone of Hilly's voice as he read the prisoner his rights. Heinri and Klausiere opened the door warily and looked out.

"Look! Media!" Klausiere exclaimed when he saw the group in the pen.

"I don't know where they came from," Heinri said, "but they're just what we need. I'll grab them. You put the bellybutton on something dark so it will photograph well."

"Right!" Klausiere started looking around the room for an appropriate backdrop.

As Heinri slipped out the door, Elphlegm wondered if she should warn him that at least one of the men outside was a police officer. Another voice was disturbingly familiar too, but she couldn't quite place it. She decided to say nothing and let the situation develop as it would.

Heinri drew his gun and walked stealthily toward the three men.

The prisoner, who was facing in his direction, spotted him. "Hey!" he said to Frank and Hilly. "I think there's something you guys should know."

"Please don't say anything until I've finished reading you your rights," Hilly admonished. "There are just nine more to go."

"But . . ."

"I'm afraid I'll have to insist that you be quiet," Hilly warned. "This must be done properly."

Heinri jammed his gun in Hilly's back. "You're all coming with me!"

Hilly let out a squawk of surprise, and Frank looked up with a dazed expression. Although he'd had the camera on both Hilly and the prisoner, his visual field had been restricted to what he was able to see through the eyepiece. He hadn't noticed Heinri until it was too late.

"I tried to tell you," the prisoner said.

Heinri spotted Frank's gun and grabbed Hilly around the neck, using him as a shield. "Drop that," he ordered, "or I'll kill your friend here!"

Frank experienced a moment of sweet temptation, but he overcame it and dropped his gun.

"What's media doing with a gun?" Heinri asked. "You must be nonunion," he told the prisoner. "You ought to join Performers' League. No director should be allowed to go that far."

Frank was offended. "We're not media!" he corrected indignantly. "We're police officers filming an arrest!"

"Oh, hell!" Heinri said. "Amateurs! Well, you'll have to do. At least you have a camera and sound equipment. Get moving! Bring that stuff into the shack over there."

Chapter Twelve
The Long Night

-1-

Frank, Hilly, and their former prisoner all took pieces of equipment and carried them to the shack. Heinri followed with his gun.

As soon as they entered the shack, Frank saw Elphlegm and let out an unearthly howl. The equipment he was holding clattered to the floor. "Shoot! Shoot! Shoot!" he screamed at Heinri.

"Who?"

"It!" He pointed at Elphlegm. "That foul creature of the night! That wereworm!"

"What're you, nuts?" Heinri asked. He turned to Hilly. "Does he have medicine he's supposed to take when he gets like this?"

Hilly looked at Elphlegm with uneasy interest. "He was saying something earlier about a series of murders in New York City being committed by a wereworm. Whatever that is over there does look something like a big worm."

Heinri and Klausiere looked at Elphlegm too.

"Now that you mention it," Klausiere said, "it is sort of tubular."

Elphlegm realized that the vaguely familiar voice she'd noticed before had belonged to Frank. He'd been a guest at one of her brother-in-law's idiotic parties a while back. She was supposed to come down and meet the guests, and she'd fully intended to. At that time, she was still trying to get along with Hilly.

But as each couple arrived, they deposited a large slab of cheese on a table in the center of the living room. It seemed to her as she hid at the top of the stairs that each cheese was ranker than the previous one. Soon the living room smelled like dirty human feet, and she knew if she went down there, she'd be sick. So she told Hilly and Yog that she wasn't feeling well and watched the party from the shadowy part of the staircase.

She'd recognized instantly that Frank was different from the others. He'd brought a boring cheese that hardly stunk at all. This evoked amused pity from the more sophisticated guests, who politely said they were allergic when Frank's cheese was passed around.

He'd also worn ill-fitting clothes that emphasized the dumpiness of his body, and throughout the entire evening, he didn't smile once. She'd admired the way he seemed to dislike Hilly, since she was just beginning to herself. She'd even admired the apparent revulsion he felt for Pusgrubs. When her sister had given in to Hilly's pleas that she demonstrate the Pusgrub mating dance, Frank had looked away and surreptitiously taken an aspirin. Elphlegm knew her people were too alien to inspire any real affection in humans, and she preferred honest dislike to dishonest friendship. Frank was probably the only human in the world that she could feel close to.

She wondered how he'd guessed she was a wereworm. Heinri and Klausiere were looking at her strangely, and she knew she'd either have to convince them Frank was lying or eat the whole lot of them, then and there. And, to her surprise, she found that she was reluctant to kill Frank. After only two brief encounters with him, he'd become more than just a dinner to her.

"Can't you see what they're trying to do?" she asked the two terrorists. "They want to turn us against one another with this absurd story. Wereworms! Good grief! It's a measure of their contempt for you that they didn't even bother to think up a plausible lie."

"Yeah!" Klausiere growled obligingly. "Lousy cops!"

"Tie them up," Heinri told him. "This guy too." He pointed at the man in the tee shirt. "They were arresting him, so he must be some kind of criminal."

"Right," Klausiere said. He looked around the room. "What am I going to tie them up with?" he asked. "There's nothing in here but sacks of feed and some old automobile parts."

"I don't know," Heinri said. "I didn't bring any rope. I didn't figure we'd need it for the bellybutton, and I had no idea all these guys were going to show up. Look in the suitcase their equipment was in. There might be some cords or something we can use."

Klausiere opened the suitcase. Then, with a bemused expression, he pulled out a ball of dusky rose knitting yarn and a partially knitted sweater.

"Be careful," Hilly told him anxiously. "Don't let it slip off the needles."

Frank forgot his fear and stared open-mouthed at Hilly. "Is that really yours?"

"Well, I have to do something when you leave me sitting alone in the patrol car while you check that madam's apartment for health code violations. Sometimes you're gone over an hour."

"That wool doesn't look very strong," Heinri said. "Aren't there any cords?"

"No. All their stuff is battery-powered."

"I guess the wool will have to do, then. Tie them up as best you can."

"Please don't unravel my sweater," Hilly begged. "I was almost at the armholes."

"Cut the yarn so you don't have to unravel it," Heinri told Klausiere. "I don't want anybody to be able to say that Lorratians are inhumane."

Klausiere examined the knitting. "Okay. I think there's enough on the ball to do the job." He took a pair of scissors from the suitcase, cut the yarn, and put the unfinished sweater aside. After he'd tied the hands of Frank, Hilly, and the other man behind their backs, there was just enough left to tie their feet as well.

Frank was a bit apart from the others. Elphlegm slithered unobserved onto his lap, stood on her tail so that her face was close to his and flashed her glittering fangs at him. He pressed back against the wall, faint with terror, but Elphlegm could feel with her tail that he had an erection. She wriggled the upper part of her body around him so that she was resting on his shoulders. Then she flicked her tail in a swift, teasing caress over his penis and dropped off him to the floor. Every time he looked up, he saw her bright, round eyes staring at him from across the room.

Klausiere was excitedly tugging at Heinri's arm. "Come let me show you what I did with the bellybutton. I think it's very effective." He led him to a pedestal, improvised from a feed sack stood on its end and covered at the top with black satin cloth. The bellybutton glowed palely in the center.

"That's beautiful," Heinri said. "It really takes my breath away. But where did you find that lovely material?"

"I made a very personal sacrifice for our cause," Klausiere told him shyly. "Those are my underdrawers." He patted his thigh. "I'm going to take this thing out of my pocket, okay? Without my undies, it's beginning to chafe."

"Sure. Make yourself comfortable."

Klausiere took a small, black, rectangular object out of his pocket and laid it on the table next to the pedestal on which the bellybutton was displayed.

"Now I want you to gag all three of those characters," Heinri told him, "so I can have their undivided attention while I tell them what I want done."

"What should I gag them with?"

"They must have handkerchiefs. You can wad them up and stick them in their mouths. Check their pockets."

Klausiere took handkerchiefs from the pockets of Frank and the man in the tee shirt and stuffed their mouths with them, but when he tried to do the same to Hilly, he backed squeamishly away. "Look, I'd rather not. I had to use that earlier tonight."

Klausiere looked at Heinri. "Now what?"

"Is yours clean?" Heinri asked him. "Yes, sure," Klausiere answered. "But, gosh, a guy's handkerchief is kind of personal. I don't want someone else's spit all over it."

Exasperated, Heinri pulled his own out of his pocket and threw it to Klausiere. But just as Klausiere was about to stick it in Hilly's mouth, they heard a noise outside.

"That sounded like a car," Klausiere whispered.

"Yes it did," Heinri agreed. "Let's have a look."

They opened the door a crack, just enough for them to see out without the light inside the shack being visible.

While their backs were turned, Hilly struggled over to the object that Klausiere had taken out of his pocket. Grunting with effort, he managed to stretch up and grab it with his teeth. He gagged several times, but finally succeeded in swallowing it. Then he flopped back to his place.

Frank made an interrogative noise.

"I saw it on television," Hilly said under his breath. "It's a good way of protecting evidence. By the time it works its way through my digestive tract, we should be out of danger. I don't know what that thing is, but it's obviously important to them."

He looked sympathetically over at Elphlegm. "Before they put the gag in my mouth, I just want to let you know that despite what my partner said, I don't believe you're a wereworm. I think it's disgusting, the way anyone who deviates from the norm is persecuted by a certain type of individual."

Elphlegm slithered over to Hilly and coiled up in front of him. "You're a saint," she said.

"Oh, not really," he protested with a self-deprecating smile. "But I do think I'm above judging a person, or whatever, by externals. Looks mean nothing to me. I married a Pusgrub woman."

"How wonderful for her," Elphlegm hissed, making sure Hilly got a look at her fangs.

His eyes widened, and he flinched away.

Heinri and Klausiere carefully shut the door and came back to where the others were sitting.

"That's Lurk's car," Heinri said. "He drove me to the locksmith's in it when I was working for him. Somehow, he managed to follow us here. And he brought another guy with him." He noticed that Klausiere was still holding his handkerchief. "Quick!" he ordered. "Gag the little skinny one before he tries to warn them."

Klausiere noticed that Hilly was doubled over and seemed to be in pain, but he didn't figure this was any time to play doctor. He stuffed the handkerchief into his mouth.

-2-

Bubby bounded out of the car and rushed to the pen. "They're alive!" he exclaimed happily. "They're all alive!"

Lurk followed more slowly. "Yeah. So they are."

Gazing over the swilling, wallowing mass of pigs, Bubby smiled with rapture. "Oh, Niemand, you don't know what this means to me. For once in my life, I've done something decent and positive."

Lurk was puzzled. "Where's the guard?" he asked. "There's always a guard on duty when there're pigs in the holding pen."

"I suppose he's around here someplace," Bubby said without much interest. He went into the pen and walked around, fondly petting the pigs.

The piglet leapt from his arms and joined its relatives. It appeared to be looking for Shirley Lee as it scampered back and forth between their trotters.

"Why don't you come into the pen too," Bubby suggested to Lurk. "They're so beautiful. This is such a peak experience for me that I want to share it with you. To think I almost had them assassinated. I'd like to kiss each dear snout!"

"I wouldn't," Lurk told him firmly. He started to get back into the car. "I have urgent business. I'll see you later."

Suddenly, Bubby noticed something on the ground and bent down to get a closer look. "Wait!" he called to Lurk. "I want you to see this. There're a knife and a gun lying in here."

Lurk got out of the car and entered the pen. Dodging the pigs as best he could, he joined Bubby in the center and looked down. "How odd. That's the knife my friend uses to slaughter the pigs. And the gun looks like a police revolver. I wonder what happened here."

"Maybe your friend just couldn't do it and threw down the knife," Bubby said.

Lurk shook his head. "He's always been able to do it before. Let's face it, Bubby, your affection for pigs is unusual."

Heinri and Klausiere stepped from the shed with their guns pointed at Bubby and Lurk.

"I don't know how you managed to find us, doctor," Heinri said with a tight smile, "but since you're here, I guess we'll have to invite you in."

Lurk tried to go for his gun, but Klausiere lunged at him and pinned his arms behind his back. "In his right pocket," he told Heinri.

Heinri took Lurk's gun and shoved it in his waistband. "Thanks. We can always use more artillery."

"Who are these people?" Bubby asked Lurk.

"I believe they call themselves the Lorratian Liberation Organization," Lurk said, rubbing his arms.

"The what?"

"See? He's never even heard of us," Heinri said resentfully. "That's why we needed media, Lurk, and you didn't give it to us."

"Please!" Lurk begged. "Let me have Basile's . . . thing. Maybe I can get back to the city before she's fully conscious. My career is at stake! My license! My sanity, even! I'm not a man who can remain inactive!"

"Sorry. You blew it. But you're just in time to watch these pigs eat the richest bellybutton in the world. That'll be a memory to treasure."

"No! Not that!" Lurk cried with horror. "Give me another chance! I'll get you all the media you want! Television! Radio! Newspapers! Magazines! Scholarly journals!"

"It's too late. The bellybutton will.start to decay in a couple of hours. There's no time now to mobilize the press."

"Let me take it back," Lurk implored. "I can get to my office just in time to reattach it. I'll call Simon. He'll be able to keep Basile there on some pretext. Please! I'll give you money. Just name your price."

"You're only a doctor," Heinri said disdainfully. "You don't have enough money to make any difference. Besides, what we really needed was coverage." He motioned for Lurk and Bubby to walk ahead of him and Klausiere to the shack. "Go in there. We have one camera at least. And sound equipment. It belongs to two cops."

"Why are the cops here?" Lurk asked nervously. "I didn't know Earwig had a police force."

"There're all sorts of people in that shack," Klausiere told him. " A regular party. You'll see. Get inside."

-3-

As soon as Lurk stepped through the door, he saw the bellybutton on its pedestal. He made a dive for it, but Heinri kicked him aside. "Please give me a break!" he wailed. "I'll do anything! Do you want an eyelift? A nose job? Do you want your girlfriend to have bigger boobs?"

Klausiere looked interested, but Heinri curled his lip with

disgust. "Decadent scum!" he spat. "Do you think soldiers care about things like that?"

"I have a lot more money than you think!" Lurk continued desperately. "You can have it all!"

"Don't try to con us," Heinri said. "If you had that much money, you wouldn't be so hysterical about the prospect of losing your license. For that matter, if you had that much money, you wouldn't be working."

"You're a fortunate man," Lurk sighed. "It's obvious that boredom is only a word to you. For me, it's been made flesh. You should cherish your ignorance."

"Is that teeny little round thing really a bellybutton?" Bubby asked. "Whose is it?"

"It belongs to the richest woman in the world," Lurk told him glumly. "Your friend, Mlle. St. Just-l'Espalier."

"Where's the rest of her?"

"Probably waking her lawyer to discuss a lawsuit."

"Tie these two up and put them with the others," Heinri told Klausiere.

"Frank! What are you doing here?" Bubby cried as he turned and saw him for the first time. "And what on earth is that? Some kind of pet?"

Elphlegm had draped herself around Frank's neck, half out of a perverse desire to frighten him and half because she thought he was the cutest human she'd ever met. Now she became embarrassed by her weakness and dropped to the floor. As she slithered behind the feed sacks, she heard him making muffled sounds through his gag. She hoped he was asking her to stay.

Klausiere had to unravel a little of Hilly's sweater to tie Lurk and Bubby, but he was careful not to let Hilly see.

"You might as well remove their gags," Heinri told him when he'd finished. "You never know. I've been thinking, one of them might have blocked sinuses and suffocate. I'd hate for that to happen, because I'm basically a humanitarian."

Klausiere took the handkerchiefs out of the mouths of the guard, the man in the tee shirt, Frank, and Hilly. Hilly was grimacing horribly.

"What's the matter with you?" Heinri asked.

"He looked a little funny before too," Klausiere said.

179

Hilly made an effort to control his twitching face. It's nothing. Just a touch of indigestion. I must have eaten something that didn't agree with me."

"So, The Boys turned on you and your partner," Frank told Lurk with a grin.

"What is this nonsense?" Lurk asked. "Are you two the cops who broke into my operating room and started raving about The Boys to my nitwit of an assistant?"

"Come on," Frank said. "The game's up. We know your friend Bubby uses you as a middleman for his contracts."

Bubby was aghast. "How could you think I'd be involved in something like that, Frank? After all the years we've known each other! After all the free spareribs!"

"It's no use, Bubby. I didn't want to believe it at first, but now I know you're in this mess up to your neck. We were arresting the hit man when these two goons grabbed us." He glared at Heinri and Klausiere.

"Hit man!" The man in the tee shirt said indignantly. "What are you? One of those militant vegetarian freaks? My work isn't easy, you know! Everyone likes to eat pig, but they don't like to think of the blood on their bacon!"

Lurk scowled at Frank. "This man's my friend. He came here tonight to do some slaughtering for me. Pigs. Not people."

"You're trying to shake my confidence!" Frank blustered. "You're all trying to destroy me! You pretend you don't believe me about The Boys! You pretend you don't believe me about the wereworm—that foul creature from the pit!" He looked nervously at the pile of feed sacks.

Elphlegm thrust her head out, hissed at him, and gnashed her fangs, even though she was more hurt than angry.

Frank flinched when he saw her, but he was too furious to be really scared. "And now you," he screamed at the man in the tee shirt, "expect me to believe you're only a pig killer!"

"Only!" Bubby gasped. "If I'd found so much as one of my darlings dead, my heart would have broken!"

Frank was taken aback by his former friend's display of passion. "You're in a funny business for a guy who loves pigs so much," he said. "How did you stand it for so many years?"

An expression of bliss stole over Bubby's face. "I've only just seen my life for the quagmire of decadence and filth it's been up to now. Shirley Lee has taught me how to love."

Frank sniggered. "Is Shirley Lee that fat old broad who was in the hall with you outside the operating room?"

Bubby stared at him coldly. "The woman's a goddess."

"Well, if you say she taught you how to love, I believe it," Frank giggled. "When we last saw her, she was giving those bodyguards a postgraduate course."

"You're out of your mind, Frank. That woman's pure and good."

"Those bodyguards didn't think she was very good. They were struggling like hell to get away."

"You wanted her for yourself!" Bubby accused him. "That's why you're saying these things! Admit it!"

"Okay! Enough of that!" Heinri said impatiently. "If you don't shut up, we'll gag you all again. Let's get to work." He looked from Frank to Hilly. "Which one of you is best on the audio-visual equipment?"

"I usually do the filming, except when the rights are being read," Hilly told him. "I have the better speaking voice. We've found that juries can relate to me."

"Untie him," Heinri told Klausiere.

After Klausiere had freed him, Hilly got to his feet awkwardly, wincing and clutching his stomach.

"What is it with you?" Heinri asked him. "Do you have an ulcer?"

"Just a nervous stomach," Hilly said weakly. "I'll be all right."

"If you say so. Now set up your cameras and lights. I want you to get a close-up of the bellybutton and then film me making a speech about the history and aims of the Lorratian Liberation Organization."

"Can I be in it?" Klausiere asked eagerly.

"Sure," Heinri told him. "You can point to the bellybutton while he's filming it. You have very expressive hands."

As they spoke, Frank became increasingly agitated. "Aren't any of you guys The Boys?" he asked piteously.

Elphlegm emerged from the pile of feed bags and balanced on her tail in front of him. It seemed to her that he didn't cringe as much as he had before. "I don't think any of these people are The Boys," she said. "But they're pretty scummy. That's something, at least."

"Not enough, though," Frank answered in a dead voice.

Elphlegm dropped down next to him and nestled against his side. He didn't draw away from her at all this time, but just stared blankly ahead.

"My hemorrhoids hurt," he said finally. "I think they're bleeding."

This information didn't have much effect on Elphlegm. She was primarily interested in arterial blood.

Hilly looked smug. "I had a feeling your hemorrhoids were behind all this. Didn't I tell you? Do any of you happen to have a tube of camphorated hog fat?" he asked the others.

They all shook their heads.

Hilly noticed that the old sink at the other end of the shack had a hot water tap. "Couldn't he have a sitz bath?" he asked Heinri.

Heinri shrugged helplessly. "I'd certainly be willing to let him. I'm a humanitarian. But there aren't any pans in here."

Hilly pointed to a rusty hubcap. "We could use that."

"Oh, all right," Heinri agreed. "What the hell! I can't help being a good person. Untie the other cop too, Klausiere."

"May Pie bless you for this act of compassion," Hilly said. He filled the hubcap with warm water and brought it to Frank.

Elphlegm unfastened Frank's trousers with her fangs and eased them and his underwear down to his knees. Then she stiffened herself into an arc so he could rest his hands on her and lift himself into the hubcap. He sighed gratefully, and Elphlegm curled up on his lap, relishing the feeling of his bare skin and the warm steam that rose from the hubcap.

"You're really not one of The Boys?" Frank asked Heinri once more.

"How many times do I have to tell you? We're soldiers of the Lorratian Liberation Organization!"

Hilly looked at him curiously. "Oh, say, are you people by any chance members of a minority group?"

"Yes," Heinri said. "An extremely oppressed one, at that."

"Lucky you!" Hilly exclaimed. "You don't have to go through all this. You qualify for our computerized atrocity scan."

"How does that work?" Heinri asked with interest.

"It's a little something we in the social sciences dreamt up," Hilly told him proudly. "You merely submit your ethnic identity to our computer, and it gives a readout of every atrocity committed against both individual members of your group and your group as a whole, the names of the perpetrators and their descendants, and the amount of cash reparation to which you're entitled."

"How far back does it go?"

"Oh, way, way back. To the accession of somebody called Charlemagne. We had to impose a cutoff date after we were flooded with claims from descendants of people who'd suffered slipped discs during the Red Sea crossing. They couldn't really provide documentation anyway. They said all the proof had been in some library at Alexandria that their enemies, aided by American military advisors, burnt down to deprive them of their settlements."

"But we're not American citizens," Heinri said. "Doesn't that eliminate us right off?"

"It makes no difference. You committed an act of terrorism on American soil, so we feel we owe you something. After all, we must have done something to upset you."

"It sounds good, I admit, but we'd probably never collect a dime. It would be tied up in red tape for years."

"Oh, no," Hilly assured him. "We don't believe in frustrating people. Waiting for something, especially money, has been proven to be a Priority A stress situation."

"So when's the payoff?"

"It shouldn't take more than a month. And there are loans available, noninterest of course, to tide you over until it comes through."

"How do we go about applying?"

"After you get your atrocity readout," Hilly explained, "you submit your claim to the main office in Potpourripolis. They pass a temporary tax so you can get your reparation immediately.

Then they sue the perpetrators or their descendants and attempt to recover the money."

"This sounds too good to be true," Klausiere objected. "How do we know you're not lying."

"Yeah. This might be some kind of trick," Heinri said.

Hilly was perplexed by their lack of faith. He had an honest face and a sincere manner. People usually believed him. "Gosh, I don't know how I can prove it to you," he said hesitantly. "Would you be convinced if you saw it in print? I think there're a few pages about it in my manual."

"I'd prefer a more reliable source," Heinri told him. "Television. A movie. Something like that."

Hilly brightened suddenly. "Why yes! Of course! As a matter of fact, there was a documentary done about our program. They rebroadcast it at least once a month, and it so happens that it's going to be shown tonight. What luck!"

"I'd accept that," Heinri said. "I'd believe anything, if I saw it in a documentary."

"You mean we have to hang around this shack until tomorrow night?" Lurk complained.

Klausiere grinned at him mischievously. "Why are you so anxious to get back? Maybe you should even think of settling here in Earwig. Why dig up the past? Wouldn't it be better to leave it buried, if you know what I mean?"

"Don't threaten me," Lurk said coldly. "I'll say you did it. And I'll see that you get sentenced to maximum therapy." Lurk was puzzled by the depth of his own rage. He'd been that angry before, but never in that way. There was a difference in quality. This anger had teeth. He wondered briefly if it were a gift from his friend Satan, but instinct told him it wasn't. It had kindled from something in himself that had become strong and violent enough to strike the initial spark. When he thought of the patient he'd killed earlier, he felt no connection to the act. Then he realized that he felt no connection to any part of his long past. He remembered it, but only as he would have remembered a biography that he'd read. He was something other than he'd been before.

Klausiere was intimidated by Lurk's steady gaze. It seemed

no more human than a lizard's. "You can't pin it on us," he said, forcing himself to maintain a bantering tone. "Who's going to believe we savaged someone's nose so efficiently? You need an education to do that."

"Whatever are you people talking about?" Hilly asked. "We're trying to be open with one another here. Let's avoid all this negative stuff."

"Yes. Let's keep things light," Klausiere agreed snidely. "I have a riddle for you."

"Fine," Hilly said. "I love riddles."

"When is a nose not a nose?"

Lurk trembled with fury, and the air in the room seemed to shake. "You've made your point," he said in a low, menacing voice. "Now shut up!"

Klausiere hugged himself to conceal the shudder that ran through his body.

Frank sighed in his hubcap. "I have a feeling something's happening," he said apathetically. "If my hemorrhoids didn't hurt so much, I'd do something about it." Then he lapsed into morose silence again.

Elphlegm huddled closer to him and watched Lurk distrustfully. The man terrified her, and she didn't understand why.

Lurk happened to look at her and caught the new image of himself reflected by her fear. He fed on it and felt stronger than he ever had in his many centuries. The earth shook very slightly, troubled by a remote frisson of excitement in Heaven.

Hilly, as always, remained untouched. "Let me see. When is a nose not a nose? When it's a runner? When you blow it? Gosh, I don't know. A nose is a nose is a nose."

"Do you give up?" Klausiere asked. He struggled to keep his voice steady. Ridiculous as it was, even though Lurk was several yards away and securely bound, he had the sensation that he was being assaulted by him.

"I give up," Hilly said with a smile. "When is a nose not a nose?"

Klausiere managed to laugh hoarsely, even though he felt something tighten around his neck. "When Lurk gets through with it!"

"That's not funny," Hilly chided. "Dr. Lurk is a great surgeon."

"I bet Lurk thinks it's funny," Klausiere persisted. "Don't you, Lurk?"

"A nose isn't a nose when it can't breathe," Lurk said softly. "Eyes aren't eyes when they can't see. A mouth isn't a mouth when it can't speak."

Klausiere, feeling his breath ebb and his eyes dim, clutched his aching chest and tried to scream. But his throat seemed to be filled with a dark muck that was slowing rising into his head. His voice couldn't get past it.

No one but Lurk and Elphlegm noticed Klausiere's discomfort. Lurk trembled with the effort of focusing his strength. He felt like he was about to pull himself over some kind of barrier. But it was a little too much for him, and he collapsed abruptly, sinking back against the wall.

Klausiere recovered at once. He glared impotently at Lurk, wanting to strike out at him, but realizing he'd look like a fool if he did. The thing he suspected him of was absurd and impossible. He hoped no one had noticed his momentary seizure, or whatever it had been. "So would you like to stay around for the documentary?" he asked Lurk, anger and triumph in his voice.

"I'm looking forward to it," Lurk answered wearily. He was flushed, like a child that'd played too hard. "What time will it be on?"

"Eight o'clock," Hilly said. He gave Lurk a searching look. "Is anything wrong? You seem uncomfortable."

"It's just anticipation," Lurk told him, rather sarcastically, now that his strength was returning. "I can hardly wait for the documentary to start."

Bubby heaved against his bonds. "No! We can't stay until tonight! What's gotten into you, Niemand? I have to save Shirley Lee! Pie only knows what she's had to endure!"

"And I have to smuggle a pork roast into a monastery for the abbot's lunch," the pig killer said. "He's a good client, and I don't want to lose him by being undependable."

"A monk? An ascetic dedicated to our Blessed Savior Pie?

And he eats pig meat?" Bubby gasped with pious horror. "Is nothing sacred?"

"Not once you get to know it," the pig killer assured him.

"I hate to be a wet blanket," the guard told Heinri and Klausiere, "but you're forgetting a very important point. There's no television set in this place."

There was a stunned silence.

"You know," Hilly said, "he's right."

"I'll run into town and buy one later," Heinri told them. "At least there's electricity. Klausiere, go through their pockets. Take everything. If we pool all the money in this room, we ought to have more than enough to buy a set."

Klausiere reached into all their pockets and pulled out bills and change, which he dumped in the middle of the floor. Then he and Heinri added their own money to the pile. Heinri counted it with an expression of growing disgust. "Only eighty-one dollars? From nine people?" He looked at Elphlegm. "Come to think of it, I didn't see you put anything down there."

"I'm sorry," Elphlegm told him. "I don't carry money when I go out for a stroll. There's so much crime."

"Now, now. We don't like to think of it as crime," Hilly corrected. "We prefer to regard it as energetic social protest."

Klausiere glared contemptuously at Lurk and Bubby. "I thought these guys were supposed to be a big deal. They had less on them than any of us."

"I never carry money with me," Lurk said defensively. "Nobody ever asks me for it, because everybody knows I'm rich."

"And I usually pay in spareribs," Bubby told them.

"Do you have credit cards?" Heinri asked.

"Don't waste your time," the pig killer said. "I happen to know the appliance store in Earwig doesn't accept them."

"Maybe we could get a used set for eighty-one dollars," Klausiere suggested.

The guard shook his head. "I can't think of anyplace in the neighborhood that would have one. Folks around here use them until they're really decrepit and then gut them and turn them into bird feeders and garbage bins. We're a thrifty people."

"Hey! I have a great idea!" Hilly told Heinri. "What if you

were to read about the documentary in *T-View?* I noticed an article about it when I got my copy earlier."

" 'If it's in *T-View,* it must be true'," Heinri said, quoting part of a famous advertising jingle. "Let me see the article."

"I don't have my *T-View* with me. I left it home on top of my set so my wife could use it. We'll have to go into Earwig first thing in the morning and pick up a copy. Does anyone know what time the stationery store opens?"

"Ten o'clock," the pig killer told him.

This was more than Bubby could bear. When Heinri had agreed to accept the word of *T-View,* he'd envisioned a quick reunion with Shirley Lee. It was too devastating to have his hopes crushed almost as soon as they were born. "That's six hours from now!" he wailed. "Can't you borrow a *T-View* from someone who lives around here?"

"What a terrific idea!" Hilly said. "Why don't you and I try to find one, Heinri. It will just take you a few minutes to read the article."

Heinri nodded. "That sounds good to me. I'm a humanitarian. I don't want you people to suffer any more than is necessary for me to get my way. Untie the guard," he told Klausiere. "We need someone with us who's familiar with the area. We can take Lurk's car."

Klausiere untied the guard, and he left with Hilly and Heinri.

-4-

After he heard the car start up and leave, Klausiere relaxed, leaning against the wall and loosening his grip on the gun. "Well, it looks like everything is going to be all right," he said. "I'm glad to get rid of Heinri and that twitchy little guy for a while. They make me nervous for some reason. Not that Heinri isn't a great soldier," he added hurriedly. "Why don't you untie the other three," he told Elphlegm. "We're going to be here for some time yet, so they might as well be comfortable. I don't think any of them will be foolish enough to try anything while I have this gun."

"I'm afraid I can't," Elphlegm apologized. "My disability,

you know." Of course, she could easily have severed the bonds with her fangs, but she was afraid the sight might upset Bubby and the pig killer more than being tied up had. Also, she was reluctant to see Lurk freed. She wanted to warn Klausiere, but she wasn't sure what to say, since she didn't know exactly what she would be warning him about.

"I'm sorry," Klausiere said. "I wasn't thinking. You untie them," he told Frank.

Frank didn't move.

"What are you waiting for?" Klausiere asked. "Go on!"

"I don't want to be bothered," Frank said listlessly. "My hemorrhoids are killing me."

Lurk glared at him. "That's a fine thing! What a selfish bastard you are!"

"Frank, untie us," Bubby pleaded. "What's the matter with you?"

Frank just stared morosely into space.

"The poor guy's really let down," Klausiere said sympathetically. "Listen," he told Frank, "if you want to think of me and Heinri as The Boys, whoever they are, it's all right with me."

"You can't think of someone as one of The Boys. They either are or aren't."

"I'm sorry you feel so bad. Heinri and I are humanitarians. That's how we got into terrorism in the first place. We hate to see anyone suffer. I wish I'd have thought to ask him and Hilly to get a tube of camphorated hog fat while they're looking for *T-View.* Most people have one lying around the house."

Frank shook his head. "It's too late. My hemorrhoids have fallen out completely. There won't be any turning back this time."

"Are you saying it's terminal?" asked Klausiere with concern.

"Yes. It's the end."

Klausiere untied Bubby himself. "You untie the others," he told him. "Would you like some more warm water in your hubcap?" he asked Frank solicitously.

"No," Frank said. "I'd have to get up while you put it in. I don't want to be bothered."

Elphlegm could sense Frank's life force ebbing. She hoped if he were going to die, he'd do it before sunrise. Then she could at least eat him, if she couldn't have him any other way. Suddenly, a compromise occurred to her.

Lurk, Bubby, and the pig killer had made themselves beds from the feed sacks and were sprawled around the shack, nearly asleep. Klausiere leaned against the wall, half asleep himself, his gun dangling loosely from his hand. Satisfied that she could be assured of some privacy, Elphlegm made her way down to Frank's feet and crawled into the bottom of one of his pants legs. As she wriggled up the inside of his calf, he gradually emerged from his depressed stupor. And by the time she thrust her head out of his open fly, he was gaping at her with wide, shocked eyes. She looked at him and ran her long tongue over her fangs and snaky lips. Then she licked his penis and sucked it deep into her throat, being careful not to snag it on her fangs. She was happy to see his stunned expression give way to a half smile of pleasure as he reached down to stroke her head.

-5-

Heinri, Hilly, and the guard climbed out of Lurk's car, which was parked in front of a battered old house with an unkempt, weedy yard.

"This is the nearest house," the guard said. "You might as well start here."

Hilly looked up at the roof. "I see an aerial. They must have *T-View*. Everyone who has a television gets *T-View*."

Heinri led the way up an overgrown path to the porch. He pounded on the front door, waited, then pounded again.

Finally, a pinched little face appeared at one of the windows. "Who on earth is it?" the old lady asked testily.

Another voice could be heard from the interior of the house. "Careful, Minnie! It might be bikers!"

"We're not bikers, ma'am," Hilly protested. "That's our car, right in front of the house."

The old lady leaned out a bit farther and looked around. "I don't see any bikes out there, Matty," she called to the unseen woman.

"You have to be careful," Matty answered. "Those boys are tricky." She appeared at the window and stared down at them too. The old ladies were so similar in appearance that it was obvious they were sisters, if not twins.

"They do look all right," Matty decided after scrutinizing the three men. "What do you want?" she called down to them.

"Do you have a copy of the new *T-View?*" Hilly asked politely.

"Is this some kind of survey? At this hour of the morning?"

"No, ma'am. I know this sounds a little strange, but we need to see one of the articles in the latest *T-View*. It's really important. You might even say it's a matter of life or death."

Milly turned to her sister, her eyes wide with alarm. "Goodness! Life or death! I wouldn't want either of those to happen! Maybe we should let them in."

"You're a soft touch and always were!" Matty snorted. "If we let you in, how do we know you won't do something awful to us?" she asked the three men.

"I swear I'd never hurt you," Hilly said solemnly. "I had a mother."

"Hmmm. He does say he had a mother," Matty told Milly. "What about your friends?" she shouted.

"They had mothers too."

"Let me make a suggestion," Heinri offered. "Why not just throw the *T-View* out to us. That way, we wouldn't have to come in. After we look at it, we'll shove it under your front door."

"Since they don't want to come in, it's probably all right to let them in," Matty told her sister.

"Yes," Millie agreed. "And if we throw our *T-View* out the window, it might get wet from the grass."

"I say we let them in."

"Might as well. I couldn't go back to sleep anyway after all this excitement."

<u>**Chapter Thirteen**</u>
Morning

-1-

It was very peaceful in the shack. Klausiere, Lurk, Bubby, and the pig killer were all asleep. Frank was still sitting in his hubcap, but he looked much happier. Elphlegm was lying at his side in a tranquil coil, her head resting on his thigh. Then, suddenly, a spasm shook her body. She realized with horror that it was dawn. Since the shack had no windows, she hadn't noticed when the sky began to lighten. She knew that in less than an hour she'd be convulsed by the agonizing rigors of metamorphosis. She had to get away.

With great effort, she overcame her sickness and began to crawl toward the door. She was nearly there when Klausiere awoke and spotted her.

"Hey! Where do you think you're going?" he shouted.

"I want to leave now," she said weakly.

"Not now. When Heinri gets back. I don't want trouble from him."

"Let me go," she pleaded. "I helped you."

"Sorry," Klausiere said. "I'm not taking any chances." He slid his foot under her and kicked her into the pile of feedbags.

"You don't have to be so rough with it," Frank complained. But he couldn't quite bring himself to get out of his hubcap and go to her defense.

An hour ago, Elphlegm could have torn Klausiere to pieces in seconds, but her fangs were already beginning to blunt. She crawled into a large burlap bag that lay in back of the feed sacks and crouched there, shuddering with pain.

Klausiere opened the door of the shack, looked out briefly, and closed it again. "It's morning," he said listlessly.

Bubby, Lurk, and the pig killer awoke, scratching and yawning.

"Did I hear you say it's morning?" Bubby asked.

Klausiere nodded.

Bubby became agitated again. "I wish they'd hurry back," he grumbled. "What could be keeping them?"

"They haven't been gone that long," Klausiere told him. "You were only asleep about an hour. It might be taking them a little while to find someone with a *T-View*."

-2-

The unexpected sound of a motorcycle broke into the morning stillness. The men in the shack froze and looked at one another nervously. Even Frank lifted his head and stared at the door.

"Could it be Heinri and Hilly?" Bubby asked.

"On a motorcycle? No. It's some kind of trouble," Klausiere said. He went to the door and opened it slightly. "Let me see what kind."

A pale young man, whose long white hair streamed behind him like smoke, was riding up the dirt road toward the pigpen. He wore a black leather jacket and dungarees.

"It's some kid," Klausiere told the others. "He's alone."

Bubby, Lurk, and the pig killer crowded around the door to get a look, whispering excitedly.

"Who is he?"

"He isn't wearing a helmet!"

"He must be crazy! He's steering that thing with one hand and drinking some kind of soft drink."

"You know, I may be wrong, but it looks like the illegal kind, that's made with refined sugar instead of honey."

"What is he wearing?"

"It's a black leather jacket. But I've never seen one cut like that before."

"Neither have I. It's weird. It's long, and it doesn't have a waistline."

Frank rose from his hubcap and walked to the door, his pants around his ankles.

The others looked at him warily.

"What's the matter?" Klausiere asked. "Are you all right?"

Without speaking, Frank pushed them away from the door and looked out at the approaching figure. When he turned back to the others, his face was transfigured. "They've come!" he said joyously. "That's one of The Boys!"

The man got off his motorcycle at the pigpen gate and walked it through the pigs to the door of the shack. He pulled it open and smiled at the curious group. As they looked at him more closely, they were all struck by his singular appearance. He was tall and thin, with big vicious hands that could circle a man's head. His hair was the color of age, yet had the springy energy of youth. Old eyes, charred and drained, were set in his boy's face. These eyes had sparse white lashes, but were totally devoid of brows. There wasn't even fuzz to mark where they should have been. His white skin was blank rather than pale. It wasn't that the blood had drained from his cheeks, but that it hadn't reached them. His face seemed to be waiting—for a beard, for shadows, for blood to find its way to his surface.

He held a can of grape soda, which was indeed the illegal kind, made with chemicals and refined sugar. When he lifted it to his mouth, they saw that his fingernails were dirty but his teeth, which were as big as a horse's, were white and strong.

"Happy to meet you all," he said. "Step aside so I can bring my bike in." His voice was perfectly average. It sounded like the voice of everyone they'd ever spoken to.

Klausiere shoved his gun in the stranger's face. "Do come in. You have some questions to answer. But the bike stays outside."

The man disdainfully brushed Klausiere's gun aside and dragged the motorcycle into the shack.

"What do you want here?" Klausiere asked him nervously. "Why are you bothering us?"

The man kicked Frank's hubcap over, splashing bloody water onto the floor. Then he dragged his bike across the room and pulled it in back of the feed sacks, piling more on top of it, until it was completely hidden.

Elphlegm, still coiled miserably in her burlap bag, felt him moving around near her. It puzzled her that, unlike the humans, he had no odor, but she was too sick to investigate.

"I have to hide out here for a while," the stranger announced when he'd finished with his bike. "There's a bunch of cops after me."

"What did you do?" Klausiere asked.

"Escaped from jail. And also I took this stuff off some guy."

Proudly, he tossed a cigarette lighter, a pen, and a wristwatch down on the table, where the bellybutton was still on display.

Klausiere was unimpressed and couldn't understand why Lurk and Bubby were shrinking away from the objects with horror. "That's no big deal," he said. "I'm a terrorist. Look what I've got!" He pointed at the bellybutton.

The stranger grabbed it, swallowed it, and washed it down with a swig of grape soda.

Klausiere let out a wild screech of anguish and tried to force the stranger's mouth open, as if he intended to reach down into his stomach and retrieve the bellybutton.

The man just laughed and pushed him away.

Lurk was nearly in shock. "You filthy cannibal!" he gasped. "Do you know what you've done? Quick! Make yourself throw up before it's digested!"

"Sorry," the stranger giggled. "You'll have to wait for it to come out the other end. But if you want to leave your address with me, I'll send it to you when it does."

Lurk staggered over to the table and leaned against it weakly. He looked down at the stolen objects with disbelief. "You are monstrous!" he told the stranger. "Where did you get these things?"

"I told you," the man said casually. "I stole them. I took them off this guy. He was standing outside the emergency room of the hospital where I went for my V.D. shot."

"I thought your serum had cured all the V.D. in the world, Niemand," Bubby said.

"I invented a new kind," the man bragged.

Lurk gave him a stern look. "Do you realize the person you robbed was a lawyer?"

"I just whacked him out and went through his pockets. We weren't introduced."

Lurk indicated the objects on the table. "A Pole-ax wristwatch. No lawyer can be admitted to a courtroom without showing his to the guard at the door. A gold-filled, monogrammed Boss pen. No legal document is valid unless signed with one. And an 18-karat Gunhill lighter. In ancient times, when people used to smoke something called a 'cigarette', they would light it with one of these. But now lawyers only flick them in unison on ceremonial occasions to symbolize the flame of truth. You've stolen the ritual objects of the Legal League! Every lawyer receives them when he passes his bar examination! These things are sacred to them! They won't rest until you've been hunted down and executed."

"What can I tell you?" the man drawled insolently. "They're going to have some awful bad insomnia." He noticed Frank, who'd been watching him with silent adoration. "How come he's got his trousers down? What kind of place is this? Are you guys a little funny?"

Klausiere was deeply offended. "He has terminal hemorrhoids. He was taking a sitz bath when you stormed in here and callously knocked over his hubcap! You have no humanity!"

Suddenly, they became aware of a commotion outside the shack. The sound of hundreds of marching feet and the grinding and roaring of heavy vehicles froze them into shocked silence. They stared at the door apprehensively.

Klausiere looked out and turned back to the others with terror written on his face. "Those aren't police!"

Lurk hurried over to the door, gasped and slammed it shut. "It's a combined force of Social Sanctuary troops and an elite strike battalion of the Legal League. They're killers!" He lashed out at the stranger. "We're not going to risk our lives to protect you! Let's turn him in now," he told the others. "Before they get here. That way they won't think we were conspiring with him." Lurk was frankly terrified. He was sure that the Legal League could find a way to kill even someone who was immortal.

The stranger grabbed the three ritual objects off the table and put the watch and the cigarette lighter in his pocket. Then he clasped Frank around the waist and held the lethal point of the Boss pen against his rectum. "Okay! Now you're going to do like I tell you, or your friend gets it right in the hemorrhoids!"

Klausiere, Bubby, and the pig killer grabbed Lurk, who had been about to run out the door and surrender.

"We have to at least take a few moments to discuss this," Klausiere admonished. "After all, the rectum of a friend is at stake. This experience has brought us all closer together and established an atmosphere of caring and mutual support."

Frank started. "For a second you sounded just like Hilly," he told Klausiere. "I wonder if it's contagious."

"It's obvious that his mind is going," Bubby said. "I like Frank, but he told us himself that his hemorrhoids are terminal."

"Yeah! It's him or us, and he's already on the way out anyway!" the pig killer added.

"He wouldn't even untie us before," Lurk whined. "We don't owe him anything."

Klausiere stepped back and pointed his gun at Bubby, Lurk, and the pig killer. "Just a minute!" he said angrily. "I'm a humanitarian! Nobody's going to get their hemorrhoids perforated while I have any say about it!"

The stranger relaxed. "At least one of you has some compassion. Now me and this guy are going to hide behind the feed sacks where I've got my bike. You get rid of those lawyers and Social Sanctuarians."

"And how are we supposed to do that?" Lurk asked him.

"Just be cool. All those pigs you got running around out there wiped away any tracks my bike made inside the pen. They'll think I came up the dirt road as far as the gate to the pen and then lit out over the hills."

"But how are we going to explain what we're doing here? It'll look suspicious, four men hanging out in a shack in the middle of a pigpen."

"What were you doing here?"

"That's none of your business," Lurk told him haughtily.

The stranger smiled his white smile. "I don't know. I come in here and see all you guys in this place with some kind of potato chip on a pair of black satin underdrawers."

Lurk and Klausiere winced.

"Weird," the stranger continued. "And I see this guy with his pants half off. You say he has hemorrhoids. I wonder how he got them."

"That isn't what we were doing here!" Lurk insisted.

"Too bad," the stranger told him. "It would have given you a reason for being in this place, and it's only a Class B misdemeanor." He looked around the room and spotted the can of soda he'd left on the table. "Hey! That's it! You can pretend you all snuck in here for a hit of that soda. A refined-sugar violation is only a Class B misdemeanor too."

Lurk sighed with exasperation. "They're on a sacrilege case. We won't be able to distract them with sugar."

"Sure you will. You know how the League is. Those guys just want to make you bleed. They don't care whether it's a drop or a gallon. With them, it's the principle of the thing. They'll write you all tickets and leave happy."

"I don't believe you," Lurk said. "They'll tear this place apart. You've spit on their gods."

"You're exaggerating. I have a friend who's a lawyer."

The others looked at the stranger with combined awe and disbelief.

"What lawyer would associate with the likes of you?" Lurk sneered.

"You'd be surprised," the stranger said without malice. Suddenly, his rough speech had become as smooth as Lurk's. "The friend I mentioned told me that only paralegals believe the old myths. Most lawyers question the divine origin of the Pole-ax wristwatch and the Gunhill lighter. And a few don't even believe in the Boss pen. God is dead."

All stared at him with shocked fascination, until the spell was broken by a change in the kinds of noises that were coming from outside. The vehicles were silent, and the muffled sound of cursing told them that the soldiers were struggling through the grunting mass of pigs.

"But even if your plan works and they only give us tickets, I'll still have a record," Lurk said.

"Don't complain," Klausiere told him. "It could be a lot worse." He put his lips next to Lurk's ear so none of the others could hear him. "They give more than a ticket for murder. You're not lucky enough to be a terrorist, so you'd be sentenced to at least ten years of intensive psychoanalysis."

Lurk blanched at the thought. To think he'd been worried about death when a vastly more horrible fate threatened. "We'll try your plan," he told the stranger.

The man picked up the can of grape soda and handed it to

Lurk, who took it reluctantly. "Go on. Drink some so they'll smell it on your breath," he ordered.

"But my teeth!" Lurk protested.

"You're asking us to commit dental suicide!" Bubby said.

"Please don't make me do it!" the pig killer pleaded. "I'm twenty-nine, and I've never had a single cavity!"

"Drink!" the man ordered.

"I'd rather not," Lurk said.

"Drink! It's good! It almost tastes like it was made from real grapes."

Lurk took a squeamish sip and handed it to Klausiere, who also drank. Then Bubby and the pig killer followed suit.

"Smear some on your lips so they'll see it," the stranger told them. "They're pretty stupid. They need all the help they can get."

The four men obeyed him.

"Now give me the can," he said. "I'm thirsty from dragging that bike in here and explaining things to you idiots." He took the can and drank from it, then handed it to Frank, who took a long, grateful draught. After he'd set the empty can on the pedestal where the bellybutton had been so the soldiers would be certain to notice it, the stranger drew Frank behind the pile of feed sacks.

–3–

The two crawled into the same burlap sack in which Elphlegm had hidden. Frank went in first, and the stranger followed, pressing his chest against Frank's back. Frank felt Elphlegm's shuddering body, which was still being twisted by the spasms that preceded her transformation. He recognized her by touch and embraced her lovingly, realizing something was wrong. When he put his hands on her, she forgot her pain enough to kiss him on the mouth and sweep her tail back and forth over his body. He rolled on top of her and felt the stranger in turn lie on him and enter him from the back. His hemorrhoids didn't hurt at all, but seemed to tingle and dissolve as the man pushed his way deeper inside him.

"I want to put it in," Frank whispered to Elphlegm. "Isn't there anyplace . . . ?"

199

In her hunger for him, she decided that if her wereworm body had no opening, she would make one. She brought her tail up to her mouth and prepared herself for the unpleasant chilly sweetness of Pusgrub blood. But as her rapidly shrinking fangs bit into her flesh, she tasted instead the warm, salty blood of a human. She was one of them! The long dormant gene of some ancient miscegenation had asserted itself and given her the right to love him as one of his own kind. She sucked him into the wound she'd made and went blank with delight.

-4-

A voice directly outside the shack hollered, "Company halt!" and someone pounded on the door.

Klausiere hid his gun in the feed sacks and nervously went to open it. A platoon leader entered, accompanied by a standard bearer and a legal secretary. The standard bearer held a flag adorned with the figure of Justice and her scales. The secretary carried a steno pad and had a sharpened pencil tucked behind his ear. The platoon leader was dressed in a sumptuous uniform with no less than three lavishly engraved gold Boss pens in the breast pocket. Through the open door, the rest of the soldiers could be seen, trying to retain their military demeanor while being jostled by the pigs.

The platoon leader addressed Klausiere. "We're looking for a tall, pale man on a motorcycle. He's wanted for a capital reverence violation, jailbreak, and inciting to rebellion."

"None of us has a motorcycle," Klausiere told him. "We walked here from Earwig."

Lurk was dodging conspicuously around the table, trying to draw the platoon leader's attention to the can of soda, but the man remained oblivious.

"You must have seen him," he insisted. "His motorcycle tracks end right outside the gate to your pigpen. By the way, is this pigpen licensed? Let me see your papers."

Bubby pulled out his wallet and showed his pig license.

"I'm sorry we can't be of more help," Klausiere said, "but we didn't hear a thing. He probably turned off at the gate and headed into the meadow."

"You're hiding something," the platoon leader accused. "It's so quiet out here, it would have been impossible for you not to have heard his motorcycle."

The secretary spotted the can of soda. "I think I know why they didn't notice anything, excellency," he offered snidely, pointing at the can. "They're all stoned on sugar!"

The leader stared into their faces and nodded. "Yes. I see. There's something all over their mouths." He picked up the can and shook it. "Empty!" he told the secretary. "You're right. They couldn't have noticed anything. Their blood sugar must be radically abnormal. Okay, junkie, who's your connection?" he asked Lurk.

"I got it from a guy named Edgar," Lurk said, trying to look guilty. "I met him on the street. He said that he got it from a counter attendant at the Earwig Soyburger Shack."

"Make a note of that," the leader told the secretary. "We'll check it out on the way back. And give all these men citations for the refined-sugar violation. Let's see some identification, you freaks!"

They all took out identification and handed it to the secretary, who copied their names onto the tickets. Klausiere was glad that Heinri had thought to get false papers for them.

When the secretary was writing out Lurk's ticket, he paused and called to the leader, "What do you know, sir! This one's a doctor!"

"Disgraceful!" the leader muttered, shaking his head.

Lurk turned purple with humiliation. How degrading it was to be accused of a misdemeanor, he thought, when any idiot could see, just by glancing at him, that he was a felony kind of person.

After the tickets were written, the leader and his escorts left with no further questions about the man on the motorcycle.

-5-

When they heard the vehicles and troops move away, the stranger and Frank emerged from their hiding place, leaving Elphlegm behind in a deep sleep. She'd completed her metamorphosis, but Frank had been first too excited and then too exhausted to notice her changing contours.

The stranger went to the door to look at the departing troops. "Come here," he told the others. "Get a load of this."

They all crowded around the door and watched the platoon marching away over the grassy hills beyond the pigpen. Either through forgetfulness or spite, they'd left the gate open, and the pigs were trotting after them like a rear guard.

"There go your profits for the month," Lurk told Bubby.

"It doesn't matter," Bubby said calmly. "I only hope they'll be all right until I get back up here with Shirley Lee. We're going to make a home for them."

"Won't all those lawyers roast and eat them?" the pig killer asked.

"No," Lurk said. "They've taken the Hypocritic Oath, by which they promise never to do anything illegal in public."

Bubby smiled. "I feel good about myself! Like I've really accomplished something!"

"You have," Lurk told him. "Your destruction. Your business is ruined. Now that you're pigless, Pie in the Sty is just another luncheonette."

"Shirley Lee doesn't care about money."

"Then she probably can't be trusted," the stranger said.

Lurk looked at him curiously. "They said you were wanted for inciting rebellion. What's that all about?"

"I'm Guido Mocha."

They all backed away from him, except for Frank.

"You were convicted of plotting against the Social Sanctuary," said Bubby with horror. "They said your depravity put you beyond the reach of social science, and you were sentenced to be executed."

"I'm also beyond the reach of their nooses. Now I'm returning to my army." He looked into Frank's tired brown eyes with his cool gray ones. "And I can always use more men."

Frank looked away.

"Come with me," Guido Mocha asked. "You want to, don't you?"

"I don't know," Frank said uncertainly.

"I'll tell you where I'll be, in case you decide to come." He whispered something into his ear.

"So far away," Frank said.

Guido Mocha pulled his bike out from under the feed sacks and lugged it across the room and out the door. "So long," he told them. "I'm going. The troops are too far away to hear my bike. I'll see you soon," he said to Frank. Then he climbed on his bike and roared away through the empty pigpen and down the road by which he'd come.

-6-

"Aren't You going to do anything?" Gabriel asked. He sat closest to God ever since Michael had begun to spend all his time skulking around the Venetian blinds.

"No," God answered. "Not at the moment."

"But they've usurped Your prerogative. You can't mean to let them get away with it."

"He'll be dealt with, just as the other one was dealt with," God said. "But for the time being, I find him amusing."

"Why? They can't even do it properly. He's missing things."

"Nothing important. Give them time. They'll get it right." God patted Gabriel's hand. "Bear with me. I find a great potential for entertainment in this situation."

"What is that?"

"You heard him a moment ago. These days the rare executions they do have are carried out by hanging. People wore crosses around their necks for so many centuries. If things go as I think they will, they'll be wearing nooses around their necks for many more centuries. What a fitting ornament for the human race!"

"So You're not going to intervene?" Gabriel asked.

"They made him. Let them kill him."

-7-

"Would you like me to put some more warm water in the hubcap for you?" Klausiere asked Frank, whose pants were still down around his ankles.

"No. Don't bother," Frank said absently. He pulled up his pants and fastened them.

They heard a car stop outside.

"Finally!" Bubby sighed. "That must be Heinri and Hilly. Now we can get out of here."

Klausiere looked out. "It's them, all right. And Heinri is smiling."

"Great!" Bubby exclaimed. "That means good news."

Heinri, Hilly, and the guard stepped buoyantly into the shack.

"He was telling the truth," Heinri said. "They have these wonderful computers and nifty laws that make weapons obsolete."

"Maybe so, but think a minute," Klausiere cautioned. "What good is the money if we can't spend it for twenty years? We'll have to do time for kidnapping."

"Not at all," Hilly reassured him. "As a recognized minority, you're immune from prosecution. Any crimes committed by minorities are considered to have redeeming social value."

"So you see, Klausiere? Everything's settled." Heinri looked around the room. "Isn't someone missing?"

"Who?" Klausiere asked.

"Our funny-looking friend."

"You mean the wereworm," Frank corrected.

"Are you still nursing that same obsession?" Hilly asked.

"But now I can prove it!" Frank insisted. "The sun has risen. She must have resumed her Pusgrub form by now."

"She?" Hilly repeated, raising his eyebrows. "The creature has a sex now? At least you're hallucinating in greater detail."

Frank flushed angrily. "I'll show you! She's right back there, in a burlap bag." He hurried behind the feed sacks and dragged the bag out into the center of the room. "Now you'll see!" he told Hilly.

"I'll see that you need therapy!" Hilly said, grabbing the bottom of the sack and shaking it.

Elphlegm tumbled out, blinking at them sleepily. She was naked, and the bite she'd made in her tail had become a nasty gash in her left instep.

Frank rushed over and took her in his arms. "Your poor foot," he said gently. He took the handkerchief Klausiere had gagged him with earlier from his pocket and used it to bind her wound. Then he draped his jacket over her shoulders.

She smiled at him gratefully.

"You're even lovelier now," he whispered.

Hilly looked as if he were choking. "That's my sister-in-law!" he managed to gasp, and for the first time since they'd been working together, he heard Frank laugh. "It's not funny!" he said angrily. "If this gets back to the Social Sanctuary, my career will be over!"

"Good!" Elphlegm told him.

He stared at her wildly. "Elphlegm, this is one of your stupid jokes, isn't it? You're not really a . . . wereworm!"

"I'm afraid I am," she said.

"Well, you'd better stop!"

"I can't. It's irrevocable."

Lurk smiled at her benignly. He was always glad to welcome a new monster on the earth.

"Please!" Hilly begged Frank. "You mustn't tell anyone about this!"

"Don't worry," he said. "Your secret's safe. I won't be around, and the others don't really know what's going on."

"What do you mean, you won't be around?"

"I'm going to meet Guido Mocha."

Lurk giggled. "Did he promise you a ride on his motorcycle? If I were you, I'd stick to hubcaps."

"You can't be serious," Hilly told Frank. "You'll be an outlaw."

"Let's hope he's better at that than he was at being a cop," Lurk said snidely. He was annoyed by the thought that someone was going to do something they wanted to do. He was much happier when people did their duty, especially if it was unpleasant for them. When Frank remained unperturbed by his jibes, he felt a rage building in him which far outstripped the provocation. "Where did Guido Mocha say he'd meet you?" he asked Frank.

"I won't tell you that."

"You said it was far away. You'll see. You'll get there and he'll have already gone. Or, what's more likely, he'll never have been there in the first place. Do you think he'd tell a cop where his army is? Even a stupid one like you?"

Frank just walked silently to the door, driving Lurk into a fury that made him rigid and pale with the effort of controlling it. "You don't even know what Mocha and his bunch are fighting for," he told Frank contemptuously.

"I don't care what they're fighting for," Frank said. "I just want to bust some heads."

Lurk threw up his hands in despair. "These are the words of a rational human being? This is the end result of man's struggle toward civilization? An idiot who wants to bust heads? To fight for the sheer, depraved joy of slaughter?"

"Not slaughter," Frank corrected. "Why not call it 'harvest'? They say God takes the good. Too early, some claim. Well, I'll take the bad. I'll be the garbage collector."

Hilly was outraged. "And where do you get the right to decide who's garbage?"

"Nobody else seems to want the job."

"Since you're going to play God, please tell me what criteria you'll be using to make your judgments," Hilly smirked. "I wouldn't want to end up on your garbage list."

"I might as well use the same criteria God does," Frank replied. "Imitation is the sincerest praise. So if I like it, it has to be good. Because if it weren't, I wouldn't like it. And if I don't like it . . . it had better watch out."

"I can't think of anything you like," Hilly told him, "except maybe The Boys and your gun."

"Okay. The Boys and my gun are safe from my wrath."

"And what isn't? Everything else?"

"Everything? Of course not! I can only do so much during my lifetime. I'm just going after a few top-priority sins. Believe me, I know what I hate."

"Judging by the look you're giving me, I have a feeling I'm at the top of the list," Hilly said with a nervous smile.

"Wrong. I don't hate you. Just that smile of yours. The only thing I hate worse than your smile is your laugh. Whenever you think there's the least danger that you might dislike something, or even like it, you laugh at it instead. By making it into a joke, you insure that it won't disturb the calm of that plateau between your ears. Your face only really relaxes when you're in the presence of the utterly banal."

"You have no sense of the ridiculous!" Hilly sniffed.

"Nothing's ridiculous until people like you make it so by laughing at it. I'm not about to laugh my feelings impotent. What I hate, I destroy if I can. And what I love . . . " Frank looked at Elphlegm. " . . . I reverence. I wouldn't waste even a second of my life on a silly giggle or a vacuous smile. I've had to wait too long for what I want, and waiting's made me impatient."

Elphlegm limped over to him and put her hand in his. "I'll come with you."

"I hoped you would," Frank told her. "I wanted to ask you, but I didn't think I had the right. It'll be a hard life. And you'll have to become a traitor. I believe Guido Mocha plans to drive your people back underground."

"They're not my people," she said.

Frank looked around the room with an expression of disgust. "I know what you mean. These aren't my people either."

He put his arm around her waist so she could favor her injured foot, and they left together.

-8-

As he watched them go, Lurk felt anger crawling like an insect up his spine. Acting on instinct, he braced himself against it and remained perfectly still until it was clawing at the nape of his neck. Then he stamped his foot sharply, and it climbed into his brain.

The other men felt the air in the room grow uneasy. It scraped on their nerves, and they drew away from Lurk, as if they sensed he was responsible.

After the troops left, Klausiere had retrieved his gun from its hiding place in the feed sacks and thrust it in the waistband of his lederhosen. Lurk's mind, which was as strong as his hands now, pulled the trigger. This served the dual purpose of drawing the attention of the others away from him and providing a little good, clean fun. Klausiere yelped with pain as the bullet grazed his thigh.

"Idiot!" Heinri shouted at him. "Are you trying to screw everything up? What if someone heard that shot and calls the police?"

"Yes, you should be more careful," Lurk admonished, hiding a smile. "The sound of gunfire carries for quite a distance." He decided not to ask Heinri to return his gun. He needn't carry one anymore, now that he could use other people's.

"I swear I didn't touch the trigger," Klausiere protested. "Do you think I'm dumb enough to want to shoot my balls off? I almost did, you know, not that anyone gives a damn."

God adjusted the screen for a close-up of Lurk, and all Heaven leaned forward eagerly. Even Michael stopped pouting and came over to watch, infected by the new mood of exhilaration. Everything seemed in sharper focus.

Tremors shook Hell, and cracks appeared in the corn popper. Satan and Pie's mother had been watching *The Blob* when, suddenly, the reception went. Mist rose from the floor and swirled into shapes more horrible than any they'd seen on television. They hastily threw a few things in a suitcase and headed for the gates of Hell.

Then Lurk lost his grip on it again, and everything went back to normal. Michael returned to his post by the Venetian blinds. Satan and Pie's mother unpacked, patched the cracks in the corn popper, and sat back down on the couch to finish watching *The Blob*. Reception was good again, and the phantasms had disappeared.

Everyone in the shack believed he hadn't felt at all peculiar until Klausiere fired his gun. None of them remembered their fear of Lurk, who was sitting on the floor, resting his back against the feed sacks. He was even more exhausted than he'd been the last time the power had left him.

"Enough bickering," Hilly said to Heinri. "I'm sure Klausiere won't do such a foolish thing again. Now let's get down to business. Is it a deal? Will you go to Potpourripolis and file an atrocity claim?"

"It's a deal!" Heinri agreed enthusiastically. "Klausiere, deactivate the mechanism."

"The what?" Hilly asked.

"Oh, we have a few of your major cities wired to blow at noon," Heinri said in a casual voice, "but don't be concerned. We have a device that shuts down all systems by remote control."

"We created a device to shut down the explosives instead of detonating them to make sure our mission wouldn't fail, even if we weren't able to carry it out ourselves," Klausiere added. "If we had been killed, three cities would have been destroyed in the name of the Lorratian Liberation Organization."

"Which cities?" Hilly asked.

"Potpourripolis, New York, and Miami."

"Potpourripolis?" Hilly gasped. "That's the headquarters of the Social Sanctuary! Where would I deliver my papers?"

"Relax," Heinri told him. "Potpourripolis isn't going anywhere. We've settled things the nonviolent way. With money."

Klausiere had been searching ever more frantically around the pedestal on the table. "I can't find it!" he said to Heinri. "You saw me put it down here when we first came in. Where the hell could it be?"

Hilly looked sick. "Was it a small, rectangular, black thing?"

"Yes," Heinri told him. "There are switches inside. Have you seen it?"

"I'm afraid I swallowed it," Hilly said weakly.

"Why on earth did you do that?"

"To protect it. I thought it was evidence."

"How long ago did you swallow it?" Heinri demanded.

"When we first got here."

"Then it should be in his intestines by now," Heinri told Klausiere.

"Maybe I ought to drive into Earwig and get a strong laxative for him," Klausiere suggested.

Lurk had recovered and stood with the rest of them again, savoring the atmosphere of impending disaster.

Heinri grabbed his wrist and looked at his watch. "There's no time for anything like that," he told Klausiere. "Those cities are due to blow in less than half an hour." He gripped Lurk's wrist more tightly and smiled. "It's fortunate we have a surgeon here with us."

Hilly started to back toward the door.

"That's impossible!" Lurk laughed. "I can't operate here.

I don't have my instruments or an anesthetic. Besides, the digestive tract is very long. I wouldn't know where to cut."

"You have to take the chance," Heinri insisted. "If we're responsible for the deaths of millions of people, it'll look bad on our reparations claim."

The thought of millions of people dying rather appealed to Lurk. Especially, since the l'Espalier woman and her lawsuit would be one of them. Simon would go too. Maybe. Lurk wasn't sure what would happen if an immortal person blew up. Would he continue to live in shreds and haunt him, like malignant, floating spaghetti, for not saving him? Would he stay in one piece and rat Lurk out to the authorities for being immoral, immortal, and unable to keep track of his patients' bellybuttons? Or was there some kind of connection between the two of them? Maybe if Simon did die, he would die too.

"It's out of the question," he told Heinri a little less certainly. "No one could survive an operation performed under these conditions."

"Losing a patient won't be a new experience for you," Klausiere reminded him.

"Will you shut up about that?" Lurk whispered furiously.

"Sure. If you get our mechanism out of this guy's gut."

"Why should I trust you?"

"Why should we make trouble for you? We'll be too busy spending our money."

"Okay, I'll do it," Lurk said.

With a long, gurgling shriek of fear, Hilly dashed outside.

"Catch him!" Heinri shouted. "Millions of lives and our money depend on it!"

The entire group rushed off in pursuit. They tackled Hilly when he'd nearly reached the pigpen gate and carried him back to the shack.

On their way, the pig killer spotted his knife lying on the ground. He picked it up and showed it to Lurk. "Can you use this?"

"Bring it in," Lurk told him. "At least it's better than my nail clippers, which were the only alternative."

They dragged Hilly, struggling frantically, into the shack.

After they'd removed the feed sack that had served as the bellybutton pedestal, they laid him on the table.

"Let me go!" Hilly screamed. "It isn't fair! I was only trying to help! I've always been an exceptionally nice person!"

"Aren't You being a little hard on him?" Gabriel asked God. "He is sort of a nice guy. Why don't You give him a break?"

"Because he shines that stupid smile of his into everything like a flashlight. He feels it's his sacred calling to analyze and explain all My mysteries to pieces. He wants to be like Me. That isn't arrogance. That's stupidity. Who in their right mind would choose to have the sun continuously in their face? He's crazy, and he's a bore. I can forgive any crime or insult, but I'm merciless to bores!"

Lurk shook his head helplessly. "I can't operate with him flinging himself around like that. He has to be anesthetized."

Heinri brought the butt of his gun down on Hilly's skull. "He's anesthetized," he said. "Get to work."

Lurk plunged downward with the knife, and a jet of blood spurted above their heads.

-9-

As Michael played with the cord of the Venetian blinds, pulling it just hard enough to move the lowest slat a bit, he felt God call him. But He was speaking in two voices wound so tightly together that Michael had difficulty separating them. One forbade him to look out. The other gently pleaded with him to disobey.

Michael dropped the cord and clutched his aching head, trying to shut out the voices. When he looked at God, he only saw His back. But although He seemed to have His attention on the screen, Michael struggled under the full weight of His mind. Unable to bear the contradictions being hurled at him, scarcely aware of what he was doing, he grabbed the cord again and yanked open the blinds.

At best, Michael had expected a shiny new universe, at worst, a void. Chaos had also been a possibility. But he found himself inches from something too alien to fit his thoughts. Compared with it, voidness was a blessing and chaos a meticulous structure. He knew the stuff he was looking at wasn't matter, since nothing could possibly be made from it. It was more like the ash of matter, numbing whatever it touched with its uselessness.

There was nothing between it and Michael. This hole wasn't like the windows on earth with their barriers of glass. Only the blinds had held it back, and now it was drifting toward him. He fought against the dry tedium that crept into his spirit and managed to turn around.

God had switched off Heaven this time, as well as the rest of the universe. The angels and the Elect sat perfectly motionless in front of the blank screen. As God approached, the stuff retreated, and He willed the blinds back down again.

He'd assumed His most attractive form, a soft golden cloud, dimpled with light. Michael felt himself change to match Him. Their thoughts became congruent, and God's mind fed Michael's the story.

God had lain, no larger than a flea, crushed and choking in that stuff out there. Then He summoned the will to force it back a little and grew stronger in the space He'd made for Himself. But, gradually, He carved away such a vastness that He became lonely in it. So He began to tear off pieces of His own expanded substance and from them create galaxies and inhabitants for them. Every time He tore a piece of Himself away, He was in pain and had to rest until the tissue regenerated. During these periods of pain and rest, His will faltered, and the stuff began to encroach on the periphery of the universe. Finally, He'd learned to push it out just a little farther than necessary when His will was strong so it never had time enough to cross the boundaries when He lay helpless. The stuff had been quiet for eons. But He didn't know how much was out there, and He was afraid it might be preparing an assault, maybe gathering itself into a tidal wave so vast that it could swallow even Him.

As Michael understood, he stopped hating God. But it had been the hatred that made him separate enough to be God's lover. When it left, there was nothing parting them anymore, and he vanished into God.

God changed back to human form so He'd have hands. He

probed His body, trying to find Michael, even though He knew it wasn't possible. The fragments were too deeply embedded and too content to be pried loose by God Himself. He returned to the screen, switched the universe back on, and called Gabriel to sit with Him.

-10-

"The incision is made," Lurk said. "I did a nice large one, since I have to cover a lot of ground. Now just let me feel around in here." He thrust his hand into Hilly's guts. "How big is the thing you want me to look for?" he asked Heinri.

"Only about an inch and a half long by one inch wide by half an inch thick. But it's hard, so you should be able to feel it."

"Don't be so sure. Bones are hard too, you know. I can see this is going to be a real production." His shoulders heaved as he fished energetically around for the object. Once in a while, he'd fling something that looked like an internal organ onto the floor.

"Doesn't he need some of that stuff?" Bubby asked squeamishly.

"I don't know," Lurk said with a shrug. "No one ever tried to live without it before." He fumbled around some more, then gave a cry of triumph. "Ha! I think I have it! I just have to move his pelvis out of the way." There was a grating noise as he wrenched Hilly's bones out of position. "One little cut! Yes! Here it is!" He held a small, bloody rectangle aloft.

"That's it, all right!" Heinri said with relief. "Thank God! We've only a few minutes to spare!" He slid the top off the object and pulled a series of tiny switches. "There. The explosives are deactivated. Now sew him up, and let's all get out of here."

"Sew him up with what?" Lurk asked. "Anybody got a needle and thread?"

"How about his knitting yarn?" Klausiere suggested.

"Perfect. Give it here."

"The only thing is, I'll have to unravel the sweater he was making. He'll feel terrible about that."

"Unravel it." Lurk looked down at Hilly. "It won't fit him now anyway."

Klausiere unraveled the sweater, winding the wool around

his hand. "There's a yarn needle in his suitcase too," he told Lurk. "Can you use it?"

"Sure." Lurk took it and the wool from Klausiere and began to sew Hilly back together in jagged, colorful stitches.

The pig killer, who thought of Lurk as a colleague as well as a friend, watched the procedure with interest.

"Seeing him," he said, looking down at Hilly, "made me remember the abbot's pig meat. Is it okay if I go? By the time I do what I have to do and get up to the monastery, it'll be one o'clock."

"Go ahead," Heinri told him.

"Can I go too?" the guard asked. "Since the pigs are gone, there's nothing for me to guard anymore."

Heinri waved him away, and the two men left together. "Do you think he'll live?" he asked Lurk, who'd nearly finished with Hilly.

"Yes, but in a considerably altered state." Lurk knotted the yarn and bit through it, then stepped back to admire his handiwork. "If it's any consolation to him," he said, "I think he's become some kind of minority. Maybe he can get money from that program he told you guys about." He grabbed Hilly's shoulders. "You get his legs," he told Heinri.

"Where are they?"

"In the usual place. Everything else has been moved around. That's what's confusing you. Just stand at the other end of him, facing me."

Heinri moved to a position opposite Lurk.

"Okay," Lurk said. "Now reach down, and what you grab will be his legs."

They carried Hilly to Lurk's car and put him in the back seat. Lurk got behind the wheel, and Bubby climbed in next to him.

"Where do we get our money?" Heinri asked.

"Social Sanctuary headquarters in Potpourripolis. Just drive due west," Lurk told him.

"But what'll we do about gas and traveling expenses?"

"Mug a few people. Pull a few stickups. Until you actually get your money, you have minority status. Make the most of it." Lurk drove off with a friendly wave.

"Let's go get our car," Heinri told Klausiere. "We'll put the audio-visual equipment those cops left in the trunk. We can hock it along the way."

"What're we going to do after we have the money?" Klausiere asked. "Return to Alsace-Lorraine and found an independent Lorratian state?"

"Shit, no!" Heinri said. "I was thinking of Freeport. They have casinos, girls. . . ."

"That sounds good, very good," Klausiere mused. "You know, I've just noticed, it's awfully hard to be nationalistic when you're rich."

"That's because the rich have a higher calling," Heinri told him sagely. "Pleasure."

-11-

He and Bubby were nearly halfway back to New York, and the exhilaration that Lurk always felt after surgery was beginning to wear off. Also, Hilly had regained consciousness. He'd managed to fall off the seat, and his moans were getting on Lurk's nerves. It depressed him that the last legal operation he'd be able to perform for at least fifty years had been such a primitive one.

Bubby, on the other hand, was ecstatic. "Just think, Niemand," he gurgled. "I'll be with her soon."

"I wish you'd shut up," Lurk said glumly. "Doesn't it bother you that one of your closest friends is a ruined man? I consider your good mood a personal insult."

"You're exaggerating. You have too fine a reputation for one little mistake to destroy your career."

"Little mistake!" Lurk fumed. "That fool Simon actually sewed the richest woman in the world shut without her belly-button. That's not a little mistake. That's a catastrophe! If only he'd waited. Even with the original gone, I could have slapped something together." He dug his fingers into the steering wheel, as if he wished it were Simon's throat.

"Why don't you turn on the radio," Bubby suggested. "Some music might cheer you up."

"It might," Lurk agreed. "Maybe I can find a good Requiem Mass."

215

"Huh?"

"There's a station that plays ancient music," Lurk explained, turning the dial of the radio. "Stuff from the preclassical era." Verdi's *Requiem* was on, and he began to relax as he listened to his favorite part, about resting in peace. He was annoyed when the broadcast was suddenly interrupted.

"I've just received a special bulletin from our mobile news team," the announcer said. "Fashion history has been made today. During a press conference in the basement of that exclusive luncheonette, Pie in the Sty, international beauty and richest woman in the world, Basile St. Just-l'Espalier, unveiled the new look in abdomens. Dr. Niemand Lurk, an eminent New York surgeon, is the innovator of this daring style, which has been christened 'The Unborn Look' and is achieved by complete removal of the navel."

A beatific smile spread over Lurk's face. He should have known better than to worry. It seemed that he was just one of those people who are born to win. Even his bad luck was good. "Did you hear that?" he gloated. "I'm saved!" He remembered Satan and added, "In a manner of speaking, anyway."

The surge of strength he'd experienced twice earlier that morning returned, but this time it had a feeling of permanence. Lurk knew he was a changed man. For the first time, his malice was completely altruistic. Theft, for instance, had become not just a means of enriching himself, but a way to cause pain. This pain could be intensified, he saw, by making it appear that a friend or relative of the victim had been the thief. And he vowed to perform his operations with just a little less than enough anesthesia, ostensibly to safeguard the patient's health. Lurk's head swam with the screams, whimpers, and pleas that he saw in his future. "I'm happy," he said.

Bubby patted his shoulder. "That's nice."

"Nice? Is that all you can say?" Lurk looked at him with faintly contemptuous pity. "You poor sap. You're still mooning over Shirley Lee, aren't you?"

"I guess so," Bubby admitted, coloring. "I can hardly wait to see her again. I want to make her forget everything she must have suffered at the hands of those animals. You know, I bet she's thinking of me too, right this minute. I can feel it."

-12-

In the basement of Pie in the Sty, naked bodies, obscenely slathered with lard, cavorted in the half light. The floor was rank with grease, and a sour smell of deviant sex and untrammeled cholesterol permeated the air. Shirley Lee Wittigrew and Basile St. Just-l'Espalier were locked in an unnatural embrace at the top of a pyramid of giggling bodyguards. Wilbur Wittigrew was filming the lard pusher while he tongued the mobile news team and did ugly things to them with half-eaten spareribs. Humanity has seldom descended to such abject wretchedness. Forgotten were piglets and innocence as Shirley Lee sucked the fruit of corruption.

Epilogue

God and the Heavenly Host were watching Guido Mocha's band raid Social Sanctuary headquarters. The screen showed a close-up of Guido Mocha, his long pale hair and beard streaming behind him and his thick white brows knit with fury as he rammed a fleeing social worker with his bike.

"You really ought to do something about him," Gabriel warned.

"Why?" God asked.

"Well, you got so upset about the other one, and this one's getting away with a lot more than he did."

"I wasn't as bored then as I am now. Boredom, not bravery, is the antidote for fear."

Gabriel looked anxiously at the screen. "But maybe each time they become. . . ."

"Stronger?"

"Yes, Lord. This is only the second they've made, and already. . . ."

"You think one of these . . . golems . . . might actually become strong enough to challenge Me?"

Gabriel kept silent, knowing that whatever he said would be wrong.

God smiled bitterly. "We'll give him a chance, then, and see what he can do. I'll tune in on another planet for a while. That way, the outcome will be a surprise. At least to all of you."

"Turn the screen to Philobilius," someone said.

"Yes," the rest agreed eagerly. "The creatures there are the funniest and crunchiest in the entire universe."

"It seems to be unanimous," Gabriel said.

God reached over and focused the screen on Krakwind, an ugly, monotonous planet, where everything dripped or crawled. "Nobody ever said this was a democracy," He told His disappointed Court.